Kate Field liv... ...y,
daughter and ... ...f
Ra...
He...

Also by Kate Field

The Man I Fell in Love With
A Dozen Second Chances

FINDING HOME

KATE FIELD

One More Chapter
a division of HarperCollins*Publishers* Ltd
1 London Bridge Street
London SE1 9GF
www.harpercollins.co.uk
HarperCollins*Publishers*
1st Floor, Watermarque Building, Ringsend Road
Dublin 4, Ireland

This paperback edition 2021
First published in Great Britain in ebook format
by HarperCollins*Publishers* 2021

A catalogue record of this book is available from the British Library

ISBN: 978-0-00-843944-6

This novel is entirely a work of fiction. The names, characters and
incidents portrayed in it are the work of the author's imagination.
Any resemblance to actual persons, living or dead, events or localities
is entirely coincidental.

Printed and bound in Great Britain by
CPI Group (UK) Ltd, Croydon CR0 4YY

To Suzannah Shaw, with thanks for twenty-five years of friendship

Mim slammed on the brakes as she rounded the bend and spotted a car already parked in her favourite layby. How annoying was that? She'd had this place to herself for the last two nights; it was *her* patch. The other car was in the best position too, so she had to squeeze her old Volvo estate into the gap next to the overflowing rubbish bin. Oh well – at least it was too cold to open the window. She would just have to close her eyes and imagine she was tucked up for the night in The Ritz…

She glanced in the rear-view mirror. In the fading light, she thought she could make out two figures in the front seats of the other car. It was one of those massive 4x4s – the sort driven by the really rich, or the pretending-to-be-rich. Surely they'd be moving on soon? She could do with going to the loo before she hunkered down to sleep but she didn't fancy nipping behind the trees with an audience.

She sat up straighter as the driver's door opened. A man got out – early sixties, she guessed, but still with a thatch of dark hair and a thick black moustache. He approached her car and she locked the door just in time before he knocked on her window.

'Hello.' His voice boomed through the glass, and he accompanied the word with a huge grin and an exaggerated wave. 'Are you free? Can you spare a moment to help some travellers in distress?'

Mim wound down the window so there was a gap of about five centimetres at the top – too small for him to get an arm through. He looked harmless enough, but she knew better than to be taken in by that. A blast of icy, late-December air slipped through the window and into the car, and she shivered, hoping she wasn't going to regret this small act of engagement.

'Don't open it too far,' the man said, bending down to peer at her through the gap. 'Are you on your own, my dear? You can't be too careful. You don't know who the dickens I am, do you? I hope my girls would be just as cautious. Let me fetch Bea. She'll put your mind at rest. Won't be a tick.'

He took a few steps away from the door, and gestured towards his own car, beckoning to someone else. The passenger door opened and a woman climbed out – around the same age as him, tall and stoutly built.

2

'Well? Have you found help?' she called, her voice carrying across the layby as she strode over. 'Please tell me it's a Christmas miracle and you've found a proper mechanic in that car.'

The woman's face loomed at Mim's window, her mouth stretched into a generous smile. Her lips were painted with bold, red lipstick that matched her chunky glasses.

'No need to worry,' she said. 'We don't bite. I suppose Bill gooned and terrified you, didn't he? Silly old sod. If he spent less time tinkering about, and more time on important things like ... I don't know, arranging breakdown cover, as a wholly random example, we wouldn't be in the pickle we're in now. Do tell me that by some lucky chance you know how to fix cars and we'll be in your debt forever.'

Mim wound the window closed and got out of the car. She'd never met anyone who spoke the way this woman did – with the sort of cut-glass accent she'd only heard on the telly, not the Lancashire twang she'd grown up with. She wasn't terrified in the least. It was the most interesting thing that had happened in days. What on earth was someone like this doing on the outskirts of Burnley?

'I don't know anything about cars,' Mim admitted, as she pulled her scarf tighter around her neck. She hoped the mild weather of the last two weeks wasn't about to turn; she was already having to wear several layers of clothes to survive nights in the car. 'Won't it start?'

'It looks like the electrics have gone,' Bill said. 'Would you believe it? Three weeks after the complimentary breakdown cover from the dealership ran out. Rotten timing, eh?'

He laughed and Bea rolled her eyes at him.

'Rotten organisation on your part. If only I'd chosen a man who was good with his head rather than his hands.' Bea turned to Mim. 'He's an inventor,' she explained, flashing a smile. 'In case you were getting the wrong idea.'

Mim could only stare in fascination as Bea leaned against Bill for a moment and they shared a private smile. Even in the lowering light of a late-December night, the bond of affection between them shone brightly and their warmth seemed to spill over and touch Mim. She didn't want to lose it yet.

'Is there anything I can do?' she asked. 'There must be some local breakdown companies. Or do you have family who could pick you up?'

'Well, there's the rub,' Bill said, running his finger along his moustache. 'We're not from round here. We live in Devon and we need to be back there tonight, one way or another.'

'It's essential that we get back. My niece is getting married tomorrow and Bill is giving her away. We can't let

4

the family down,' Bea said. Her voice cracked. 'We've left Lia in charge at Vennhallow. All the relatives are descending and I dread to think what chaos she's creating, even with Corin to supervise. It's imperative that we make it home. We'll have to ring Corin,' she said to Bill, rummaging in her bag for her phone. 'He'll know what to do.'

She dialled and for a minute Mim heard only one half of the conversation.

'We're still in the north, darling... No, he's fine, but the car has broken down... I know, but we diverted to collect the engine this morning and you know what he's like when he meets a fellow enthusiast... He couldn't resist looking at the whole railway... I'll put you on loud speaker...'

'... a nightmare, like the circus has moved in.' The reception was crackly, but the words were clear enough as they were flung out of the phone. The voice was male, posh, and sounded grumpy to Mim. 'How much longer will you be?'

'That's the problem,' Bill said, leaning towards the phone. 'We've no way of getting back.'

'Haven't you tried a breakdown service?' Corin asked.

'No one will take us down to Devon, not when it's New Year's Eve tomorrow and there's a forecast of snow up here,' Bill replied. 'The best they would do was drive us to the railway station.'

'That will do, won't it? There must be trains down to Exeter.'

'The west coast line is closed for maintenance until January,' Bea said. She sagged against Mim's car, looking older and suddenly vulnerable. Mim felt a flash of annoyance with this Corin person. Would it kill him to show more sympathy? 'I can't see how we can make it back for tomorrow.'

'I'll have to come and pick you up.' It sounded like a grudging offer. 'Can you send me details of where you are?'

'You can't do that, son. It will be five hours each way,' Bill said. 'You'll be shattered.'

'I'll have ten hours of peace. Ten hours without being asked when it will be my turn. Shattered is a small price to pay.'

Mim had heard enough. The solution was obvious, wasn't it?

'I'll drive you home,' she said.

———

Why not? It wasn't as if she had anything else to do; it was a hopeless time to be looking for a new job and she could make this journey and be back ready to start the job search again in January. Besides, it would be an adventure. She'd never been to Devon; it was one of those mythical places down south she sometimes saw on the telly and struggled to believe was on the same island where she lived. Perhaps she'd even see the sea at last. And even if she didn't, she wanted to help. She felt drawn to these people, despite knowing nothing about them. Bea's worry about letting her family down had touched a nerve with Mim; it wasn't going to happen if she could do anything to prevent it. She might not have much in this world, but it cost nothing to be kind – something the posh man on the phone would do well to remember. And look at Bea now – she was rejuvenated. It had been an impulsive offer, but Mim didn't regret it one bit.

She opened the boot to try to make room for two suitcases. The boot was a mess, stuffed with bin bags and supermarket bags-for-life that were, quite literally, holding Mim's entire life. Her swimming costume and towel were draped over the top of everything else, in the vague hope that they might dry out before she used them again tomorrow. Well, she didn't need to worry about that now. It was unlikely she'd make it back to Burnley in time for the free swim at the leisure centre tomorrow morning. She swept everything over to one side of the boot, just as Bill and Bea wheeled over two expensive looking cases.

'Gracious, have you been having a clear out?' Bea asked, as Bill hoisted the first suitcase into the boot. He dislodged a towel that Mim had used to strategically conceal the bag containing her toiletries. Mim tugged it back in place quickly, hoping that Bea hadn't seen the toothbrush and deodorant poking out of the top. Perhaps she hadn't reacted quickly enough. When she glanced at Bea, there was a strange expression on her face – part surprise, part curiosity.

'We simply can't start this road trip without proper introductions,' Bea said. She held out her hand to Mim. 'Beatrice Howard. After the Shakespearean heroine, of course. Call me Bea. And this is Bill. A William! Isn't that perfect?'

Mim shook the hand that Bea offered.

'Miranda Brown,' she said, and immediately wondered why she had said that. No one had called her by her full name for years. Perhaps it was Bea's accent; at least she hadn't done anything really stupid like curtsey. 'Usually Mim,' she added, but her words were lost as Bea crushed her in a hug.

'Miranda!' Bea exclaimed, calling over Mim's shoulder to Bill. 'Did you hear that? She's one of us!'

Mim stood awkwardly while Bea squeezed her. She hadn't been brought up with hugs and didn't know what to do with them. It felt unfamiliar and strangely comforting. But what was all that about being one of them? From what she'd seen and heard of Bill and Bea so far, her life couldn't be more opposite to theirs.

'One of you?' she asked, as she stepped back from Bea's embrace. No point in getting too comfortable there. 'What do you mean?'

'The name. Miranda. It's from Shakespeare, isn't it?' Bea said. 'That's how we chose the names for all our brood. We have Corin, the son and heir, then Rosalind, known as Ros, then Orlando – or Olly – is number three, and Ophelia – Lia – is number four. So you see, my dear, our meeting was meant to be.'

'Really? In that case, I wish it could have happened on a warm beach somewhere.' Mim shivered as a gust of wind blew across the layby. The weather was turning and there was hardly any light left. She slammed the boot shut. 'Are we ready?'

'Hold fire,' Bill said, as he dashed back towards his car. 'I can't go without my Hornby Dublo. It's a St Paddy!' he called to Mim in a baffling aside.

'It's a model engine,' Bea explained, smiling affectionately after Bill. 'We've been in Carlisle on an emergency mission to visit Bill's brother; he fell on Christmas Day and ended up in hospital. We should have been safely home yesterday, but Bill was determined to detour for this engine while we were in the north. Apparently it's a rare piece. Don't you think a man of his advanced years should have grown out of playing with a train set?' Bea laughed, a peal of laughter that seemed to brighten the gloom like a firework.

At last they were all in the car.

'Shall I set the sat nav?' Bill asked. He peered at the dashboard. 'Ah. This motor's too old, isn't it? Do you have a portable one?'

'No.'

'Use your phone, do you? It's the answer to everything for you young people, isn't it?'

'Not me,' Mim said. 'I don't have a phone at the moment.'

'No mobile phone?' Bea peered forward from between the seats. 'Oh my, dear, have you lost it? What a nuisance.'

'Sort of.' She hesitated, but couldn't lie. 'It came with a job that I don't have anymore.' She turned on the engine, conscious that both Bea and Bill were staring at her in the gloom, as if waiting for her to say more. She pulled onto the road.

'And we're off!' Bill said. 'This is an adventure, isn't it?'

This *was* an adventure for Mim. She'd never travelled further than the Lake District before, on a school trip where everyone else had paired off, leaving her to sit with the teacher. Now, as she drove down the motorway in the dark, passing signs for places she'd heard of but never been to, it felt as if with each mile she was figuratively as well as literally leaving the past behind. Chester, Stafford, Stoke-on-Trent... Had anyone ever been so excited to spot signs for Birmingham before?

Bill and Bea were like a comedy double act and

hardly stopped talking and laughing for the entire journey. Mim loved hearing them, and their stories made her laugh even though she had no idea who or what they were talking about. Bea occasionally slipped in a sneaky question and Mim admitted that she'd worked in a hotel for the last ten years, but it was easy to distract her again before she could ask more. People judged, didn't they? She was enjoying being herself and not her past for once.

It felt like they had travelled across a continent, never mind a country, and Mim was desperately trying not to fall asleep at the wheel when Bill eventually directed her off the motorway. It was too dark to see any of her surroundings and the road signs now pointed to places Mim had never heard of: Exmouth, Budleigh Salterton, Sidmouth. She hunched forward, gripping the wheel as Bill directed her onto roads that seemed to become twistier and narrower with each turn. She finally turned left onto what seemed no better than a farm track; in the full beam of the headlights, she could see tufts of grass sprouting through the centre of the road ahead and bare hedge branches loomed alarmingly close on either side.

'What do I do if a car comes the other way?' she murmured, half to herself. There were no signs of any passing places. Bea only laughed in response.

'It's highly unlikely at this time of night. Everyone will be on the Champagne,' she said. 'Be careful here; there's a sharp turn to the right and then you can pull in on the left. There, do you see, behind those other cars.'

She tapped Bill on the shoulder. 'It looks like everyone has arrived. We must have a full house!'

A security light came on as Mim parked behind eight or nine other vehicles that were lined up in front of a huge barn with three garage doors built into the wall. A tall conifer hedge surrounded it, but there was no sign of a house – and surely, if all these cars belonged to visitors, it would be bulging at the seams rather than merely full? But it was none of her business, Mim reflected with a tinge of regret as she hopped out of the car and opened the boot so that Bill could retrieve the suitcases. Her part in this adventure was over.

'Now, what are we going to do with you?' Bea said, as Mim hurriedly tried to stuff her knickers back into one of the carrier bags that had tipped over – probably as they bumped along the lane to this place. She hoped Bea couldn't see what she was doing. 'It's standing room only in the house, so that won't do. Ros might have a spare sofa bed, but she'll never forgive me if I ring and wake the children at this time. If only I hadn't pressed the Essex cousins on Corin. He'd rather have had you than those awful twins. Perhaps—'

'Don't bother about me,' Mim interrupted, before Bea could go through her entire address book. 'I'll be heading back first thing in the morning. I'm sure I can find somewhere.' If she could find a quiet picnic area to park up for the night, it would be an upgrade from a layby. Devon was holiday country, wasn't it? Or even better –

could she find her way to the sea and be lulled to sleep by the sound of the waves? That would be the best ending to what had been an unexpectedly fun day.

'The local hotels and B&Bs will be full of wedding guests,' Bea said, 'the ones that open at this time of year. There must be somewhere we can put you.'

'What about the caravans?' Bill asked, his voice coming out of the darkness as the security light switched off. 'They've not been used for a while, but they should be watertight.'

'That's it! The perfect solution.' The lights flashed on as Bea spun back to Mim, a huge smile filling her face. 'You can stay in one of our caravans. You're one of us. We're not giving you up so easily.'

Chapter Two

Mim was woken by the tinny sound of knocking on metal. She jolted upright, fearing that she was about to be moved on from the layby... And then she realised, as a mattress spring prodded her buttock and she breathed in the slightly musty air, that she wasn't in her car after all. She was in one of Bea's caravans: cold, dusty, and with some damp stains on the curtains, but still the most luxurious place she had slept over the last fortnight.

There was a longer knock at the door and Mim hurried to answer it. She shielded her eyes with her arm as the visitor shone a torch straight at her face.

'Sorry, darling. I didn't mean to blind you.' The visitor – a girl in her mid-twenties, wrapped in a huge wool coat and wearing floral wellington boots – at last switched off the torch. 'Hello. I'm Lia,' she said. She leaned forward and air kissed Mim's cheeks. 'You must be Mim, the saviour of the day. We've heard all about you and how amazing you are. Mummy didn't mention that you have such fabulous hair. Is it all natural?'

'Yes.' Mim flinched as the girl reached out and touched a strand of her hair. She hadn't brushed it yet, and she suspected that the usual waves might have turned into corkscrew curls overnight. The sooner she could tie it back, out of the way, the better.

'You are so lucky,' Lia continued. 'You wouldn't believe how much I have to pay for extensions or else my hair looks literally as thin as tissue. Yours is a gorgeous colour too, not exactly red, but like the most beautiful autumn leaves. I'd love to paint you. You could be a contemporary Pre-Raphaelite. You will let me, darling, won't you?'

'I won't be here. I'm going back today.' Not back home. She had no home – not a bricks and mortar one, at any rate. She had an area of the country where she'd spent most of her life. It wasn't quite the same, was it? 'What time is it?' she asked, peering out of the door and seeing that the sky was much lighter than she'd expected.

'Almost nine.' Lia rolled her eyes. 'I know. I said it was too early to disturb you, but the house is in pandemonium because of the wedding.'

'Nine?' Mim hadn't slept so late since … well, she couldn't remember when. The springy mattress must have been more comfortable than she'd expected. Disappointingly so – she'd planned to be on her way back to Lancashire by now.

'Speaking of the wedding,' Lia carried on, 'Mummy sent me over to ask you an enormous favour. She'd have come herself but she's in the middle of having her highlights done. Two of the village girls who were supposed to be waitressing for the caterers have phoned in sick this morning, so we're short staffed. Apparently you mentioned having hotel experience, so is there any chance you could help out, darling?'

The request was accompanied by a charming smile. Lia really was an extraordinarily attractive girl, with her heart-shaped face and ash-blonde hair piled into a messy bun. There was no malice in the words, but that 'staff' was a reality check after the 'one of us' talk of the day before. Still, Mim didn't take offence. What other place could she ever have among these people, with her background, her flat northern vowels, and with her home address being a clapped-out Volvo?

'I've brought you some clothes – a black skirt and a white blouse – and some toiletries. I'd say we're a similar size, wouldn't you?' Lia carried on. 'You poor thing, having to sleep in your clothes. I wanted to bring you some pyjamas last night but Mummy thought you'd prefer some peace and quiet after the long drive. I do tend to talk a lot. Just ask Corin.' She laughed. 'Tell me to shut up. Everyone else does. So what do you say? Will you be our saviour again and help out?'

'Yes, of course.' Mim was happy to help. It made no difference whether she returned to Lancashire today or tomorrow. She'd much rather be busy here than twiddling her thumbs in the car until she could start job hunting again.

'Fantastic.' Lia seemed to take Mim's agreement as an invitation as she slipped past Mim and into the caravan. 'Hurry and change and then I'll show you the way to the house. The caterers have laid on a huge pile of sandwiches for breakfast.'

'Breakfast?' Mim laughed. 'You should have mentioned that in the first place. I'd have agreed to anything for a bacon butty.'

Lia's clothes were slightly tight, but as Mim studied herself in the tarnished mirror on the back of the wardrobe door, a recognisable version of herself stared back: smart, professional, clean, uncrumpled – a far cry from the figure that had unfolded from the back seat of the Volvo for the last couple of weeks. For twenty-four hours, she could be someone useful again, someone respectable. She was going to enjoy it.

Mim stepped out of the caravan and took her first look at her surroundings in daylight. It had been dark when she arrived here last night, but now she could see that she was in a field that was set out like a residential cul-de-sac. A gravel road entered in one corner and swung round in a wavy circle, leading to six static caravans that were scattered through the field, spaced well apart and tucked away between trees to give each an impression of privacy. Each caravan was parked at a different angle and was surrounded by a large veranda.

It was a blissful location, even on a crisp winter morning when the bare branches of the trees danced in the wind and the grass shimmered with a layer of frost. But as Mim turned back to lock her caravan – the first one, nearest the gate leading out of the field – first impressions gave way to reality. The exterior of the caravan, once a pale cream, was now stained with green leaf residue and streaks from dirty rainwater. The veranda was in desperate need of a lick of paint too, and some of the spindles around the edge looked rotten. The plant containers which should have brightened the veranda were either overgrown with leggy plants or empty. As Mim looked across the whole site, she saw that the other caravans were in a similar condition, and weeds sprouted up through the gravel drive.

'What is this place?' she asked Lia, as she followed her towards the gate. 'Why is it empty?'

'Daddy,' Lia said, as if this one word could answer all possible questions on the subject. 'It wasn't one of his most successful schemes. I think people came to stay when the caravans first opened, but no one has been near here for years. I'd forgotten all about them until Mummy mentioned you were here.'

Forgotten all about a collection of caravans that must be worth tens of thousands of pounds? What sort of world was she living in? A very different one than she was used to, Mim realised a few minutes later as they passed the garage where her car was parked – now surrounded by an army of vans belonging to caterers, florists, and beauticians – and followed the track round the tall conifer hedge she had noticed the night before. Lia carried on towards the front door of the building in front of them, while Mim stopped and stared.

'Come on,' Lia called, glancing back. 'Don't let breakfast go cold.'

'Breakfast is here?' Mim asked. She gestured towards the building before them. 'This is your house?'

'Of course.' Lia laughed. 'This is Vennhallow. What did you think it was?'

Mim shrugged. A hotel, maybe? Although it was larger than the hotel where she had worked for the last ten years with her friend Gordon. This building was... Words failed her. It was the most beautiful place she'd ever seen. It was a long two-storey building, at least as wide as six or seven terraced houses if measured against the houses that Mim was more used to seeing. The white painted walls were broken up with a regular series of high, wide windows that she imagined must allow the light to flood in, and it was all topped with a grey slate roof and half a dozen tall chimneys. There was a pleasing lack of symmetry about the house that made it feel approachable rather than too perfect. Even so, could Mim really go inside? It looked like she had no choice; Lia was already at the door, waiting for her to go through.

'Everyone's in the kitchen,' Lia said as Mim tentatively followed her through the wooden front door and into a spacious hall. There was hardly time to take in much detail beyond the staircase that was twice as wide as any Mim had seen before and the massive Christmas tree, as Lia rushed along a corridor and through a door that opened into what could only be the kitchen. It was an enormous space. The first section contained the kitchen cupboards and cooking equipment, and a team of aproned caterers were moving around here with quiet efficiency. Beyond that, a huge table seating at least a dozen people stretched across the centre of the room. It was laden with plates, tea pots, and cafetières, and a number of people flocked around it.

But there was no time to study them, and no more thought about food, despite the tempting aromas wafting around. The furthest part of the room was a modern extension, furnished with squashy sofas and constructed of floor-to-ceiling glass walls. Mim was irresistibly drawn over until her nose was pressed to the glass. Beyond a lawn filled with a cream marquee, beyond another field, she had her first glimpse of the sea. It was only a tiny strip before the headland curved round and cut off the view, but it looked magical as it sparkled as the winter sun rose in the sky.

'Mim? Mim.' Lia tapped her on the arm to get her attention, and Mim reluctantly tore her gaze away from the view. Lia smiled.

'Admiring the view?' she asked.

'How could you not?' Mim smiled back. 'It's amazing.'

'You sound like Mummy. She insisted on building this extension so she could see the sea. None of the other rooms have much of a view because of the angle at which the house was built.' Lia shrugged. 'I can't say it bothers me. Half the time it's obscured by mist anyway. Besides, it's not exactly the Caribbean, is it?'

'I haven't a clue,' Mim said. 'I've never been.'

'The Mediterranean, then. You know what I mean. It's not like holiday sea, is it? You don't want to rush out and bathe in that, do you? Unless you're seriously weird, like Corin,' she added, almost as an afterthought. 'He loves all that cold, wet, outdoorsy stuff.'

'I've not been to the Mediterranean either,' Mim said. She looked out of the window again, wanting to take in every detail in case this was her one and only chance. 'I've never seen the sea before.'

'What, never ever? Darling, where do you go on holiday? The desert?'

'I don't go on holiday.' A memory slipped into Mim's mind of her six or seven-year-old self, begging to go away, to visit the seaside like all of her friends had been doing in the summer holidays. Another memory was inextricably linked with it, of how she had been punished for whining and for being an ungrateful child. She shivered, unconsciously rubbing her left forearm, and the ugly scars that were hidden beneath the fine silk of Lia's blouse. She turned her back on the view and on the shadows of the past that had no place here. She smiled.

'Didn't you mention breakfast? I'm sure I can smell bacon.'

Lia introduced Mim to the catering team and when Paula, the lady in charge, had quizzed her about her waitressing experience and finally welcomed her to the team, Mim grabbed a plate of bacon butties and ate them with relish while Lia pointed out the various aunts, uncles, cousins, and friends who drifted in and out of the kitchen. It was impossible to keep track; there seemed to be dozens of people, all talking and shouting over each other so there was never a quiet moment. Bill came in at one point and made a beeline for Mim.

'Good morning, good morning,' he said, grinning widely so that his moustache quivered. 'How was your night in the old caravan; not too bad? Sorry we had to put you in there, but we're full to the gills as you can see. Not what you're used to, eh?'

Mim smiled and shook her head. It was a million times better than what she had been used to lately but the owner of this house was never going to understand that.

'I hope you didn't mind being asked to help today?' he asked. 'It's all hands on deck when it comes to an event like this and what with your experience it seemed the perfect solution. Bea would have asked herself, only she's in the middle of her preparations and you know what it's like. These things can't be interrupted.' He laughed. 'I hope Lia hasn't driven you to distraction with her chattering yet.'

'I've been on my best behaviour,' Lia said, dropping a kiss on the top of Bill's head as he sat down at the kitchen table. She placed a bowl of muesli in front of him and he sighed.

'The old fish food again, eh? I thought I might have been allowed special dispensation today. I've important duties ahead.'

'And you've important duties ahead for years and years,' Lia replied, draping a casual arm across his shoulders. 'So you'll be sticking to the healthy diet.' Lia smiled at Mim and rolled her eyes. 'Are all parents so impossible?'

Mim couldn't answer that and she was glad when Paula called for her to start work. The first job was to set up the tables in the marquee where the wedding reception would be held. After seeing the house, it came as no surprise that the marquee was vast; it even had separate rooms, so a porch led to an entrance lobby which then opened out into a space for dining, with a dance floor at one end and a bar set up in another room at the far end.

The dining area was already filled with tables and chairs but Paula had brought crates of cutlery, china, glassware, and table decorations that all needed to be laid out and given a final polish so that they would sparkle under the lights of the candles that graced the centre of each round table. It was easy work for Mim; she'd laid the tables for breakfast and dinner in the hotel every day, and Paula soon recognised her competence and stopped hovering over her shoulder. It was good to be working again and doing something familiar. Even better, the wait staff were allowed an advance sample of the soup that would be served to the guests later. Two hot meals in a day and both free! Mim could hardly believe her luck.

The afternoon and evening whizzed by in a blur as Mim helped to serve the wedding breakfast and then set out the evening buffet. It felt like she'd stepped inside the pages of one of the celebrity magazines they'd had in the hotel and found herself caught up in a proper society wedding. There was serious wealth and pedigree in this room: she could hear it in the accents, see it in the shimmer of the expensive fabrics and the sparkle of jewels, and smell it in the waft of perfume as she dipped down to remove or deliver plates. Even more intoxicating was the heady atmosphere of love in the room – and not just the bubble of romance that floated around the bride and groom. There were families here: children dancing in the arms of their parents; young people crouched next to old, building a bond between generations; friends laughing as they danced together. Mim soaked up every detail of this mesmerising world that was a million miles away from the one she knew. She loved every bit of it.

When it was almost midnight, the guests were ushered outside for a fireworks display to mark the end of the wedding and the start of the new year. Paula had allowed the waiting staff a break to watch the fireworks. Mim grabbed an abandoned glass of Champagne and hurried outside. The garden looked stunning, lit by braziers and warmed by fire pits, but she veered away from the crowd on the lawn and headed for the shadows created by a group of trees, from where she could watch in peace.

The display started with an explosion of colour as rockets of red, blue, and green fizzed through the sky. Mim was in the wrong place for the best view and she stepped backwards to find a better position, crashing into something warm and solid. She spun round, her heart thumping. It was too dark to see clearly, but she could make out the tall figure of someone leaning against a tree trunk and could hear their steady breaths.

'Sorry to startle you,' the person said. It was a man's voice, and a posh one – although all southern accents sounded posh to her. Why he thought he should apologise was a mystery when she had bumped into him. 'I wasn't expecting anyone else to hide out under the trees.'

'I'm not hiding,' Mim said. 'Are you?'

'I'm stealing five minutes' peace. That's not too much to ask, is it?'

The sky lit up with a kaleidoscope of colours and Mim caught a glimpse of her companion: tall, strong, dazzling smile. He was wearing black trousers and a white open-necked shirt, the uniform of the male waiters, and his sleeves were rolled up to show muscular arms that looked like they'd known hard graft. He was holding a bottle of Champagne. No wonder he was hiding. He must be one of the bar staff and have grabbed the bottle as he left. And she'd felt guilty enough for taking an abandoned glass!

'Have some more Champagne,' he said, sloshing the liquid in the general direction of her glass. Most of it trickled down her hand and, in the flickering light between fireworks, he reached out and brushed it away. His touch was warm and felt extraordinarily intimate.

'Did you pay for that?' Mim asked, whisking her hand away quickly.

'No.' He took a long swig from the bottle. 'You're not from round here, are you?'

'What gave it away?'

The only reply was a quiet laugh which echoed in the darkness.

'It's a strange time, New Year, isn't it?' he continued, his voice clear despite the backdrop of fireworks. 'It makes you reflect too much. About the ways the old year didn't work out as you'd hoped. About the emptiness of the year ahead. About how different things might be, if you'd been born into another life. Don't you think?'

He was drunk. Mim wondered why she hadn't realised that before. Perhaps he'd been helping himself from the bar all night. If there was one thing she couldn't stand, it was a maudlin drunk feeling sorry for himself.

'No,' she said. 'There's no point envying the people here. If you don't like what you've got in life, change it. There's always something you can do. You can't stop trying, however bad it gets.'

'Are you one of those relentlessly cheerful people for whom the glass is always half full?' he asked.

'I'm one of those relentlessly poor people and I'm always grateful to have a glass.'

Fireworks flashed over their heads again. He was closer than she'd realised and looking right at her. She could feel heat radiating off his body and see curiosity in his face. She raised her Champagne glass to him, in a mock toast, and that smile shone out again, so luminous that it was hard to look away. The moment was broken when cheers rang out from the garden and the guests started to sing a ragged version of 'Auld Lang Syne'.

'Happy New Year,' the man said, and he clinked his

bottle against her glass. 'Let's make the most of that glass and have another drink.'

'I have to go.' Her break was over and presumably his was too. There was still a huge amount of clearing up to be done and thirsty guests to serve.

'Disappearing on the stroke of midnight?' He laughed. 'Who are you, Cinderella? Will you leave me your shoe as you escape?'

'I'd better not.' She smiled. 'It's the only pair I've got.'

Chapter Three

I t felt like déjà vu when Mim was woken the next morning by a knock on her caravan door. This time, Bea was standing on the veranda wearing a large pair of sunglasses despite the mist swirling around her and the general dreariness of the day. Mim stifled a pang of disappointment at this Lancashire-like weather. Shouldn't it always be glorious down south?

'Aha, you're still here,' Bea said. 'Can I come in?'

She didn't wait for an answer, but brushed past Mim and sank down onto the sofa that ran along the wall in the lounge area of the caravan.

'Sorry, I must have overslept,' Mim said. Overslept again. This Devon sea air was knocking her out more effectively than sleeping tablets. 'I can be gone in ten minutes, if that's okay?' Bea didn't seem to be listening. She was rubbing her head and groaning quietly. Mim swallowed a huge chunk of pride and forced herself to carry on. 'I don't think I have enough petrol to get me back to Lancashire and I'm short on cash at the moment. Would you mind filling the car up?'

'Why is it so cold in here?' Bea asked. She was wearing an oversized camel cardigan that Mim suspected was worth more than her Volvo, but still shivered and wrapped it more tightly round herself. 'Are the heaters broken?'

'I didn't switch them on.'

'Whyever not?'

'Because they would have cost money to run.'

'Pooh! Pennies.' Bea dismissed this with a flap of her hand. 'You can't put a price on being warm.'

Mim could. She remembered all too well the places she'd lived before finding work with Gordon at the hotel. There had been many days when she'd had to choose between putting 50p in the gas meter or buying food. The price of warmth had been hunger. Whatever happened, whatever it took, she wasn't going back to those days again.

'So, about the petrol?' Mim asked again.

'Yes, you don't need to worry about that, my dear. Bill will take you to the garage. It's hard to find your way down the single-track lanes if you're not familiar with them. It may be open tomorrow, or perhaps the day after. It's always tricky to know at New Year.'

'Tomorrow?' Mim repeated. 'But I was planning to go back today.'

'Were you?' Bea raised the sunglasses off her face and peered at Mim, before wincing and letting them fall back to the bridge of her nose. She patted the sofa seat beside her. 'Stop hovering by the door. Come and sit down and let's have a chat.'

That sounded ominous, but nonetheless Mim crossed the caravan and sat down next to Bea.

'I'm not being judgemental, my dear,' Bea said, 'but there's clearly more going on than you're telling us. Have you run away from home? From a husband or partner or whoever?'

'No. I don't have any sort of partner. I haven't run away.'

'I see. Only, it looked as if all your worldly goods were stashed in that car of yours. I'm sure I saw your toothbrush in one of those bags you tried to cover up. And then I found a blanket on the back seat, and it may sound silly, but I had the absurd notion that you might actually be sleeping in your car. Tell me that's a ridiculous idea, Mim. I can't bear to think of it.'

'It's not ridiculous,' Mim said. She hadn't wanted to volunteer the information but she wouldn't lie about it now. 'It's true. It's only been a couple of weeks, though. Not long. And it won't be for much longer. Something will come up soon. I'm lucky, really, having the car. Many people are much worse off.'

Bea leaned forward and grabbed Mim's hands.

'How can this be?' she asked. 'How did you find yourself in such dire straits?'

'Quite easily.' It had been frighteningly easy. Mim had never realised what a fragile divide lay between being employed and being homeless. 'I told you I worked in a hotel. I'd been there for ten years and I lived there too. Four months ago, Gordon, the owner, died.' Mim took a deep breath to calm the sob that was lurking. She still missed him dearly. 'His daughter inherited the hotel and left me to carry on running it while the probate went through and she looked for a buyer. She told me the week before Christmas that she'd sold it to a property developer to turn into flats and that the business was closing with immediate effect. I lost my home and my job.'

She hadn't been the only one affected. There had been Beryl, who had taken on a cleaning job at the hotel when her husband had been made redundant six years earlier. Then there was Robbie, who Gordon had taken on as chef despite his spell in prison, and who had been about to celebrate his first Christmas with a new baby. There had been the local businesses who supplied goods and services to the hotel, from laundry to fresh eggs, the guests who had rooms booked, and the locals who had arranged to come to the hotel to enjoy Christmas lunch. Mim had been given one day to cancel all the contracts, break the bad news to staff and guests, and close down the business. There had been no time to think of her own plans. When all the work was done, she had grabbed her bags and driven off, not looking back. It wasn't the first time she had been moved on at short notice. She would survive it, just like she had done before.

'Surely you must have had family or friends who could put you up for a while?' Bea said.

'No.' Mim shrugged. She'd seen the extent of Bea's family and friends last night. Their worlds were so far apart that it would be hard for Bea to understand. 'No family and no friends. I'm on my own.'

'No you're not. You have us.' Bea squeezed Mim's hands. 'If you have no home, no job, and no one waiting for you in Lancashire, why are you going back? You might as well stay here.'

Mim stretched her leg and turned on the tap with her toe, letting more hot water gush into the enormous roll-top bath in Bea's en suite bathroom. It was utter bliss. The bathroom itself was huge, bigger than the attic bedroom where Mim had lived at the hotel, and it was beautifully decorated with glossy white tiles and hints of sea green to reflect the coastal location. Underfloor heating made the room toasty warm, and a fluffy bath sheet hung on the towel rail, waiting for Mim to step out of the bath. If she ever did. She could live in this room forever.

It was a couple of hours since Bea had visited her in the caravan, wrung her story out of her, and suggested she should stay in Devon. As it seemed that she was stuck here at least until tomorrow, when Bill would pay for her petrol, Mim had agreed to think about it. From there, Bea had made short work of persuading her to the house for lunch, and inviting her to use her bathroom when Mim had admitted that the hot water in the caravan was tepid at best.

She lay back and let the water cover up to her chin, soothing the aches in her muscles and joints that were a lingering legacy from her cramped sleeping arrangements in the car. Bea's question had touched a nerve. Why was she going back to Lancashire? She couldn't be homesick for somewhere when she'd never had a proper home. All that was left for her there were sour memories, and the three months she had left on the leisure-centre pass that Gordon had bought for her birthday so she could indulge her love of swimming; it had been a godsend over the last few weeks, providing access to toilets and showers.

Once the Christmas break was out of the way, her top priority was to find a job and somewhere to live, but couldn't she do that just as well here? Maybe there were more opportunities down here in tourist country for someone with hotel and bar experience. She took a deep breath and immersed herself in the water. She needed to make an objective decision and not be swayed by luxuries such as orange-scented bubble bath and a roast dinner. These were temporary treats, not a real part of the life she might lead in Devon. And yet, as she eventually strode out of the bathroom wrapped in the warm towel, and let her toes sink into the deep pile of the bedroom carpet, she couldn't resist dancing across the room and pretending that all this was hers.

She paused by the window, looking out across the lawn. The mist still hung low in the distance, over where Mim guessed the sea to be, but the garden was clear and she could see a team hard at work dismantling the marquee. Voices and laughter drifted up, stirring a memory. There were two men standing below her window, one wearing a sweatshirt with the marquee company logo on it, and the other a dark-haired man wearing jeans and a woolly jumper. She pressed closer to the glass for a better look, and as she did, the man in the jumper turned and she glimpsed the bewitching smile of the waiter who had hidden under the trees the night before. She was surprised to see him again; perhaps he worked for the family and was expected to help with whatever needed doing around the house. It was certainly big enough to need staff. She felt a flash of sympathy; she knew what it was like to juggle a multitude of random jobs, trying to make ends meet. Before she could move away, he glanced up and caught her watching, and his smile grew. She pulled the towel more tightly round her and retreated into the bedroom.

The kitchen was busy when Mim eventually found her way back downstairs. Bill was kneeling on the rug between the sofas, helping two small children build an elaborate construction with coloured bricks which looked far too advanced for their ages. A couple around her own age, who Mim didn't know, lounged on one of the sofas, chatting. Lia was perched on a chair at the table, sketching, and an unfamiliar man in his twenties was helping Bea in the kitchen. Classical music flowed out from hidden speakers. Mim hovered in the doorway, relishing this picture of contented family life. She couldn't imagine anything more perfect.

'Mim's here!' Bill called, looking up from the bricks and spotting her. 'Come in, come in. Don't be lurking there. Olly, pour Mim a glass, there's a boy. She deserves it more than the rest of us. She did a day's work yesterday while we were enjoying the party. Make it a large one and you can top up the rest of us while you're at it.'

The young man in the kitchen – presumably Olly – filled a Champagne flute from one of several bottles resting in an ice bucket and handed it to Mim.

'Good to meet you, Mim,' he said. 'Although from the way Mum and Dad have been talking, I'm disappointed you don't have wings and a halo.'

'I only wear them on special occasions.' Mim smiled

in response to Olly's infectious grin. It was easy to see the connection with Lia; he had the same delicate features and expressive eyes, although she guessed he was a year or two older. He was immaculately dressed in striped trousers and a floral sprig shirt, which probably shouldn't have worked together but somehow did. Like everyone else she'd met in the family, his outfit shrieked of designer labels and expensive price tags.

'I knew that bath would do you good,' Bea said, smiling at Mim. The sunglasses had now been replaced with a pair of normal glasses, with half green and half blue frames, that co-ordinated with her jumper and chunky necklace. 'You're glowing. You look more relaxed already. See how Devon life suits you! Now, who don't you know? That's Olly, number three, and over by the window you'll find Ros, number two, with her husband Jonty. The little ones are their children Jeremy and Maisie. We're just waiting for Corin, the son and heir, and then everyone's here. First born, but generally the last to any gathering!'

'Is there anything I can do to help?' Mim asked. There were pans on every ring of the large induction hob, and three ovens were blasting out welcome heat. Everything looked under control but she would prefer to be doing something useful than idling about making small talk. How would they ever find common ground?

'You're a darling to offer, but certainly not. You're a guest.' Bea laughed. 'Don't be fooled, my dear. I'm not actually cooking. Paula brought the whole meal round yesterday. All I'm doing is heating it up in accordance with her detailed instructions.' Bea waved a typed sheet of paper at Mim. 'On the subject of Paula,' she continued, 'she left this for you.'

She opened a drawer and passed an envelope to Mim. There was a stack of money inside, more than double what Mim had in her purse at the moment.

'What's this for?' she asked Bea.

'It's your wages for yesterday. It seemed light to me, but Paula assures me it's the going rate.'

'That's brilliant. Thank you.' Mim flicked through the notes. Light? She felt suddenly weighed down by riches. She'd thought the work yesterday was a favour to Bea. She hadn't realised she would be paid for it. Her mind whirled with images of what she could do with the money. She could treat herself to a hot meal every day for a couple of weeks. Or pick up a warmer coat and some boots from a charity shop. Or pay for her own petrol back to Lancashire so she didn't have to beg Bill. If she was even going back to Lancashire...

'Do you think Paula would have any more work available?' Mim asked. This might help her make a decision. The going rate in Devon seemed much better than in Lancashire, judging by the notes in her hand.

'There's no harm in asking. She said you were an excellent worker.' Bea smiled and held out her glass for

Olly to refill. 'Does this mean that we've persuaded you to stay in Devon?'

'I'll go wherever there's work. And a place to live,' Mim added.

'Plenty of spare rooms here now the mob have gone,' Bill called over. 'Don't worry on that score.'

'Oh no.' Mim cringed at how her words must have sounded. 'I wasn't hinting about staying here.'

'Wouldn't have minded if you were.' Bill laughed. 'We rattle around this old place. We'd be happy to fill it up again. The more the merrier.'

'Thanks, but I really couldn't.' Mim gulped at the Champagne that Olly had given her, wondering how she could explain without sounding ungrateful. It was an extraordinarily generous offer, but she couldn't accept it, not after the trouble she'd had at the hotel. Gordon's daughter had accused Mim of taking advantage of him when she'd first moved in, even though it had been his idea, and had never overcome her initial suspicion and hostility towards Mim. It had been the only blot on life at the hotel. She wasn't risking that again. 'I need my own space.'

'Of course you do,' Bea agreed, but Mim thought there was a touch of wistfulness in her reply. 'You can stay in the caravan for as long as you like until you find somewhere better.'

'Oh Mummy, have you seen the caravan?' Lia

exclaimed, looking up from her sketchbook. 'It's hardly fit for anyone to live in.'

'It's perfect for me,' Mim said. She wandered over to the table and looked at what Lia was drawing. It was a pencil sketch of the two children, and though Mim knew nothing about art, it seemed an impressive likeness. 'If you're sure you don't need it? But I can't stay there for nothing.'

'We certainly won't take any money,' Bea said. 'So please don't offend us by suggesting it.'

'I can't afford to give you any money.' Mim wracked her brains, but there was only one solution she could think of. 'What if we agree on a barter? I'll do jobs for you in exchange for staying in the caravan. Is there anything you need doing? I've turned my hand to most things over the last few years. I can clean, drive, do some gardening or general labouring, manage basic accounts, cook a mean English breakfast...'

'Sounds like the perfect woman, eh Jonty?' Bill said with a grin. Ros silenced their laughter with an exasperated sigh.

'You don't need to do any of that, my dear,' Bea said, giving Mim an apologetic look. 'We already have a housekeeper, and a cleaner, and a handyman who deals with the garden.' That explained the man in the woolly jumper, Mim thought. 'You do too, don't you Ros?' Bea continued.

'Yes, although I might be glad of a hand with these

two sometimes when Jonty's away.' Ros smiled at Mim. She was a few years older than Lia and Olly, and had dark hair to their blond mops, but her smile was wide and friendly – and oddly familiar. 'Corin doesn't have a cleaner, does he, but we all know Corin's views on such matters.'

The family's laughter was interrupted by the sound of paws skittering across the wooden floor, swiftly followed by a posh male voice.

'You know my views on what?'

Mim turned to look at the new arrival. Tall, strong, dazzling smile … and apparently not a Champagne-stealing handyman, after all, but Corin, Bea's son and heir.

Chapter Four

Mim couldn't believe she'd been so daft. How likely was it that a member of staff had stolen a bottle of Champagne and got hammered in the middle of a shift? But hang on … when they'd met under the trees, hadn't he been grumbling about his life? She tried to remember what he'd said. Something about an empty future and wishing he'd been born into a different life, wasn't it? She sank down onto a chair next to Lia and watched all the fuss that was being made over Corin's arrival. Bea was giving him a hug as if she hadn't seen him for a year, never mind since yesterday, and everyone else was laughing and talking over each other with evident warmth and unity. It looked like a pretty good life to her. What could he possibly have to complain about?

She looked away, trying not to make eye contact with

him, and spotted a dog sitting at her feet. It was small and squat, with wiry hair that was mainly white but with the odd gingery patch on its body and around one eye. It was completely still, gazing up at her. She smiled at it – she'd never had a pet and didn't know what else to do – and it jumped onto her knee, sniffed her trousers, circled a couple of times and curled up.

Lia laughed.

'Wow. How have you managed that? Dickens is far too aloof to give me the time of day.'

'Dickens?' Mim repeated.

'Corin's idea of a joke,' Bea called over. 'He doesn't appreciate Shakespeare.'

The man in question had wandered over to the sofas and was bending down to tickle one of the children – Maisie, Mim guessed from the floral dress, although they both had angelic blond curls that made it hard to tell them apart. He looked towards Mim and smiled. Did he recognise her? Mim couldn't tell.

'I'm glad to see you still have a glass,' he said. That answered that question. 'A worrying lack of shoes though.'

Reluctantly, Mim smiled. She'd left her shoes in the hall, wary of leaving footprints through the house.

'Good job I don't have holes in my socks,' she said. She looked pointedly at Corin's feet. He wasn't wearing shoes either and the heels of both his socks were almost threadbare. In fact, now she studied him properly, all of him looked shabby – at least in comparison to the rest of the family; his jeans were frayed at the bottom and his jumper sported a hole above the left elbow. Unless he'd paid a fortune for the distressed look, his clothes must be even older than hers.

He laughed but had no chance to reply as Bea called them to the table for lunch. Mim let the conversation drift on around her as she tucked into thick slices of roast lamb, roast and mashed potatoes, and heaps of fresh vegetables. Vegetables! After two weeks of living off sandwiches, nothing had ever tasted so good. She was so absorbed in her food that she barely noticed that the conversation had turned to her again.

'And she's insisting on a barter system until she has enough money to pay rent,' Bea was explaining to Corin. 'Quite unnecessary, of course, because it's not as if we're doing anything else with those caravans.'

'Quite understandable, too,' Corin said. He put down his knife and fork. 'There's nothing wrong with wanting to pay your way, rather than having everything handed to you.'

'So you won't mind if Mim comes to clean your house?' Bea persisted. 'We can't upset Mrs Dennis and her team by letting her help here and Ros has Anya.'

'I'm perfectly capable of cleaning my own house. How is she supposed to find a job and earn money if she's always doing favours for us?' Corin leaned forward and peered down the table at Mim. 'Sorry to talk about you as if you're not here. What sort of work are you looking for? What qualifications do you have?'

'I have an A level in maths.' It sounded a bit pathetic on its own but Mim was proud of it. It had been an achievement against the odds. 'My experience is in working in a hotel but I'll do anything. I don't mind cleaning, or shop work, or bar work. I can't afford to be choosy. As long as it pays, I'll do it.'

She felt a number of curious gazes land on her as she said that. How could they understand, sitting around a table piled with wasted food and bottles of wine, what it was like to have nothing? She saw a flash of sympathy on Corin's face and quickly looked down at her plate. She didn't need anyone's pity.

'I've nothing vacant at the moment but Janet's your answer if that's the sort of work you want,' Bill said, setting down his glass with a decisive thump. 'She owns the shop and the pub in the village, and has a couple of holiday cottages. It's quite the business empire. She might have something for you.'

'Oh Daddy, you can't send Mim to work for Janet,' Lia replied, pulling a face.

'Does she have a vacancy?' Mim asked. It sounded perfect, if she ignored Lia's ongoing grimaces and whatever they meant.

'She always has vacancies.' Corin smiled. 'This is one occasion where you might decide to be choosy.'

'Nonsense,' Bill said. 'Janet's a character but harmless enough.'

It wasn't a gushing recommendation but was good enough for Mim.

'Will she be open tomorrow?' Mim asked. 'Could you show me the way?'

'Go with Corin,' Ros suggested. 'She once let him off a penny when he didn't have enough money for sweets. It's her only recorded act of kindness. He might be your lucky charm.'

'But we were going out for petrol anyway,' Mim said, appealing to Bill.

'Oh, Corin can deal with all that. You don't want an old dog like me when he's around. Besides, if all goes well with Janet, you may not need that petrol, eh?'

This time Mim was ready when the knock came on the caravan door the next morning; she wasn't going to let another member of the Howard family catch her in her pyjamas. She opened the door and Dickens trotted in while Corin leant on the veranda balustrade with his back to her, looking out over the field of caravans. A fine drizzle hung in the air and was making the ends of his hair curl out at the nape of his neck but at least he was properly dressed today in boots and a thick coat that looked like an old favourite but didn't have any obvious holes. He certainly didn't share the sartorial elegance of his family from what Mim had seen so far. He turned and smiled.

'Ready?' he asked. She nodded. 'Come on, Dickens. Time to go.'

The dog obediently scampered out of the caravan and ran at Corin's heels as they followed the track towards the garage where Mim's car was parked.

'You don't have to come,' Mim said, matching his pace as he strode along. 'I can manage if you tell me how to find the petrol station and Janet's shop.'

'That's no good. I have instructions to pay for your petrol.'

'I can pay myself now, with the money I earned at the wedding.' It was one thing taking the money from Bill – she'd driven him down from Lancashire, after all. She felt more uncomfortable about Corin paying, however short of money she was. That felt more like charity and she wasn't a charity case. She'd hit an unlucky patch but there were thousands worse off than she was. 'You said it yourself. I'd prefer to pay my way, not rely on handouts.'

'Don't be so prickly. This isn't a handout. Filling your car with petrol is simply putting you back in the position you were in before you met Mum and Dad.' Corin picked up a stick and threw it for Dickens. 'You shouldn't be out of pocket for doing them a favour.'

'Prickly?' Mim repeated. She was prepared to admit –

grudgingly – that he had a point with everything else, but not about that. 'It's not prickly to have principles.'

'Principles or pride? There's no shame in accepting help when you need it.'

As that was exactly what Mim would have said herself if their situations were reversed, she didn't give him the satisfaction of a reply and they were soon on their way to the petrol station, which was in the nearby village of Littlemead. They followed the drive past Vennhallow and various outbuildings until they reached the main road, where the end of the estate was marked by a fine pair of stone pillars and a small lodge. Corin explained that these were all that remained of a much grander mansion that had occupied the estate before being destroyed in a fire and replaced by the current house.

The narrow roads were much easier to navigate in daylight than they had been in the dark. After they'd stopped for petrol at an old-fashioned garage with an attendant who insisted on filling the car himself, the road wove downhill through what Mim guessed must be the centre of the village. Grey stone buildings lined the sides of the street, some with thatched roofs that Mim stared at in delight; she hadn't realised such things still existed apart from on jigsaw puzzles and biscuit tins. Most of the buildings appeared to be residential, although Mim spotted a café, a butcher's shop, an art gallery and a B&B. The village looked as if it hadn't changed in years, and it was particularly pretty at the moment with the Christmas decorations still in place. Oak barrels that might have been washed up from a shipwreck were positioned at regular intervals along the pavement, each containing a Christmas tree strung with bright fairy lights. Coloured lights blazed from some of the windows too, and almost every door was adorned with a wreath of holly, ribbons, and baubles. It was an utterly charming place and Mim couldn't stop smiling as she absorbed it all. Could she really have the chance to call this place home?

The road came to an abrupt end at a turning area at the bottom of the hill where a weathered wooden sign pointed pedestrians left or right for the South West Coast Path or straight down a cobbled path to the beach. Corin directed Mim to a small car park on the left. There was a surprising number of cars already there, and walkers were setting off in anoraks and boots, many with eager dogs pulling on their leads. Corin took a lead out of his pocket and clipped it to Dickens's collar.

'Don't get excited,' he told the dog. 'We're not going on a walk yet.' Dickens thumped his tail in reply.

'You don't need to come with me,' Mim said, getting out of the car. 'If you point me in the right direction, I'll be fine.'

'Let's see how you get on with Janet first.' Corin smiled and pointed at the end building on the opposite side of the road. It was a solid stone pub called The Boat

Inn, three storeys high but fairly narrow, with only two windows on either side of the central entrance. In contrast to the rest of the buildings in the village, the pub looked dark and uninviting, except for the tinsel stars that hung in the ground-floor windows, swinging in the draught. 'That's Janet's pub and the shop is next door.'

The shop was attached to the pub and looked as if it had been converted from several cottages knocked into one. As they crossed the road and got nearer, Mim could see that the large feature-window was filled with an eclectic mix of goods including boxes of fudge and biscuits, plastic toys, teddy bears wearing 'I heart Devon' jumpers and a selection of local walking guides. The sign above the window read, 'The Littlemead Deli'.

'It's gone upmarket since I was a boy,' Corin said, gesturing at the sign and grinning. 'Believe it or not. It was only a convenience store then. Are you ready?'

He tied Dickens to a bracket on the wall and went into the shop, holding the door for Mim. It was bigger inside than she'd expected, stretching back across almost the whole ground floor of the cottages. The shop was divided into two distinct areas. On the far left, there was a section for tourists, with more guidebooks, postcards, armbands, buckets and spades, flip flops, and souvenirs. The centre and right-hand side housed the food, with tinned goods and cans of beer rubbing shoulders with wicker baskets of fruit and vegetables and shelves of bread and cakes. At the far right-hand end there was a counter doubling as a refrigerated display filled with a selection of cheeses, pies and pasties, and cooked meats.

Apart from Mim and Corin, there were two other people in the shop: a woman behind the counter and a little boy filling a bag at the pick 'n' mix sweet display. As Mim watched, the boy took his bag and handed it to the woman, who inspected the contents carefully before announcing it would cost fifty pence. The boy stretched across the counter with his money, but the coin must have slipped out of his hand and there was a clunk as it hit the glass surface of the counter before rolling to the floor.

The boy dropped to his knees and after a few seconds of fruitless searching, Mim hurried forward to help, but there was no sign of his coin; it must have gone beneath the counter.

'I don't have any more money,' the boy said.

'No money, no sweets.' The woman turned to put the bag of sweets on a shelf behind her. The boy looked at Mim with tear-filled eyes.

'Hang on,' Mim said. She pulled her purse out of her bag, counted out fifty pence in change and carefully placed the coins on top of the counter. 'There's your money. Now can we have the sweets?'

The woman handed over the bag and as soon as it was safely in the boy's hands, he ran out of the shop, throwing a thank you over his shoulder.

'You're a soft touch,' the woman said. She was around

sixty, short and stocky with long steel-grey hair, and she was wearing the most extraordinary navy fleece with rabbits all over it. 'I dare say he tries that on regularly. Mark me, his coin will be safely in his pocket.'

'Well if that's true, you both benefit, as my coins are now safely in your till. Are you Janet?' Mim asked.

'Miss Thaw to strangers. What do you want with me?'

'I'm looking for work,' Mim said. She was beginning to understand why Lia had grimaced so much. If Corin thought Mim was prickly, what did he make of Janet? 'I heard you might have a vacancy here.'

'Did you indeed? And who's been telling you that? I haven't advertised a position.'

'I told her.' Corin stepped forward from the doorway and the transformation in Janet was instant. Her suspicious frown was replaced with a beaming smile and she tucked her hair back behind her ears. 'You're running a successful business empire, Janet. You must be in need of some help. You need to be careful not to wear yourself out.'

'Too true,' Janet agreed. 'Success like this takes hard work and no slacking. Not many could have done it on their own. When I read about today's snowflake generation, I despair.' She looked Mim up and down. 'What sort of work are you after? Shop or bar?'

'Either. Or both,' Mim said. 'I'll take whatever you're offering.'

'I haven't decided if I'm offering anything yet.' Janet heaved herself onto a stool behind the counter, revealing a pair of green corduroy trousers and white Crocs. 'Are you from the north?'

'I am. Well spotted.' Mim smiled. 'I expect some of your customers are too, if they come down here on holiday. They might be glad to meet someone who speaks their language.'

Janet ignored this.

'What experience do you have?' she asked.

'I've spent the last ten years managing a small hotel.' It wasn't exactly a lie – she had acted as manager even though she'd never officially been given the title. Mim decided that Janet didn't need to know all the ins and outs. 'I dealt with customers every day and ran a small bar at night. I have up-to-date food safety and hygiene certificates.'

'That's all well and good, but I'm more interested in whether you're a hard worker. Do you have any references?'

'No, I don't.' Janet shook her head, but Mim wasn't going to be defeated yet. 'I can't get one. My last employer died; that's why I'm looking for work.'

Not for the first time, Mim regretted her honesty – stupidity, more like. On that final day of packing up the hotel, she'd wondered whether she should write her own reference, while she still had access to the letter-headed paper, but she'd shied away from the deception. More fool her. But before she could explain further, Corin stepped forward and gave Janet a lazy grin.

'Don't worry about that, Janet. My family will vouch for Mim. She's honest and will pull her weight.'

Janet smiled back and nodded. Mim stared. Was it that easy? What must it be like to sail through life with the right name and the right accent, having doors automatically open for you? A streak of stubbornness kicked in. If she was going to get this job, she wanted to earn it on her own merits, even if it meant the door would slam in her face.

'Why don't we do a test?' Mim suggested. 'Corin can pretend to be a customer and I'll see if I can manage to serve him. If I pass, then you'll give me a trial run at the job.'

Janet agreed and Corin pottered round the shop, bringing back a basket containing six or seven items.

'The till can be temperamental,' Janet said, before Mim had taken the first item from the basket. 'Let's pretend it's not working today. How will you manage now?'

'I suppose I'll have to add it up in my head.' Mim took the items out of the basket and checked the prices. The extortionate cost of some of the goods almost distracted her from the task, but after checking the last packet of fudge she looked back at Corin. 'That will be £16.74 please.'

Janet slithered off her stool, took a calculator out of the drawer and added up the items.

'£16.74,' she repeated, with a grudging nod. She looked Mim up and down. 'You'll do. Thursday through Sunday, eight til six. Start this week on a two week trial. Take it or leave it.'

'I'll take it.'

'You're not bad looking, though you could do with making a bit more of yourself,' Janet said. Mim held back a smile at this damning appraisal. Should she buy herself a rabbit fleece? 'Howie is short staffed in the pub. What about the same nights in the bar, seven til close, if he's happy to take you on?'

'That would be great. Thanks.' Better than great. They would be long days but Mim was used to that. She'd rarely been off duty when she'd worked in the hotel with Gordon. Four days on the hours Janet had offered was a week's worth of regular work. It was a start, and she might be able to find other work for the free days. 'How much will you pay?' she asked.

'Minimum wage. You'll find me a fair employer.'

Mim wasn't convinced of that yet, given Janet's reaction to the little boy, but as long as she was paid on time for the hours she worked, she was sure she could put up with Janet's quirks. Janet was blunt, but Mim didn't mind that. She could be blunt herself. Perhaps they would get on in time. 'Is there any staff discount?'

'Five per cent off purchases over £30 in the shop,

excluding alcohol. I know how to look after my staff. I'll always reward hard work.'

It wasn't a tempting offer, but Mim still left the shop thrilled with the outcome of the encounter with Janet. She couldn't believe how her luck had changed in the course of a few days. She had somewhere to stay and she had a job. There was only one thing missing: somewhere to swim. It was her one indulgence, the only break she had regularly taken at the hotel. Powering through the water made her feel strong and in control, made her feel equal to everyone else, as if the past couldn't touch her. She couldn't manage without it. She glanced towards Corin who was strolling at her side, an amused smile on his face.

'Are there any swimming pools nearby?' she asked. 'Cheap ones, I mean. Council owned – I don't want a fancy gym. I just want to swim.'

'You like swimming?' Corin's smile widened. 'The nearest pool is in Sidmouth but there is a cheaper option.'

'Is there? What's that?'

Corin pointed down the path that was signposted to the beach and Mim headed that way. The cobbled path ran between a high wall then turned abruptly to the left where it met the beach. Dickens ran off without a backward glance, tearing along the beach and occasionally jumping up and barking at nothing. Mim wasn't so sure-footed. She took a few tentative steps onto the pebbles that made up the ground between the land

and the sea, slipping and sliding and stumbling on the unfamiliar terrain under her feet. It wasn't what she had expected.

'What sort of beach is this?' she asked. 'Shouldn't there be sand?'

Corin smiled.

'This is part of the Jurassic Coast. Many of the beaches are shingle along here. The geology is incredible. There's over 185 million years of history along the coast, from the Triassic, Jurassic, and Cretaceous periods. It's a fascinating place to live.'

He certainly looked enthusiastic but Mim hadn't understood half of what he'd said.

'Sorry.' He laughed. 'I don't suppose you're interested. What do you think of this? Is it a big enough swimming pool for you?'

He gestured across the sweep of the bay. Behind them, the land rose steeply on both sides of the village, creating tall cliffs that jutted out towards the sea in the distance, forming the crescent shape of the beach. In front of them, the sea was a shimmering expanse of grey that merged into the sky on the horizon.

'It's magnificent,' Mim said. She walked down to the edge of the shore and dipped her hand down to an incoming wave. She took it out again quickly. 'It's freezing!'

'It's not for the faint-hearted,' Corin said. 'Perhaps you'd be better in a proper pool.'

'No. This will be perfect. I'm not a soft southerner,' Mim said with a grin. 'I'm tough enough to cope with some cold water.'

'After seeing the way you handled Janet, I think you probably are.' Corin smiled at her. 'Ask Mum if you can borrow a wetsuit. She'll have a stack of our old ones somewhere. And don't go out on your own – at least until you're used to it. It's quite a different experience to swim with the current and the waves. Try asking Lia. She's rarely busy.'

Mim nodded, without much intention of following his advice. She didn't need a minder. She'd survived far worse than a few waves and pebbles underfoot. She wandered along the shore, her cheeks stinging with the cold, and stopped occasionally to scoop up stones and to admire how smooth they were and how much variety there was in the colours and shapes on close inspection. She'd expected the beach to be the yellow sand she'd seen in photographs and on television but she wasn't disappointed. The raw, natural beauty of this place tugged at her heart in a way she couldn't explain.

She looked up from a curious, heart-shaped stone and found Corin was studying her, while Dickens raced back towards him with a stick.

'Do you think you'll stay here?' he asked.

'For now,' she said. 'If I can pass Janet's two week trial.'

'There's no reason for you to go back to Lancashire? No family or friends pulling you back?'

'No. It's up to me where I go.'

'You're lucky.'

He spoke the words so quietly that Mim thought she must have misheard him. His earlier enthusiasm was gone, replaced by a sigh of resignation so that for a moment he was once again the man under the shadows of the trees on New Year's Eve. But he wasn't that man and the connection that Mim had imagined between them had never really existed. How could he say that *she* was lucky? He had the dream life, as far as she could see. Family. A home. Stability. Money. Everything she had craved throughout her life.

'It's a curious definition of luck to have no one and nothing,' she said. 'I wouldn't wish it on you.' She slipped the stone into her pocket. 'Can you tell me the way back now?'

Chapter Five

I t was almost a disappointment when Mim wasn't
woken by a member of the Howard family the next
morning. Almost a disaster too: if it had been Thursday,
she would have been late for work, she realised, as she
grabbed her watch and noticed that it was after nine-
thirty. She had the feeling that Janet wouldn't tolerate
unpunctuality. It answered her question about what she
should do today. Shopping would have to be her top
priority, and an alarm clock was now added to her
mental list.

Despite the late hour, she stretched out like a
starfish, enjoying the luxury of a proper bed. A double
bed too – she'd only had a single in the hotel, in a room
squashed up in the eaves that had been too poky to
rent out to guests. It might have been tiny, but that
room had been the world to her for the ten years she'd

stayed in it. She had knocked on the kitchen door of the hotel one teatime, weary and ragged after a day of fruitlessly begging for work, and found that she had called at the perfect time. Gordon's waitress had resigned that morning, his chef had called in sick, and he had been juggling every job himself. Mim had donned an apron, washed her hands and winged her way through the hardest shift of her life. By the end of the night, Gordon had offered her a job and a room, and the next day she had packed up her few possessions and left the hostel she'd been staying in. She'd spent the subsequent ten years repaying his kindness and his faith in her by working until she was exhausted and refusing a wage most months to help keep the hotel afloat. She'd never imagined that it would come to such an abrupt end.

Mim wiped away the tears that memories of Gordon provoked, even four months on. He'd taught her never to look back and that everyone was entitled to be judged on what they did today, not on the past. She wasn't going to waste another minute. She jumped out of bed, endured a quick, lukewarm shower, and dressed in the warmest jumper she owned; despite Bea's encouragement, she was still reluctant to use the fire, at least until she started paying some rent. She found a pen and pad of paper in a drawer and began a thorough inspection of the caravan. She hadn't paid much attention to the details over the last few days, when it had only been a roof over her head. Now she was going to stay, she would look at it with a new perspective.

It was a great space – the largest place she'd ever had to herself. The main external door was on the side of the caravan, and it opened into an open-plan living area, with a dining table, a television and a built-in L-shaped sofa that ran along the wall and under a large bay window at the front. One part of the room contained a compact kitchen, equipped with everything Mim could need. The rear half of the caravan was divided into a double bedroom with small en-suite, a twin bedroom and a family bathroom.

It had probably once been smart, as the upholstery and soft furnishings looked to be in a quality fabric in tonal shades of beige. Close inspection revealed the signs of neglect. Dust covered every surface, save for patches where Mim's movements had wiped it clean. There was a stain down one wall where water had leaked in from somewhere and there were some black patches of mould on the sofa fabric and on the lining of the curtains. There were green marks around the sinks and taps, and enormous cobwebs filled almost every corner. Mim wasn't daunted by any of it. It was hers. It was safe. It certainly wasn't the worst place she'd ever stayed. She settled down at the dining table and made a list of all the shopping she needed, with tea bags and milk topping the list and cleaning products filling the rest of it. Now all she needed to do was find a shop, as she had no intention of paying Janet's prices, even with the five per cent staff discount.

She wandered up to Vennhallow and was surprised when Bea answered the door herself; she'd half expected that they might have a butler to do that.

'Mim. Perfect timing,' Bea said, standing back and waving at her to enter. 'I was about to have morning tea, so you can keep me company. I've been abandoned.'

Mim followed Bea through the hall, where the Christmas tree was in the process of being dismantled, past the entrance to the kitchen and into a cosy room overlooking the garden at the back of the house. A log burner was blazing in the fireplace and Mim gravitated towards it while she studied the rest of the room. Like the kitchen, it was decorated in a modern style and looked recently refurbished. A sapphire-blue velvet sofa ran along the length of one wall, and two patterned armchairs were arranged next to a coffee table near the fire. It was all done with exquisite taste and, Mim guessed, an eye-watering amount of money. As she was admiring it all, a lady in a brown housecoat carried in a tray and set it down on the table.

'Thank you, Mrs Dennis. That looks lovely, as always.' Bea sat down on one of the armchairs and gestured for Mim to take the other one. 'Tea? Help yourself to cake.'

Mim didn't need telling twice. As well as a teapot and two cups and saucers, the tray also contained a platter containing slices of fruit cake, lemon drizzle cake, and what looked like homemade shortbread fingers. She started on a slice of fruit cake while Bea poured the tea.

'Are Lia and Olly not here?' Mim asked.

'No, Olly lives in London and headed home after breakfast. He's a lawyer and carries out pro bono work,' Bea replied. Mim had no idea what that meant, but nodded anyway. 'Lia went with him. She's going to spend a couple of days shopping before flying off to the Maldives with the girls. It's beautiful at this time of year. We were there last winter but couldn't risk going long haul this year with Bill's health as it is.'

'Isn't he well?' He looked hale and hearty enough to Mim, but then she remembered on New Year's Day how Lia had fussed over his diet.

'Oh, he had a scare six months ago, and worried us all senseless,' Bea said, picking up a biscuit. Her hand trembled. 'It's time he remembered he's not as young as he was and stepped back. Thank goodness Corin's come home to take over. I don't know what we'd do without him.' She smiled and made light of it, but Mim could see the worry was still close behind the surface. She wasn't surprised. She'd seen with Gordon how quickly an apparently active man could be cut down.

'Enough of that,' Bea continued. 'Let's not spoil our tea. Did you come over for anything special, my dear?'

'Only to see if you had a map I could borrow.'

'A map? Oh Mim, you've not decided to go home

after all, have you? I hope you haven't had second thoughts about Janet. Corin said you handled her wonderfully well.'

'No, I just need to go shopping and I don't want to get lost,' Mim said.

'Oh, you don't need to bother with that. Waitrose delivers.'

Mim chose a piece of lemon drizzle.

'I can't afford Waitrose,' she said.

'Ah yes, I didn't think.' Bea sipped her tea. 'Well, I'm sure there must be some other supermarkets in Sidmouth. Ask Mrs Dennis. She'll know the best places to go. But don't buy any vegetables. The garden produces more than enough for everyone.'

'I couldn't—'

'Nonsense.' Bea cut off the protest. 'Bobby delivers a box to all the family. I'll ask him to add the caravan to his list.' She leant forward as Mim picked up a biscuit. 'Forgive me for asking, my dear, but you did have breakfast this morning, didn't you?'

'No. But I will do, once I've been shopping.' Mim couldn't wait. She'd longed for a bowl of warm porridge every morning when she woke up in the car. Tomorrow she would have some and it would seem like the biggest treat in the world. Bea reached over and gave her hand a brief squeeze.

'Make sure you do. Come over for supper tonight. Mrs Dennis is making a casserole and there will be far too much for the two of us. You must come. We don't want you wasting away.'

Armed with an old road map from Bea and directions to the nearest discount supermarket from Mrs Dennis, Mim spent the next few hours eking out what cash she could spare on basic food rations and essential cleaning products. She then cleaned the caravan from top to bottom, until every cobweb and speck of dust was gone and every surface sparkled. It was good to get stuck into some hard work again, after too many idle days living out of her car.

After a day of physical labour, she woke up the next morning longing to have a swim, to loosen her muscles and free her thoughts. It was Thursday tomorrow, her first day working for Janet, and the long shift in the shop and the pub would leave her with no time to swim for the next four days. Corin had advised her to take Lia, but that was impossible now that Lia had gone off on holiday. She looked out of the big bay window at the front of the caravan. It was a grey but dry day, and the branches of the trees in the field were barely moving. There wasn't even the hint of a storm, as far as she could tell. She was a strong swimmer. She'd be perfectly safe on her own, wouldn't she?

Twenty minutes later, she was on the beach, shivering

in a towel and wondering whether she should have listened to Corin's suggestion that she borrow a wetsuit. Her old swimming costume offered little protection from the cold air that grazed her bare shoulders and sent goose bumps racing up her legs. There was more of a breeze down here on the shore than she'd anticipated and she watched the sea for a few minutes, trying to assess the size and strength of the waves, but without much idea. It wasn't calm but it didn't seem rough either. There was only one way to find out.

She packed the towel in the bag with her clothes, hoping that no one would steal her car keys, and picked her way over the stones to the water's edge. An incoming wave licked her toes and she shuddered at the temperature of the water, but it spurred her on; the sooner she was swimming, the sooner she would warm up. She clenched her fists and waded forward, gasping as the waves hit her thighs, until the water reached her waist and she ducked down and started swimming.

It wasn't like the swimming she'd been used to at the leisure centre in Burnley, and not only because the water was so cold. It was strange to taste the salt as the water touched her lips, rather than the chlorine. She felt more buoyant here than she did in the swimming pool too. The waves were stronger than they had appeared from the beach, and tried to buffet her back to the shore. She swam on, parallel to the beach, relishing the challenge and the feeling of power that came with each stroke forward. She loved every second. She had never felt more alive.

Then, as she paused and looked back to see if it was time to turn round, a sharp spasm of cramp pulled at the calf muscle in her right leg. She doubled over and a fierce wave caught her off guard, splashing over her head and into her ears. She scrabbled to put her feet down, but she was further out than she'd realised and slipped forward, swallowing a mouthful of water, before another large wave rushed over her back, pushing her down below the surface. She kicked her left leg and fought to reach the surface again, but her throat was burning with the sea water, her lungs were straining with the effort of not breathing, and as her limbs tired, she felt herself sinking lower down rather than rising up. Everything started to turn black.

She couldn't hold her breath for a second longer. She had no energy left to kick. This was it. The glorious new life she'd glimpsed here, the promise of a future so much brighter than her past, was over before it had begun. But as the panic faded away and Mim was filled with a peaceful acceptance of her fate, she felt a tug across her shoulders. Her head breached the water and she gasped in huge gulps of air as she was towed back to the beach and deposited on the pebbles.

Mim lay still for a moment, relishing the discomfort of the stones jabbing her bottom and the backs of her legs. Discomfort was good. Discomfort meant she was alive. Then coughs wracked her body, and she rolled over and threw up.

'That's good. Get it all out.' It was a female voice and the words were followed by a gentle pat on the back. Mim opened her eyes. A woman wearing a wetsuit was standing over her. She was aged around fifty and her chin-length hair was slicked back with water.

'Thank you,' Mim said, but she was overtaken by another bout of coughing before she could say more.

'Should I ring for an ambulance?' Another woman appeared and studied Mim – a younger woman, aged around forty, also wearing a wetsuit. Hers was dry.

'What do you think?' the first woman asked Mim. 'How do you feel? Do you want to be checked out?'

'No.' Mim didn't want to make a fuss or to shatter the peace of the morning by bringing an ambulance screaming through the village. 'I'm fine. Thank you.' Her words trailed off on a shiver.

'You're cold. Do you think you can walk? Take her other arm, Heather, and let's get her back to the camper to warm up.'

Without waiting for a reply, the two women took one arm each and hoisted Mim to her feet. She stumbled and coughed again – her legs felt boneless and her lungs ached – but she managed to stay upright. They staggered slowly across the beach towards her bag of clothes, and Heather, the younger of her two rescuers, picked it up and wrapped Mim in her towel before they carried on back up the path to the village car park. Every step felt like a marathon to Mim and she hadn't stopped shivering, even with the towel.

A racing-green VW camper van was parked at the far side of the car park, and the women helped Mim towards it. The gravel of the car park jabbed into the soles of her feet. The older woman unlocked the door, climbed inside, and drew the curtains across the windows.

'There you go,' she said, gesturing for Mim to enter the van. 'Go in and get dry and dressed. Can you manage on your own?'

Mim nodded. She took her bag from Heather and stepped into the camper van. She stripped off her wet swimming costume and threw it in the washing up bowl, then rubbed vigorously with the towel, trying to generate some heat. Her limbs still felt cold and clammy as she pulled her clothes back on. She was just struggling to pull her socks over her numb toes when the door slid open.

'Are you decent?' The older woman peered in. 'Budge up on to the driver's seat a minute. I need to get this wetsuit off.' She paused. 'I'm Karen, by the way, and that's Heather outside. It seems polite to exchange names before you see me in the buff.'

'I'm Mim.' She scrambled across the tiny floorspace to the driver's seat, which was rotated to face the interior of the van. Karen peeled off her wetsuit and threw it out of the open door before getting dressed. She opened a deep drawer that was concealed beneath a bench seat and took out a couple of blankets. She passed one to Mim and wrapped the other round her own shoulders.

'Here. Wrap yourself in that. I'll make you some tea.'

Karen produced an old-fashioned singing kettle and placed it on the small gas hob that formed part of the kitchenette running down one side of the van. As she opened the curtains, and Heather stepped in and slid the door shut, Mim took a proper look at her surroundings. It was a compact space but well kitted out, and gorgeously decorated. The upholstery was covered in luscious green velvet to match the exterior, and the kitchen cupboards were painted with a glossy cream coating and finished with gold handles. The colour scheme was reflected in the cushions and curtains as well as the rug on the floor. It was a wonderful, cosy space. Mim couldn't help a pang of envy. This would have made a perfect place to sleep in instead of the Volvo.

Karen handed round three mugs of tea and then sat on the bench seat next to Heather, facing Mim.

'Let's get one thing straight,' Karen said. 'Did I stop you or save you?'

'Stop me…? Oh!' Mim took a moment to realise what Karen meant. 'No, it was an accident. Of course I didn't mean to…' She shook her head and sipped her tea. It seemed to be half sugar, but she drank it gratefully, feeling the warmth returning to her limbs at last. 'I would never do that.'

'Good. In that case, you can have a biscuit.' Karen opened a kitchen cupboard and pulled out a packet of chocolate biscuits and offered it round. 'Life's precious to both of us. We don't like to see it wasted.'

For the first time, Karen smiled, and the atmosphere in the camper van relaxed; concern took over from the tension that Mim had hardly registered before.

'I'm sorry I ruined your swim,' Mim said, looking at Heather.

'Don't worry about it.' She smiled. 'This is our first time back after the Christmas break. I wasn't sure I could face the cold again. Now I can feel pleased with myself without having got wet. It's win-win.'

Mim's laugh turned into another cough.

'Do you swim here regularly?' she asked, when the cough subsided.

'Every Monday, Wednesday, and Friday,' Karen said. 'I've been doing it for a year now and Heather ... what is it? Four?'

'Just over.' Heather nodded. 'I started five months after we lost Carmel.' She looked at Mim. 'My daughter died of meningitis when she was two. I needed to get away from the house with all its reminders and do something that was physically and mentally exhausting. That probably sounds silly but it worked. It kept me sane.'

'And I started about a year ago,' Karen said. 'Similar reasons. My partner, Susie, had been diagnosed with breast cancer. She was going through hell and I couldn't make it better. I needed some time to myself, selfish though it sounds. Swimming was a way to get rid of my frustration and fear. I could then appear strong in front of Susie.'

'I met Karen on the beach one day, cursing at the sky.' Heather laughed. 'We've been friends ever since and now we swim together. Friends who swim together, stay together.'

They squeezed hands and the strength of the bond between them was obvious to Mim even though she'd never experienced anything like it herself. She had no friends, not the way these two were. Growing up, she'd never stayed in one place long enough to form close ties, and working all hours in the hotel had left no time for friendships. She hadn't missed it, because she hadn't realised what it meant, not until now. Perhaps this new life could bring new friendship? She wished it would.

'How is Susie doing?' she asked Karen.

'Well. She's finished the course of treatment and the prognosis is good.' Karen put her mug down on the kitchen worktop. 'So what's your story? You're not from round here any more than I am. I'm Derbyshire but I reckon you're further north. Lancashire?'

'Yes. I've always lived there. I only arrived here a few days ago.'

'Have you brought your family with you?' Heather asked.

'I don't have any family.'

'No children?' Karen said. 'You're young. There's plenty of time to decide if that's what you want.'

'No family at all,' Mim said. Karen and Heather both stared at her, looking aghast. Perhaps they imagined some horrific accident had wiped them all out. It was much less dramatic than that. Although she didn't dwell on the past, she didn't think it fair to conceal it now, when these women had shared far worse stories with her.

'I was brought up in care,' Mim explained. 'I never knew my dad and I was taken away from my mum when I was eight. She had a history of violent relationships and couldn't keep me safe. I lived in a series of foster homes and care homes until I was moved to a hostel when I was eighteen.'

'You poor soul,' Heather said, and she took a couple of steps across the camper and gave Mim a brief half-hug. 'Where's your mum now?'

'I don't know. She abandoned any attempt to keep in touch years ago.' Mim met the women's looks of pity and smiled. 'Don't feel sorry for me. I was rescued from a bad situation. I kept my head down, worked hard, and didn't get into trouble. And then ten years ago I was given a second chance by an amazing man who didn't care about the past and who gave me stability for the first time in my life. It all worked out for the best.'

'The best?' Karen repeated. 'I'm not sure I could be so sanguine about it.'

'Come swimming with us,' Heather said. She inched forward on her bench seat until her knees were almost touching Mim's. 'Be part of our little group. If you want to, I mean. We swim for a while and then come back here for a cup of tea and a chat. It helps.'

'Are you sure?' Mim asked. She couldn't think of anything she'd like more. 'You two have been through terrible things. I don't want to get in the way.'

'You won't,' Karen said. 'We've suffered because we have people we love. I'd take that pain any day over having no one to love at all. You're more than qualified to join us.'

Chapter Six

It was like old times again when Mim heard an abrupt bang on the caravan door on Thursday morning. At least it didn't wake her up this time. She'd invested in the cheapest alarm clock she could find and it had done the job of waking her up in perfect time to have her breakfast before going to the village shop for her first day of work.

She was surprised to see Corin on her doorstep, wearing his scruffy old coat teamed with what looked like an expensive cashmere scarf. Dickens trotted in and jumped onto the sofa where he sat and stared at Mim. Corin stared at her from where he stood outside.

'Is something the matter?' she asked. 'I'm in the middle of breakfast. Don't forget I'm on probation with Janet. I can't be late on my first day.'

'From what I hear, you almost didn't make your first day at all,' he said.

'What are you talking about?'

'I warned you not to go swimming on your own.'

'Urgh.' Mim sank down on to her chair, and scooped up a spoonful of porridge. She couldn't face this on an empty stomach. 'Have you tramped over here to say I told you so? That's such an annoying habit.'

'Not as annoying as someone who deliberately ignores good advice.'

Mim swallowed her porridge.

'I didn't ignore it. I was going to ask Lia to come with me but she's on holiday. Didn't you know that?'

He shrugged. 'It's impossible to keep up with her social diary. There are other people besides Lia in the world.'

'Not in my world. I didn't know anyone else. Apart from Janet, I suppose, but I think it's too early in our relationship to invite her on a swimming date.'

'She'd scare the current away.' Corin laughed grudgingly but stopped when Mim gave a throaty cough, a lingering symptom of her immersion yesterday; she'd tried to hold it in but hadn't managed it. Corin pulled out some sheets of paper from his coat pocket and tossed them on the table in front of Mim. 'Here. I've printed out some details about the swimming pool in Sidmouth. It's not that expensive if you only want to swim and it would be safer.'

Mim carried on eating her porridge while she read the information. She must have been fairly close to the pool when she went shopping, so she knew it wasn't too far away, and it looked a similar set up to the leisure centre she had used in Burnley. But … Gordon had given her the membership in Burnley for her birthday last year. She'd have to pay for this one herself. Corin had a very different idea of 'not that expensive' than she did.

'Thanks, but I can't afford it,' she said, folding the pages back up and sliding them towards Corin. 'The monthly membership would buy me food for at least a week.'

'Okay.' Corin made no move to pick up the sheets again. 'I'll pay for your membership.'

'Why would you do that?'

He sighed.

'Don't sound so suspicious. Can't we say it's because I'm a kind and generous soul and want you to stay alive?'

Mim pushed her chair back and took her bowl over to the sink. She filled it up with water to soak.

'You mean because you're rich,' she said, turning at last. 'It's easy to be kind and generous when you won't even notice the money leaving your account.'

'You don't mince words, do you?'

'What's the point?' Mim said. 'You can hardly deny how rich you are. You live in an enormous house. You holiday in places like the Maldives. You drive cars that cost as much as a house where I'm from. I don't know why you pretend to be something you're not by wearing a scruffy coat and shoes.'

'I don't pretend to be anything. You're talking about my family, not me.' Corin looked down at himself. 'And I happen to like this coat. It's covered my back through some tough times.'

Tough times? Mim wondered how tough his life had ever been; had he once had to drink fizzy wine instead of Champagne?

'Look, I get that you mean well,' she said, 'but I've already told you I don't want to be treated as a charity case. I have a job – if I ever manage to get to it. I can pay my own way for anything I need. Membership of a swimming pool is a luxury I don't need, especially when the sea is free. But thanks for looking into it,' she added, thinking that she may have sounded too ungrateful. They came from such different worlds. He'd probably been brought up to believe that money was the answer to everything. She knew that hard work and a lot of luck were the real answers.

'Fine,' Corin said. 'If you won't accept my charity, what about my company? I'll go swimming with you.'

'You?'

He smiled.

'Was that an enthusiastic yes? Just checking in case I misunderstood your accent.'

Mim grinned. He was persistent, she had to give him credit for that.

'You don't need to bother,' she said. 'I met two women on the beach and we've arranged to swim together. You can use the free time to go clothes shopping.' He laughed. 'Now I've really got to go. If Janet sacks me for being late, I'll be heading straight to your door with my begging bowl.'

'I thought you weren't coming,' Janet said, as she unlocked the door for Mim.

'I'm ten minutes early,' Mim pointed out. She'd waited in the car for five minutes, worried she might annoy Janet if she turned up too early so it was galling to face criticism.

'You start your shift at eight. I need to train you before you can do the job properly and start earning money.' Janet stood back to let Mim enter the shop. 'I'll have to dock your wages for the first hour. I'm not paying while you're learning. It's not a good start, is it?'

It wasn't, and Mim gritted her teeth and made a mental note to arrive at the pub half an hour early that evening in case training was needed there too. She had a horrible suspicion that Janet had deliberately not told her about the required training to put her on the back foot. Besides, what training could there possibly be? How to spot the difference between a tin of peas and a tin of carrots?

Forty minutes later, Mim had discovered that the training consisted of a brief introduction to the till and the slicing machine, and the delivery of a lengthy list of rules. These were varied and extensive: no giving away samples of cheese; no letting customers off the correct money, even for a penny; no more than three unaccompanied children in the shop at one time; names and addresses to be taken from any child who ate a sweet while filling a bag at the pick 'n' mix; more than three visits to the toilet each day would be viewed with suspicion. Janet had thought of everything.

'Will we both be working in the shop at the same time?' Mim asked, when Janet had finally exhausted the regulations. She hoped not. She liked plain talking but Janet might test that to the limit.

'I'll be observing for a few days to see how you get on.' Janet heaved herself onto the stool behind the counter. 'You won't be on your own until I'm satisfied you're a hard worker. Don't forget you're on trial.'

It was a long morning. There was a steady flow of customers in the shop and Mim would have enjoyed it if Janet hadn't been there, scratching away with her pencil and paper as she made a note of something Mim had done wrong.

'You chatted too long to Mrs Windsor,' was Janet's

first complaint. 'She'll not stop once you give her an opening. You can't risk a queue forming.'

'The man who bought that map was probably a tourist,' was the next comment. 'You should have upsold some fudge or biscuits.'

'You need to be more careful when cutting a piece of cheese.'

Mim had bitten her tongue at a lot of the feedback, but she couldn't let this last one go.

'What do you mean?' she asked. 'The customer wanted 250g and I cut 246g. I thought that was pretty good for my first go.'

'It was under. You never cut under. You'll find you can go over by up to ten per cent and the customer will still buy it. I didn't get where I am by giving away easy profit like that.'

In the thirty minute break she was allowed for lunch, Mim wandered down to the beach and let the sea breeze blow away the clouds of frustration that hung over her shoulders. The job was straightforward and she was enjoying meeting more of the villagers, but Janet was testing her patience already. Unfortunately, she needed the money too desperately to do anything but nod and bite back a sigh as Janet picked her up on some other spurious pretext or insisted on checking the change she was giving a customer for the umpteenth time. Mim couldn't wait to make it through her probation period and lose her chaperone.

In the middle of the afternoon, a man in his early thirties came into the shop, browsed around and then dumped a pile of biscuit packets on the counter next to the till. He was wearing muddy trousers and, despite the cold weather, a T-shirt which showed off the huge muscles in his arms. Blond hair framed an attractive face that still boasted a slight tan.

'Hello,' he said, giving Mim a friendly smile. 'You're not Janet.'

'Well spotted.' Janet was on a bathroom break; she was apparently allowed more than three each day but Mim wasn't complaining as it gave her at least ten minutes without scrutiny. 'Do you want her? She'll be back in a minute.'

'No.' He shuddered. 'Are you Mim?'

'Yes. How do you know that?'

'The accent. We don't hear many northern ones down here, not out of holiday season. I'm Bobby. You met my sister Heather yesterday.'

'Heather the swimmer? Yes, I did.' Mim smiled and then realised that Bobby was likely to have heard the story about her disastrous swimming attempt if he'd spoken about her with Heather. 'It's all a bit embarrassing. I was lucky she arrived with Karen when she did.'

'It hasn't put you off the sea, has it?'

'Not at all. I'm not giving up after one go. I was fine until I got a cramp.'

'Try warming up before you go in,' he said. 'You'll soon get used to it.'

Mim smiled and rang the biscuits through the till. Why couldn't Corin have been so relaxed instead of barging in with his 'I told you so' attitude and his offer of charity? Sometimes kind words were needed more than actions.

'You'll let me know if you have a favourite veg, won't you?' Bobby continued. He held out a crumpled ten pound note to Mim.

'Veg?' Mim was confused by the abrupt turn in the conversation. 'You've walked past it.' She pointed to the baskets of over-priced fresh produce. Bobby pulled his face.

'You've not bought any of that, have you? I'll be bringing you a box tomorrow. I thought Bea would have mentioned it.'

'Bea? Oh – you're Bobby the gardener?' That explained not only the muscles, but also the roughened hands that were ingrained with earth. 'Are you sure you don't mind?'

'No, there's loads to go round and it's better quality than anything you'll find here. More variety too. You'll probably get some cabbage, carrots, sprouts, parsnips and Jerusalem artichoke tomorrow.'

'Jerusalem artichoke?' Mim laughed. 'I wouldn't have a clue what to do with it. You can leave that one out.'

'All the more for Lia then. It's her favourite.'

A faint colour crept over Bobby's cheeks as he said this. That was interesting.

'Lia's away at the moment,' she told him. 'Didn't you know?'

'No. Where's she gone?'

'The Maldives. I don't even know where that is.'

'It's outside my price bracket,' Bobby said. 'That's all I need to know.'

He said this with such a glum air that Mim's suspicions were heightened even further. Did he like Lia? She wondered if he would stand any chance if he did. Bill had given the impression that her love life was like a constantly revolving door, with a new man entering as soon as the old one was on his way out. And would Bill and Bea approve if Lia did show an interest in their gardener? He probably ranked higher than Mim on the social ladder, but they were both well below the Howards. There was quite a leap from letting someone like her stay in an unused caravan to welcoming them as a member of the family.

'What's all this, Bobby Knight?' Janet asked, shuffling back into the shop and clearly catching only the tail end of the conversation. 'If you've not got the money for those biscuits, you can put them back.'

'He's already paid for them,' Mim said, and while Janet checked the till Bobby made a cowardly escape and dashed out of the shop.

'What are you doing here so early?' the large, gruff man behind the bar asked, when Mim turned up at the Boat half an hour early for her first shift later that night. 'You won't get paid until seven, so you don't want to be working a minute before that.'

'Don't I need training?' Mim asked.

'Have you pulled a pint before?'

'Yes.'

'Can you work a till?'

'Yes.'

'Can you carry a tray of empty glasses?'

'Yes.'

'That's good enough for me.' The man held out his hand. 'I'm Howie. Pleased to meet you. You've been in the shop all day, haven't you? How'd you find that?'

'It was busy,' Mim replied. She had no idea who Howie was and whether he was related to Janet, so she decided to be careful. He guffawed at her response.

'I'll bet. Janet worked you until you were ready to drop, I expect. You'll find we operate differently here. Have you eaten?'

'I had an apple.' There hadn't been time for much else.

'That'll never do,' he said. 'You're no use to me if you faint away. Go to the kitchen and get a bowl of soup down you.'

'I can't afford to buy soup.'

Howie laughed again.

'Who said anything about buying it? I'm the boss here. It's a perk of the job as far as I'm concerned.'

Mim headed in the direction he pointed, through the kitchen door, thinking she was definitely going to enjoy her nights in the pub more than the shop work. The chef gave her a steaming bowl of tomato soup and a couple of slices of bread, and Mim took them through to the bar. It was fairly empty at this time, and she found a quiet table near the toilets from where she could look around at her new workplace.

The Boat was an old-fashioned pub which had apparently escaped any urge to modernise it. It felt friendlier inside than it had looked from the outside. The floor was stone-flagged and a defined groove had been worn from the front door to the bar. A huge fire blazed in a hearth on one side of the pub. Brass lights hung on the walls, which were otherwise covered in old photos of boats and fishermen, and with pieces of equipment that Mim guessed came from ships although she had no idea what they were. A banquette covered in red velvet ran along the main stretches of wall, and an assortment of mismatched tables and chairs filled the centre of the pub. Looking round, Mim wondered what sort of customers came here. It was the only pub in the village, as far as she had seen, and it certainly had a cosy warmth to it, but she couldn't imagine that many young people would come in. The three customers in at the moment couldn't have seen sixty for some time, but that suited Mim. Most of the visitors to Gordon's hotel had been middle-aged and upwards. She was going to feel right at home here.

As soon as seven o'clock came, Mim joined Howie behind the bar and he quickly showed her where everything was. Thursday night was traditionally quiet, he explained, except for the book-club ladies who were due in half an hour; they met here every week, although they opened more bottles of wine than books. Friday and Saturday night were always packed, with even more customers visiting over the holiday season.

Mim was pleased to see a familiar face when the book club arrived. Heather was one of the dozen or so ladies who invaded the pub in a cloud of perfume and noise. She waved at Mim and approached the bar while her companions occupied the table that had been reserved for them by the fire.

'Hello,' Heather said, unwinding her scarf. 'I didn't expect to see you in here. When did you start?'

'Tonight is my first shift. I work in the deli by day and the pub by night.'

'It's a shame you're working. I was going to ask if you wanted to join the book club. It would help you to get to know more people.'

'Thanks, but I'm not much of a reader,' Mim said.

'Really?' Heather looked shocked. 'You mustn't have

found the right book yet, that's all. You need to keep trying.'

'I've tried enough. The books were either too grim or too happy. I've seen enough grim, and I don't believe in happily-ever-after.'

'Well we'll have to see what we can do about that. Have you met my brother Bobby yet?'

Mim laughed. She couldn't accuse Heather of subtlety – although if her suspicions about Lia were correct, Heather wasn't very observant.

'I have,' she said. 'He seems nice. But please don't even think about matchmaking. I'm not into all that love and romance stuff. It's the last thing I'm looking for.'

Heather gave a resigned shrug and joined her friends. Mim was kept busy for the next hour or so serving their drinks and food, and dealing with the other customers who gradually wandered in over the course of the evening. By nine o'clock she thought the bar had reached its peak and Howie had just suggested she take a fifteen minute break when the door opened and another cluster of seven or eight people hurried in out of the cold, Corin, Bobby, and Dickens amongst them. They dragged a couple of tables together and settled down on the opposite side of the pub from the book club.

What were the chances? Almost half of Mim's acquaintances in the village seemed to have descended on the pub tonight. She stared at Corin's back as he shrugged off his coat and scarf and threw them on the banquette. Was it a coincidence? He knew she had started work here tonight. Was he checking up on her? His reputation was on the line, after all, as he had vouched for her with Janet.

He turned before she could avert her gaze and smiled at her. She looked away quickly and shuffled the beer mats along the bar, wishing she had taken that break when she'd had the chance.

'How has your day been?' Corin materialised in front of her at the bar. 'I'm delighted to see that you survived your first day with Janet. Are you the best of friends now?'

'I wouldn't go that far.' Mim responded to his laughing smile with a reluctant grin. 'But I haven't been sacked yet so I'm taking that as a successful day.'

'Very successful. Her record is thirty minutes, but that wasn't so much a sacking as a mutual parting of the ways.' He laughed. 'It was Olly. He took it into his head to obtain work experience to enhance his university application. I don't think he made it beyond the rule that he had to cover his carefully curated outfit with an apron.'

Corin's easy laugh was infectious and it was impossible not to join in.

'That was never going to be an issue for me,' Mim said. 'The apron was probably the most expensive thing I was wearing.'

Corin looked her up and down – or as much as was

visible over the bar.

'You look perfectly charming to me.'

'What can I get you?' Mim asked. 'I assume you're here to get the drinks, not to make cheesy comments.'

He reeled off a list of orders and Mim lined up the glasses on a tray.

'And one for yourself,' Corin said, as he held out his bank card to pay. Mim picked up the card machine and hesitated.

'Do you buy Howie a drink?' she asked.

'Sometimes, but he's fond of a double whisky so it can be an expensive business.' Corin smiled. 'Let me guess. You think I offered out of charity.'

Mim smiled.

'Did you?'

'No. I was being polite, not rich, and to prove it I'm now limiting my offer of a drink to a maximum spend of £2.50.'

'In that case, I'll have half a pint of bitter.' She held out the card machine. 'Thanks.'

She watched as he carried the drinks back to his group, and took a seat in the centre of them all. It was easy to make friends if you were wealthy and could buy the drinks, she supposed, although he seemed to have chosen an odd selection of friends. They were a group of men across a broad age range, with Bobby probably the youngest and the oldest one a similar age to Bill. They all looked like working men, not posh ones, and she wondered what Corin could possibly have in common with them. Clearly something – he looked entirely at ease, in the thick of the group, and there was lots of laughing and chatting going on.

The book club left around ten and Heather popped over to remind Mim of the arrangements for their first swim together on Monday. Some of Corin's friends gradually drifted out, until by closing time only he and Bobby were left. As Bobby left the pub, Corin joined Mim at the bar.

'It's closing time,' Mim said. 'Didn't you hear the bell for last orders?' She'd be amazed if he'd missed it. Very appropriately, there was an old ship's bell behind the bar and to her great delight, Howie had let her ring it.

'I did,' he replied. 'You rang it with such gusto they probably heard it at Vennhallow.' Mim grinned. Perhaps she had been rather hearty with it. 'I came over to see if you can manage to get home safely.'

'I expect so. I've figured it out now. Left at the top of the hill, then right then left. That's it, isn't it?'

'Spot on. You're like a local already.'

'As long as I don't open my mouth and reveal the flat vowels.' She smiled and Corin laughed.

'In that case, I'll wish you goodnight.'

He'd taken a few steps away when Mim called out.

'Corin?' He turned, still smiling. 'Thanks for checking.'

'Any time,' he said.

Chapter Seven

It was late January before Lia returned from the Maldives. She burst into the shop late one Sunday morning, startling Mim who was cleaning the shelves during a lull in trade. Although, from her experience so far, the whole of Sunday seemed to be a lull. She rarely had more than a dozen customers, and she wondered why Janet paid her to mind the shop when even her slim wages must outweigh the profit. Not that she would ever ask. The wages might be slim but they could be made to stretch surprisingly far with some clever shopping.

It helped, of course, that she was living in the static caravan rent free and bill free. Bea had even insisted that Mim should use the washing machine at the main house when she'd caught Mim handwashing her clothes in the sink. Bobby delivered a box of fresh fruit and vegetables twice a week, so Mim was eating well. It was hard to believe that a month ago she had been sleeping in her car and eating the cut-price food from the supermarket that was about to be thrown away. She owed Bill and Bea everything and her only complaint was that they wouldn't let her do anything in return. Her debt to them was mounting by the day.

Lia bounded round the shelves and air kissed Mim's cheeks. She looked amazing: her skin glowed with a natural tan and her hair had been transformed into a sheet of ash blonde.

'What do you think?' Lia asked, swishing her hair around her shoulders. 'I had it done in London yesterday at the most divine salon. I won't tell you how much it cost because you would be horrified, darling, but some of the top models go there so you can probably guess.'

Mim thought she probably couldn't. Her last haircut had cost £15 over a year ago and she felt she'd been robbed at that price. But there was no doubt that Lia looked gorgeous and was wanting to be told that, so Mim obliged.

'Did you have a good time?' she asked, as she ran a damp cloth over the shelf to pick up the dust.

'The. Best. Time. Ever,' Lia said. 'There was such a fabulous crowd there this year. We had a blast.' She stopped and peered towards the counter. 'Janet isn't here, is she? This might not be fit for her disapproving ears.'

'She'll be here in ten minutes to cover my lunch break.'

It had taken almost three weeks but at last Janet had decided that she could trust Mim to run the shop on her own. It had made the hours in the shop a lot more fun, although Mim still had to be on her guard. She'd discovered that Janet lived in the flat upstairs and she still popped in for occasional spot checks.

'Perfect,' Lia said now. 'Come home with me for lunch and I can tell you all about it.'

'There isn't time. I only have half an hour.'

'Oh, she really is so mean. I'm amazed you've managed to bear it here for so long, darling. What do you usually do? Go to the Boat?'

'I walk along the beach if the weather's fine.'

Lia glanced out of the window. It was one of the best days that Mim had experienced since arriving in Devon and a weak sun was bathing the village with the illusion of warmth. Lia sighed.

'Very well. The beach it is, although it really won't compare to Constance Halaveli.'

'Is she one of your friends?' Mim asked, confused. Lia's laughter pealed round the shop.

'It's a beach, darling; one of the most fabulous places in the Maldives. I'll show you a picture in a minute.'

Mim finished stacking the shelf while Lia wandered round touching and inspecting everything in the shop. She paused at the pick 'n' mix sweets and helped herself to a couple. She put a finger to her lips, her eyes sparkling.

'You'll get me sacked,' Mim said, laughing. 'She probably knows—'

She broke off just in time when she heard a warning creak from the stairs.

'Swallow quickly,' she hissed to Lia, who obliged and stuck out her tongue to show her mouth was empty. She was still laughing when Janet shuffled in.

'What's going on?' Janet asked. 'Why aren't you working?'

'I am.' Mim waved her duster. 'I've cleaned and restocked all the tinned soup and vegetables. What do you think?'

'Hmm.' It wasn't high praise but Mim had realised by now that it was the best she was going to get from Janet. Janet looked at her watch. 'Your thirty minutes has started. Don't be late.'

Mim grabbed her coat and hurried Lia out of the shop. They headed across the road to the footpath that led down onto the beach.

'What happened there?' Mim asked. 'Janet didn't acknowledge you at all. I thought the Howards were her favourite family. She gushed when Corin went in.'

'It's a mystery, isn't it?' Lia laughed. 'I can't explain why I don't have the same effect on women as my gorgeous, unattached older brother. '

'Urgh.' Mim pulled a face. 'You're not telling me she fancies him?'

'Of course she does, darling. Who doesn't? Apart from me, obviously, because that would be totally gross.'

'I don't.'

'Oh, are you a lesbian?' Lia looked at Mim with interest as they walked across the pebbles. 'You should go and visit Olly in London. His boyfriend manages one of the best gay bars in town.'

'I'm not a lesbian,' Mim said, and immediately regretted the confession when Lia grinned and carried on.

'So what's wrong with Corin?' she asked. 'I mean, have you seen his eyelashes? I would literally die to have those long, dark lashes. He'll get under your skin in the end. He always does.'

'He won't be getting under, over, or anywhere near my skin, thank you very much,' Mim replied. 'I'm not looking for anything like that.' And if she were, she wouldn't be looking in Corin's direction. He was friendly enough but she wasn't convinced that any substance lay beneath the surface charm. He didn't seem to do much apart from take Dickens for a walk and drink pints in the Boat. She supposed he didn't need to when he had family money to rely on. Yet he seemed totally unaware of how privileged he was, judging by his words at New Year. He made her laugh but she could never be seriously interested in someone like that. She smiled to herself. It was never going to be an issue. Why would the son and heir look twice at her?

'It's probably just as well,' Lia said, 'because he's shown no sign of finding a partner. He's a confirmed bachelor, to Mummy's great despair. She's been waiting for him to carry on the family name for years.'

To Mim's relief, Lia changed the subject and spent the next twenty minutes talking non-stop about her holiday while Mim munched on the sandwich and banana she'd brought for her lunch. Lia's exploits were totally alien to anything in Mim's experience. The only beach she'd ever known was this pebbly one under her feet, not the endless stretches of white sand that Lia described. The only hotel she'd known was Gordon's, where the age of the average guest was sixty and no one had asked for a cocktail in the ten years that Mim had worked there. It was endlessly fascinating to hear about such a different type of life.

'You must go one year, if you can,' Lia said, when she finally reached a break in her stories. 'You'd adore it, darling.'

'I probably would,' Mim agreed. 'But I've never had a holiday, so I'd love anything. When I was growing up, it would have seemed like the best adventure in the world to stay in your parents' caravans for a few days.'

'Would it?' Lia looked thoughtful as they made their way back up to the village. 'It is a shame they're standing empty in that case.'

'Why does no one use them?'

'Oh, it was one of Daddy's Grand Ideas,' Lia said,

giving the words definite capital letters. She laughed. 'He always has a scheme on the go, of one sort or another. For the past few years, he's been determined to become the Dyson of irons. I don't know what went wrong with the caravans. I'll have to ask Mummy.' She paused as Mim reached the door of the shop and opened the door. Twenty-nine minutes had whizzed by in Lia's company. Mim couldn't risk being late. 'You're not working tomorrow, are you?' Lia asked. 'I'll pop round after breakfast. I've had the most brilliant idea!'

Mim had enjoyed a swim with Heather and Karen, eaten breakfast, stripped and washed her sheets and made a start on cleaning the outside of her caravan by the time Lia showed up the next day. It was technically after breakfast, she supposed, even though hers had been several hours ago and she was already thinking about lunch. Perhaps time ran at a different pace in the big house?

'What *are* you doing?' Lia asked, as she joined Mim at the front of the caravan. Mim looked at the sponge in her hand and the bucket of soapy water at her feet. Wasn't it obvious?

'I'm cleaning,' she said. 'The windows are filthy.'

'I'll mention it to Mummy. Our window cleaner can do that for you. It will ruin your nails.'

'Too late for that,' Mim said cheerfully, inspecting her short nails. She'd spent ten years at the hotel putting her hands in much worse than soapy water. It was no use being vain now. Lia looked horrified.

'I've had the most amazing idea,' she said, while Mim continued to wash the windows. 'We can rent out these caravans to poor people, who can't afford a holiday abroad. People like you – didn't you say you'd have loved to stay here?'

'Yes, I would,' Mim said, dropping her sponge in the bucket and wiping her wet hands on her jeans. 'But we couldn't afford a holiday at all, not just a foreign one. And then I was living in care, so it was never an option.'

'You were in care?' Lia stared at Mim. 'But you're so … normal.'

'Thanks.' Mim smiled. 'And so are many other people brought up in care. Who'd have thought it?'

'Oh yes, of course.' Lia grimaced. 'Sorry, darling. That was awful of me, wasn't it? Shall we forget I said that?'

'With pleasure. Have you spoken to Bill and Bea about your idea?'

'Not exactly.' Lia grinned. It was impossible not to like her, however tactless she was. 'I asked Mummy why they stopped renting out the caravans. She said they were only a diversion, really, when Daddy was between inventions. They'd tried to target an upmarket customer but then glamping became all the rage rather than traditional static caravans and bookings trailed off. They couldn't compete with the huge caravan parks along the coast for the general holidaymaker, as we didn't have a pool or a bar, so it all fizzled out.'

It was astonishing to Mim that they had let it fizzle without a fight. Gordon's hotel hadn't been a huge success when she'd arrived but they'd started trying out new ideas and promotions and had never thought of giving up. Perhaps it was simply a matter of motivation. Some people needed a living and some people needed a hobby.

'So what do you suggest?' Lia asked. 'Is there a way we can use the caravans to help people who can't afford a holiday? I thought it was such a good idea.'

'It is,' Mim said. 'But I'm not sure it will really make a difference unless you start giving away holidays.'

'Well why shouldn't we?' Lia clapped her hands. 'That's the answer. We give the holidays away. I mean, it's not as if we need the money. It's perfect, isn't it?'

'You might want to speak to Bill and Bea about that.'

'I have a better idea,' Lia said. 'Let's go and speak to Corin.'

'Corin?' Mim repeated. 'Why him?'

Lia was already striding away across the grass.

'Because he's sure to know how to do it,' she called over her shoulder.

Mim wasn't sure what made Corin so qualified on the subject but she abandoned her bucket, locked the caravan, and dashed after Lia.

To Mim's surprise, they walked past Vennhallow and on down the track that led out to the village. She was about to ask where exactly they were going to find Corin when Bobby crossed their path, pushing a wheelbarrow full of cut logs. Despite the cold late-January weather, he was wearing a vest top that showed off thick muscles in his arms. He stopped when he saw them and wiped his face with his arm, making his hair stick up at the front.

'I've been cutting logs,' he said, gesturing at his barrow. 'It's hot work.'

'But it gives you the most fantastic muscles,' Lia said. 'We're so grateful to you for keeping us warm.'

'No bother,' Bobby said. The colour rose in his cheeks and he nodded and walked on with his barrow. Lia groaned.

'Why did I mention his muscles?' she said, turning to Mim with a look of despair. 'Now he'll think I was ogling him.'

From where Mim was standing, it had looked very much as if Lia had been ogling Bobby.

'Would that be a problem?' she asked.

'Yes. I don't want him to think I'm an airhead. He had to rescue me from a tree when I was thirteen – Olly had dared me to climb up and I was too scared to climb down. I'm sure Bobby has thought I'm the family idiot ever since. Why do I always say such inane things when he's around?'

Why indeed? Mim filed away an interesting suspicion

about that while they carried on down the lane until they reached the small gatehouse at the end. Lia opened the rusty gate that led on to the front path.

'Corin's here?' asked Mim. It seemed an unlikely place for him to be.

'I hope so.' Lia checked her watch. 'He should have finished work by now.'

'He works?'

Lia laughed.

'Did you think we all spent our days reclining on the sofa eating caviar? That's only on weekends, darling.'

It was actually very close to what Mim had thought and she gave herself a mental telling off. She hated it when people made assumptions and judged her for her background, so why shouldn't the same apply to the Howards?

'Is he an artist, like you?' Mim asked. 'Is this his studio?'

'No, this is his house.'

'Corin lives *here*?' It was a small stone building, all on one level, and – though Mim was trying not to judge – first impressions were that it was quite shabby. It was up the property ladder from her caravan but well below the opulence of Vennhallow. Why hadn't he told her he lived here when she had accused him of being rich for living in an enormous house?

Lia paused at the front door.

'It's baffling, isn't it?' she said. 'Can you believe he

chooses to live here instead of at home with us? He moved in when he was eighteen. He likes his own space. He's always been odd like that.'

The front door had opened while Lia was talking. Corin stood in the doorway, wearing his trademark jeans and a woolly jumper.

'I can hear you through stone walls.' He looked at Mim over Lia's head and smiled. 'Back me up here. How is it odd to want to get away from someone so loud?'

'You won't win Mim over to your side,' Lia said. She linked her arm with Mim's. 'We're the best of friends and she won't hear a word against me. Aren't you going to invite us in? We'll literally freeze to death if we stay out here much longer.'

'You literally won't,' Corin said, but he stood back and held open the door. 'Stop crushing Mim and let her in.'

Mim flashed him a smile as Lia released her arm and she stepped inside the house. She hoped it wasn't too obvious how awkward she still found physical contact. It was unfamiliar rather than unpleasant. She hadn't been brought up with kind touches or with the hugs and kisses that Lia and her family exchanged so easily. She didn't know how to respond – but she wanted to learn, and that was progress, wasn't it?

The inside of the lodge wasn't at all what she expected after the scruffy exterior. A small hall led through to a surprisingly spacious open-plan room containing a smart grey sofa and armchair, a table for four, and a compact, modern kitchen. The walls were painted a pale shade of grey that made it seem bright but warm, and a log burner in a stone hearth was pumping heat into the room. Dickens was curled up in a basket close to the fire. He opened his eyes briefly to inspect the new arrivals and Mim could have sworn he took one look at Lia and closed them again.

Lia immediately threw herself onto the sofa and wrapped herself in a blanket that had been folded neatly on the seat.

'Is there any chance of a cup of tea?' she asked, turning to smile at Corin.

'Will you literally die of thirst if you don't have one?' he said. Lia laughed. 'You wouldn't be so thirsty if you didn't talk so much.'

Lia stuck her tongue out at him.

'It's so unfair being the youngest in the family,' she said. 'I'm the butt of everyone's jokes. Do you have any brothers or sisters to endure, Mim?'

'No. It's just me.'

'That sounds delightful.' Lia grimaced. 'Sorry. I'm totally putting my foot in it today, aren't I? Corin, did you know that Mim was brought up in care?'

'No.' He looked up from making the tea. 'But perhaps it's not something she wants to talk about.'

'It's not a secret,' Mim said. She wasn't sure how to take his tone. Was he closing down the subject because he found it embarrassing? She met his gaze. 'I'm not ashamed of it. It wasn't my fault.'

Corin crossed the room and held out a mug to her.

'We're the ones who should be ashamed,' he said, 'for having so much privilege and doing so little with it.'

It was the last thing she'd expected him to say, and she couldn't interpret the look he gave her. It certainly wasn't embarrassment or pity but something she didn't have a name for, something that loosened knots inside her that she hadn't even known existed. Lia broke the moment.

'Now do you see why Corin is the perfect person to help?' she said. Corin sat down on the armchair, long legs stretched out towards the fire and crossed at the ankle.

'Help with what?' he asked. 'Or should I be afraid to ask?'

'Our amazing plan to offer free holidays in the caravans to people who can't afford a break. What do you think?'

'I think you're becoming more like Dad by the day with your ideas and schemes,' Corin replied. 'He must be thrilled.'

'She's not asked Bill and Bea yet,' Mim said. 'They might object.'

'They won't,' Lia said. 'Besides, Corin is the son and heir. All this will be his one day, including the caravans, so they won't object if he's behind us.'

'But what about the rest of you?' Mim asked Lia. 'It seems unfair if everything goes to Corin. But I should keep my nose out,' she added quickly. She didn't want to sound like Janet, butting in with her blunt opinions.

'I agree with you,' Corin said. 'It is unfair. But none of the others want it. Now, why don't you tell me what you have in mind for the caravans?'

Mim sat back and drank her tea while Lia did all the talking. Her attention drifted as she looked around the room and noticed a few things that she had missed when she first walked in. There was a small bookcase in one corner, filled with books with colourful spines; she couldn't read all the titles, but a couple of them mentioned South America. A roughly carved wooden bowl sat on the bookcase, and a couple of photographs stood on the mantelpiece, one showing a group of four people in front of a jeep and the other an amazing sunset. Neither looked like Devon, from what she had seen of it so far. She stole a look at Corin. Was there more to him than the shallow, rich man she had mentally labelled him?

'Mim? Mim darling? Are you falling asleep?' Lia's voice pulled her thoughts back into the room.

'Sorry.' She smiled. 'Perhaps I was drowsing after my swim this morning, and with the tea and the warm fire.' She saw Corin open his mouth. 'And no, I didn't go swimming on my own before you ask. One of the women I swim with is Bobby's sister.'

She had the satisfaction of seeing a look of interest flash over Lia's face.

'I know,' Corin replied. 'That wasn't what I was going to say. You look as happy as Dickens when he settles in front of the fire. Are you finding the caravan cold? Does the fire not work?'

'Are you saying I look like a short, hairy dog? No offence,' Mim said to Dickens, as she noticed that he had sat up in his basket and was staring at her.

'Only in the expression of contentment,' Corin said. 'But don't dodge the question.'

'I don't know if the fire works,' Mim admitted. 'I haven't tried it.'

'You've been living in the caravan without heating?' Lia pulled the blanket more tightly round her. 'How have you not frozen to death, darling? Why would you do that?'

'It's still warmer than sleeping in the car.' The surprise on Corin's face stopped her. Perhaps he hadn't heard that she had been homeless when Bea and Bill found her. She hurried on. 'You know I told Bea that I'd only live in the caravan if she let me do some jobs to pay my way. She's not given me anything to do, so I'm not running up expenses.'

'That's ridiculous,' Corin said. 'Next you'll be telling us that you never switch a light on.' Mim shrugged. She wasn't daft enough to tell him that. The cheap torch she'd bought was surprisingly powerful. She only needed the lights on when she was cooking. Corin sighed. 'I don't think I've ever met anyone so stubborn.'

'Stubborn and looks like a dog?' Mim smiled. 'Steady on, I might get big-headed.'

Corin laughed and refrained from further scrutiny, just as Mim had hoped. She turned back to Lia.

'Did I miss something?' she asked.

'Yes, you did. Corin thinks we should set up a charity and do it all officially.'

'Does he?' Mim pulled a face. 'That sounds complicated. And expensive.'

'It's not too difficult,' Corin said. 'Olly can arrange the legal side. He's done it before. You two need to come up with a name.'

'I've already thought of the perfect name.' Lia sat forward, grinning in excitement. 'I came up with it last night. Mummy will never object when she hears it.' She paused to build the moment. 'As You Like It holidays. What do you think? Isn't it the most perfect title, darlings?'

Chapter Eight

I t had taken Mim a few weeks to get used to swimming in the sea, even with the benefit of one of Ros's old wetsuits, but now she couldn't imagine going back to a swimming pool again. The sea was alive, sometimes helping her in the direction she wanted to go and sometimes making her fight against it. Her confidence and her strength were growing with every swim. No two days were ever the same and she relished the challenge of facing and conquering the unknown.

She also relished the growing friendship she shared with Karen and Heather. They had nothing obvious in common: they were different ages, came from different backgrounds, and had very different family circumstances. It was hard to say why it worked, but it did. For the first couple of times Mim had been reluctant to join them in the campervan, wary of interfering with an established relationship. Karen and Heather had swiftly put an end to any doubts and dragged her into their circle. Mim had never enjoyed female friendship before, never had any confidantes to talk to and with whom to share mutual support. It was one of the most precious discoveries of this new life in Devon.

She told Heather and Karen about the idea to use the caravans when they met up the following Wednesday.

'Who will it be for?' Karen asked. She was always the more practical of the group. 'People on low incomes? You'd need to think how low. And how would you find them?'

'I don't know,' Mim admitted. She'd been swept up in Lia's enthusiasm for the idea, and they hadn't worked out the practicalities yet. 'It's a good point. It seems arbitrary to set an income limit. Income doesn't tell a whole story, does it?'

'My second cousin went on a holiday with a similar charity a few years ago,' Heather said. 'I think it was in Wales. She was a single mother at the time – she's married since then – and was struggling to manage because she was looking after a disabled father and her little boy with chronic asthma. A four-day break meant the world to her. She was nominated by a social worker.'

'I like that idea,' Mim said. 'It would be good to have an objective assessment of who would benefit from a break. I wonder who could get involved. Teachers? Doctors?'

'Health visitors?' Heather suggested. She passed round a Tupperware box of cupcakes – another reason why Mim enjoyed these swimming sessions. The cake supply could keep her going until teatime.

'You should open it up,' Karen said. 'Not just for low-income families. What about young carers? Or anyone with a caring role who needs a break? You should make one of the caravans accessible.'

Mim thought about the layout of the caravan field. There was already good access for vehicles, but each caravan was surrounded by a veranda that had only step access. Her caravan was fairly open-plan inside, but she hadn't been in the others to see what they were like. She didn't even know what condition they were in and how much work it would take to make them fit for use. She didn't mind the cold and damp patches in hers but holidaymakers would deserve a higher standard. She sighed.

'The more I think about it, the more impossible it seems,' she said. 'Lia's enthusiasm hardly seems enough to carry us through.'

'Is Lia behind this?' Heather asked. She looked surprised. 'I didn't realise she was enthusiastic about anything other than fashion and holidays. She always seemed the weak link in the family. A bit flaky, if you know what I mean.'

'Is that what Bobby says?' Mim asked. Perhaps her suspicions were wrong, after all.

'No, he never mentions her. That's my point. He's always had something good to say about the rest of the family. He was delighted when Corin came back. But he's never said anything about her.'

Interesting. Perhaps Bobby didn't mention Lia because he knew his sharp-eyed sister would see straight through him. Mim was about to ask where Corin had come back from when Karen interrupted.

'It's not impossible if you have the money. You'll need some to get all this off the ground. Where's that coming from?'

It was another good point and one Mim couldn't answer. She'd asked Corin and Lia the same thing when they had first discussed the charity and they had told her not to worry about that. It was a pointless instruction, as worrying about money had been one of her chief occupations for so long that it was as automatic as breathing.

'Don't build your hopes up too much,' Heather said, sending Mim a sympathetic look. 'Bill seems a lovely man, from what I've seen, but he's well-known for having ideas that seem the next big thing and then fade away. He once renovated a land train to attract tourists to Littlemead and it caused chaos on the roads. It probably wasn't even legal. Then there was the caravan park. We all thought it would be great for the village at the time. But all the work was done by people from outside, not locals. It was abandoned after a few years.'

It was more or less the same story that Lia had told. Was the charity another idea that would produce initial enthusiasm and then be cast aside for something else? Mim hoped not. Corin had seemed genuine enough, but perhaps she should tread cautiously before thinking up too many ideas and getting her hopes up that the scheme might actually happen.

Bea flagged Mim down as she drove towards the caravans later on, by standing in the middle of the track and waving her arms as if she were delivering a semaphore message. Mim slammed on the brakes and jumped out of the car.

'Is something up?' she asked. Bea laughed.

'I do love your accent, my dear,' she said. 'No, nothing is "up". Quite the opposite. Bill is down in his workshop, tinkering with his latest invention and doesn't have time to take me to Exeter to pick up my new glasses. Are you busy, Mim dear? Would you be able to take me?'

'Yes. We can go now if you want.'

'Lovely. Give me thirty minutes to make myself presentable.'

Presentable? Bea already looked smarter than Mim did. But Mim agreed and spent the thirty minutes having a lukewarm shower to wash away the salt water on her skin and in her hair before returning promptly to the house and waiting outside for Bea.

'Whyever didn't you come inside?' Bea asked. 'You didn't need to sit out here like a taxi driver.' She peered into the car and brushed at the passenger seat before getting in. A burst of intense perfume filled the car, improving its fragrance considerably. Bea looked at Mim. 'Did you not have time to dry your hair? You should have said. We could have set off later.'

'It's no problem. I don't have a hairdryer.'

'Why didn't you ask? We probably have dozens of spare ones littering the house. Come in later and we'll find you one. What would we do if you perished of pneumonia?'

'Scatter my ashes in the sea, if it's not too much trouble.'

Bea laughed and they set off towards the road that would lead to Exeter. Bea directed Mim at every turn.

'Didn't you fancy driving yourself, then?' Mim asked. There was clearly no issue about Bea getting lost on her own. 'Not that I mind taking you,' she added quickly.

'I don't drive,' Bea said. 'I had a go once but I didn't take to it. Besides, Bill loves driving so much that he would hate me to take a turn. I found that my services were better employed navigating, until the sat nav came along and made me redundant.' She gave Mim the next couple of directions. 'Of course, when Bill had his little health scare last year, I did wish I'd kept on with the driving but now we have Corin back with us so we can always call on him. He's infinitely safer behind the wheel than Lia,' she added, leaning close to Mim. 'She took six attempts to pass her test.'

Mim had passed first time, but then she'd had the best and most patient teacher. Gordon had taught her when he'd realised she'd never had lessons, and he had taken her out whenever they'd had a spare half hour in the hotel. It was only one of the many gifts he'd given her.

Bea talked all the way to Exeter, where they finally parked in a multi-storey car park and climbed up a steep hill into the city centre. Bea collected her glasses – a vibrant black and yellow pair – and led Mim down a passageway which unexpectedly opened onto a grassed area, with the largest church Mim had ever seen at the centre of it. A cobbled road ran round the edge of the grass and was fringed with a variety of old buildings, some with black and white timbering, others made of stone, but all stunning in their own way.

'You don't get this in Burnley,' Mim said, spinning round. Even on a dull winter's day, the place basked in peace and beauty, as if the bustle of the city was far behind them. Mim loved it.

'It's very special, isn't it?' Bea replied, smiling at Mim. 'I never tire of coming here, in all seasons, whether it's quiet and cold like today or warm and sunny so the grass is packed with students and tourists. Bill and I were married over there in the cathedral.'

'In there?' Mim pointed. It looked like the sort of place where members of the Royal Family would marry, not ordinary people. Although, she supposed that the Howard family weren't ordinary by her standards. 'Wasn't it terrifying?'

'It was wonderful. I'd do the whole thing again in a heartbeat.' She smiled at Mim. 'You'll understand when it's your turn.'

'Oh, I won't be taking a turn,' Mim said. 'I don't want to be half of someone else. I'm happy being all of me.'

'I'll look forward to seeing whether you stick to that when you meet the right man or woman. But do you know what I'm looking forward to now? Lunch in the café over there, facing the green. It's my treat, before you argue, as a thank you for driving me here.'

Bea was clearly a regular in the café as she was greeted with smiles and given one of the best tables in the bay window.

'Don't even think about the price of anything,' Bea said, holding up a warning finger to Mim when they were given the menus. 'But bear in mind that they make delicious cakes and you'll want to save room for one.'

Cakes twice in one day? Mim decided she deserved it after her swim this morning. It always gave her an appetite and so she tucked into a huge bowl of soup, a plate of sandwiches, and a slice of chocolate fudge cake without even a pang of guilt.

'This is one of the things I like about you, Mim,' Bea said, as she poured them both another cup of tea. 'You enjoy your food and don't mind showing it.'

'Is that a polite way of saying I'm greedy?'

Bea laughed.

'You are very naughty, twisting my words. And on the subject of being naughty, there's something we need to discuss.'

Mim froze, the last piece of chocolate fudge cake halfway to her mouth. What had she done wrong? She'd tried to live as frugally as she could in the caravan but she couldn't avoid the cost of using the cooker and the water. Were the bills mounting up? Or was it something worse? Had she left a pair of coloured knickers in Bea's washing machine and ruined some expensive clothes? She ate the piece of cake quickly and put down her spoon.

'If I've done something wrong and you want me to move out, please just say it,' she said. 'You've already been kinder than you needed to be by letting me stay so long.'

'Move out?' Bea repeated. She shook her head. 'Only if you've found somewhere you'd rather be. You misunderstand, Mim dear. I'm concerned, not cross. Corin told me that you're still not using the heating in the caravan.'

Mim sighed. Not that again.

'He had no business mentioning it,' she said. 'He's a tell-tale.'

'He's also sensible. He reminded me that the fires in the caravans haven't been checked for years and might not be safe. So actually I'm asking you *not* to use the fire until the gas engineer has been. I've booked him in for Friday. You'll be at work, won't you, so it won't disturb you.'

Easy for Bea to say; she hadn't lived in the sort of places that Mim had, where rooms and possessions were considered common property. Even here, it would disturb Mim to know that a stranger was in her space. She tried to protest.

'You don't need to do that for me. I'm happy without the fire. It's not that cold down here compared to what I'm used to. It will be safe enough if I don't use it.'

Bea dismissed this with a wave of her hand.

'We'll need to have them all serviced before we use them again, so it makes sense for yours to be done too.'

'Before they're used again?' Mim forgot her own concerns and grinned as she realised what Bea meant. 'Does that mean you've agreed to Lia's idea about the holidays?'

'Of course. How could you doubt it? It's a wonderful idea. I'm only ashamed we didn't think of it ourselves.' Bea smiled. 'We need to all come together and make plans for how it will work. What about Sunday? We can combine it with lunch.'

'I'll be in the shop.' Mim couldn't hide her disappointment. She may have just eaten a hearty lunch, but the thought of missing a Sunday roast was a huge blow. 'You don't need me there,' she said reluctantly. 'It doesn't really have anything to do with me.'

'Nonsense,' Bea said. 'It has everything to do with you. We'll make it for Monday evening instead, after dinner. This is going to be a huge success. We won't let it be anything else.'

Mim hoped so but she couldn't help wondering if the same words had been spoken when the caravans were launched the first time – and that hadn't been much of a success, had it? She was going to do everything she could to make it a success this time. Bea checked her watch and raised her hand for the bill.

'I've delayed us too long. We're going to be late.'

'Late for what?' Mim asked, pulling on her coat. She hadn't realised they had another appointment that day.

'I told Ros that you would babysit the children. She has a meeting this afternoon and has asked me to go with her. You don't mind, do you?'

'Me? Babysit?' Mim stared at Bea. 'I don't know anything about children. Don't I need qualifications for that?'

'It's not a permanent job.' Bea smiled as she tapped her payment card against the machine. 'I thought you'd run a hotel? I think you can manage a couple of toddlers for an hour or two. It's all perfectly simple.'

It took Mim less than an hour to conclude that babysitting wasn't simple and it definitely wasn't perfect. She'd encountered children in the hotel occasionally but never had any direct dealings with them and hadn't been left in charge of any. Although she soon realised that it was a mistake to imagine she was in charge. Jeremy and Maisie seemed to have an inexhaustible supply of energy and, though only one and three years old, a strong determination that they should get their own way.

Mim was looking after them at Vennhallow. After an hour of covering the kitchen with paint and bricks faster than Mim could tidy up, she decided the only safe option was to take them outside and let them run around until they wore themselves out. She helped them put on wellies and anoraks and shooed them out into the garden.

Jeremy didn't need any encouragement. As soon as he was out of the front door, he shot off across the lawn, with Maisie tottering behind on her chubby toddler legs. Mim chased after them and for the next twenty minutes it did seem simple, after all. She chased, they ran. They ran, they laughed. But then Maisie sank down onto the grass and started to suck her thumb and wouldn't move another centimetre.

Mim looked down at her, wishing she'd had the sense to bring a pram. Maisie stared back and lifted her arms. What was that supposed to mean? Mim tried to lift her and set her back on her feet, but Maisie wriggled until she had wrapped her arms and legs round Mim and was clinging on like a monkey.

Mim lifted her higher on to her hip, and Maisie rested her head on her shoulder. She was heavier than Mim had expected, softer too, and she smelt of something sweet and fruity. Mim cuddled her closer, savouring the unfamiliar sensation.

'Uncle Corin!'

Mim hadn't realised they'd run so far; at its end, the Vennhallow garden backed onto the lawn that surrounded Corin's gatehouse. Corin was walking round the house from his car to the front door, looking unusually smart in a formal shirt and trousers, and with a jacket and tie dangling over his arm. Jeremy ran through a gap in the hedge and straight at Corin, who picked him up and tucked him under his arm.

'I've caught a monster in the garden,' Corin said, tickling Jeremy who squealed with delight. Maisie noticed what was going on and slid down Mim so she could toddle after her brother. Corin soon had a giggling child under each arm, while his jacket lay in a heap on the floor. Mim followed the children into the garden.

'Have you been landed with looking after these two terrors?' Corin asked. 'What did you do to deserve that?'

'I don't know. It must have been really bad, mustn't it?'

Corin lowered the children to the ground. Jeremy tugged his hand.

'Mim isn't bad,' he said, with the earnestness of his full three and a half years. 'She's fun. But she has a strange voice.'

'It's called an accent,' Corin explained. He caught Mim's eye and smiled. 'It's because she comes from a land far away in the north.'

'The North Pole?' Jeremy asked.

'Not quite as far as that,' Corin said, stifling a laugh. Jeremy still regarded Mim wide-eyed, but then another thought distracted him. He tugged Corin's hand again.

'Can we have some hot chocolate?' he asked. 'Please?'

'Go on then, as you asked so politely.'

Corin unlocked the door and pushed it open. The children rushed in and Mim could hear them squealing over Dickens.

'Poor Dickens,' Corin said. 'He won't thank me for this invitation.'

'Doesn't he like children?'

'I think he agrees with me, that our family is far too large and best tolerated infrequently and in small doses. You can't go anywhere without running into a cousin or

128

an aunt or a godparent. It's like being surrounded by all Rabbit's friends and relations.'

'You have a rabbit?' Mim was confused. He didn't look like a rabbit man. Did he have a rabbit fleece like Janet? Perhaps that explained why he was such a favourite with her.

'It's a *Winnie the Pooh* reference,' Corin explained. 'Don't you remember? It was always my favourite bedtime story.'

'I didn't have bedtime stories.' It was a fact, not a plea for sympathy, but Mim caught the flash of compassion on Corin's face. 'Stop feeling sorry for me,' she said. 'It's very annoying. The past is gone. I'm alive and I'm healthy. Everything's fine, okay?'

She brushed past him into the house and found the children sitting next to Dickens's basket, stroking the dog, while Dickens curled up with a resigned expression on his face. Corin followed her in.

'Give me five minutes to change and then I'll make a drink.'

He wasn't gone that long, and Mim was glad when he came back wearing his usual jeans and scruffy jumper. He'd seemed different in his suit, less approachable and more like the businessmen who used to stay in the hotel, the ones who either paid her too much attention or failed to notice she existed.

'Let Dickens have some peace,' Corin said, and he lifted up the children one by one and deposited them on the sofa beside Mim. He threw the blanket over them. 'Here, use this until the fire gets going.'

He lit the fire, switched on the lamps, and made hot chocolate, while Mim snuggled on the sofa with two children who seemed suddenly exhausted by the effort of running round the garden earlier. When Jeremy asked to watch television, Corin said he had a better idea. He plucked a book from the bookcase and started to read a story about a bear of little brain called Winnie the Pooh... Maisie fell asleep, leaning against Mim's shoulder, and Mim couldn't blame her. With the flickering fire and the cosy glow from the lamps, the warmth of the blanket, and the soothing rhythm of Corin's voice, she was beginning to doze herself. Peace crept beneath her skin and filled her bones. She couldn't remember ever feeling so content in her life.

A knock on the door disturbed the idyll and a moment later Ros entered the room. She looked around and smiled.

'This looks a picture of perfect domestic happiness,' she said. 'Thanks for stepping in, Mim. I see you have everything under control. It seems a shame to disturb you all.'

'It's been fun,' Mim replied. Then, because she didn't want either Ros or Corin to think she was making herself too comfortable, she added, 'I don't mean this bit. We had fun before this. We did some painting and chased each other round the garden.'

'Thanks for clarifying which part was fun,' Corin said with a smile. 'I'm sorry *Winnie the Pooh* wasn't entertaining enough. I'll choose something more exciting next time.'

Next time? That wasn't likely to happen. Mim was about to point that out when Corin sprang up from his chair and joined his sister.

'How did it go?' he asked in a low voice.

'Everything's good. Number three will be joining us in late July. I couldn't be happier.' Her words were backed up by an enormous smile. She was an extraordinarily beautiful woman and now her evident joy made her even more so.

'I'm delighted for you.' Corin dropped a kiss on Ros's forehead and pulled her into a hug. Mim marvelled at how similar they were, with their elegant frames entwined, dark heads bent together, matching smiles of pleasure. 'Mum must be thrilled.'

'She is. She had no idea what was happening until we arrived at the hospital. You know that she's longing for as many grandchildren as possible.'

'I do know.' That sounded a heartfelt comment from Corin. 'And I love you for sparing me the job.'

'You will never be spared, son and heir.' Ros laughed and squeezed his hand. 'I've bought you some time, that's all.'

Mim had been listening to this exchange with open curiosity. Ros was pregnant again? Mim was exhausted after a few hours of looking after two children; she couldn't imagine how Ros would manage with a third – or, frankly, how she'd found the energy to be expecting a third at all. Mim was ready for bed and sleep was the only thing on her mind. The thought made her yawn.

'Sorry,' Ros said, smiling at Mim. 'Have they worn you out? I'll take them off your hands and you can carry on without them.' She flicked a mischievous look between Mim and Corin, and Mim caught the resemblance to Lia in it. She struggled out from under the blanket and stood up.

'I'd better be going anyway if you don't need me any more,' she said, looking round for her shoes. She spotted them by the front door, lined up between Corin's and the children's. How had that happened? Her coat was hanging above them on the pegs. She pulled it down.

'Shall I walk you home?' Corin asked. 'It's dark now.'

'You're all right. I can manage.' She opened the door, and a gust of wind blew in and broke the spell of the cosy room inside. She smiled at Corin. 'Thanks for the story.'

Chapter Nine

Mim didn't see any member of the Howard family over the next few days. There were no early morning knocks on the caravan door, no encounters on the lane, no visits to the Boat, no more stories in front of the fire. She was surprised how much she missed them, after only knowing them a few weeks. But contact didn't completely stop. She found a carrier bag outside her door one morning, beside Bobby's box of vegetables. There were two paperback books inside it, one about an attempt to climb Mount Everest and one about an expedition to the North Pole. They looked like well-thumbed books. There was a sticky note stuck on the cover of one with a few words written in a neat hand:

A couple of my favourites. You might find them more fun than Winnie. Corin.

She'd told Heather she wasn't a reader and that was true. But she picked up the book on Mount Everest one breakfast time, intending only to flick through the pictures, and she was soon so engrossed that she only made it for her shift in the deli with a minute to spare. She read it in her lunch break, huddled in the car when it rained and on the beach when it was dry; she read it in the gap between shifts at the shop and at the bar; and even at the end of an exhausting day, she devoured more pages as she curled under her duvet at night.

She sought Corin out as soon as he arrived for dinner at Vennhallow on Monday evening, even though he was the last to arrive and Bea was trying to usher everyone towards the dining room.

'Thanks for the books,' she said. 'I've started the one about Everest. It's brilliant.'

'You like it?' He looked genuinely pleased. 'I hoped you might. The author showed incredible resilience, carrying on to the summit despite the initial difficulties. That's why it reminded me of you.'

With that cryptic comment, he let Bea lead him to the dining room. Mim hadn't been in here before and it was as impressive as the rest of the house. A long wooden table filled the centre of the room and was set with seven places. An array of crystal glasses and ornate cutlery glittered in the light cast by a modern chandelier over the table, and the whole scene was reflected back in the dark windows along one wall. Mim thought of the tables she had set in the hotel dining room, with bulk-buy glasses and budget cutlery and china. She'd done her best with it and been proud of the results, but it had never looked as magnificent as this. She would have loved to have laid this table, never mind sitting at it to eat.

Mim was seated at one end of the table with Bill and Lia, while Corin, Bea, and Ros took the other end and Jonty occupied the middle. Corin and Bea carried in the food: platters of thickly sliced roast beef, crisp roast potatoes and Yorkshire pudding, and bowls of steaming vegetables. They refused Mim's repeated offers to help.

'We've not started a diplomatic crisis, have we?' Bill asked, pointing at the pile of golden Yorkshire puddings in front of Mim. 'Are we allowed to serve Yorkshire food to a Lancastrian?'

'There would have been a bigger crisis if you hadn't,' Mim replied. 'I'm impressed. I didn't know you ate Yorkshires down south.'

'Are we southerners a more civilised breed than you expected?' Corin asked. He set a jug of gravy on the table in front of Mim, and laughed as she took a deep breath, inhaling the rich scent. 'Your nose is twitching like Dickens's would.'

'Where is Dickens?' Mim said, leaning back to check the floor in case she'd missed him. 'I thought you took him everywhere.'

'They are totally inseparable,' Lia called across the table. 'Is it surprising that Dickens is his only friend when he repeatedly compares people to a dog? You are so mean to poor Mim, Corin. Will Dickens be your date for the Valentine dinner?'

'I think he might be washing his hair that night.' Corin sat down next to Bea. 'I'd do the same if I could.'

'Don't be such a misery,' Bea said. 'You haven't been for years. Everyone will be looking forward to seeing you again. We'll be there en masse this year, as Olly is coming back for the weekend and all the cousins will be attending. It will be like a huge family party. What could be nicer?'

'Being hung, drawn, and quartered?' Corin suggested.

Bea laughed and slapped the back of his hand.

'You are silly. You'll have a wonderful time. It will be such a treat to show off the son and heir again.'

Corin smiled but, glancing down the table at him, Mim noticed a shadow pass over his face at Bea's words. She didn't have time to work it out as Bea turned her attention to Mim.

'That reminds me, Mim dear,' Bea said. 'Are you busy on the Saturday after Valentine's Day?'

'I'll be working at the shop and at the Boat.' Mim helped herself to a spoonful of roast potatoes. There didn't look to be many on her plate, so she took a second helping.

'But no date? That's good. Paula asked if you'd be

free to work at the Valentine dinner as you were so helpful at the wedding.'

'I'd have loved to but I can't if it's on a Saturday.' It was a shame. She'd earned more at the wedding than from a couple of nights at the Boat.

'Don't worry about the Boat,' Bea said. 'Paula is married to Howie. She'll persuade him to let you have the night off. Good. I'm glad we could sort that out.'

Was it sorted? Mim didn't think she'd agreed to anything.

'Perhaps Mim would prefer to make up her own mind,' Mim heard Corin say in a low voice.

'Nonsense! The Valentine dinner will be much more fun than that gloomy pub. You don't mind, do you Mim?' Bea called.

'No.' She smiled. 'If it pays, I'll do it.'

It wasn't until after dinner that the conversation turned to the caravans. Mim had barely spoken during the meal as she was too busy savouring the delicious roast, and equally savouring the atmosphere in the room. There was never a quiet moment. At least one member of the family was always talking, and quite often several were speaking at the same time, bickering or teasing or encouraging each other. Mim had never felt so much love and laughter in a room. This was what she had always imagined having a family would be like. She was happy to eat and watch and she wished that the night could go on and on.

Everyone moved to the sitting room after the meal, another new room to Mim. Enormous, squashy sofas were scattered around the room, all facing towards each other to encourage conversation. Mim sank down next to Lia – literally sank, as Lia would have said, as the sofa was so soft that her bottom sank lower than her knees and she wondered how she was ever going to get up again.

'Here you are, Mim dear,' Bea said, passing her a notebook and pen.

'What do you want me to do with these?' Mim asked.

'Make notes of our plans,' Bea replied. 'You've managed a hotel so I can't think of anyone more qualified to manage this project. You don't mind, do you? Besides, apart from Ros, I suspect you're the most sober person in the room.'

Mim could easily believe that. She'd been amazed at how many bottles of wine had passed around the table that evening. She'd tried some but the red wine they were drinking had clearly been too expensive to appeal to her common palate and she hadn't managed much of it. Now Bill was pouring out balloons of brandy from a drinks cabinet in the corner of the room.

'Actually, Dad, do you have any beer?' Corin asked, declining a glass of brandy. Mim wished she could ask for some too but a couple of minutes later, Corin came up to her, holding a pint of beer in one hand and a half in the other. He moved the half pint glass towards her.

'Fancy a proper drink?' he asked. She smiled.

'Thanks. I'm gasping.' She reached out and took the pint glass from him, and he laughed and sat down on the neighbouring sofa.

Any concerns Mim still harboured that Bill and Bea might not like the plans for the caravans were swept away within minutes. They both spoke about As You Like It holidays with enthusiasm and excitement, and Mim could hardly keep up with scribbling down their ideas. Bill was on top of all the practical arrangements, such as making sure the gas, electrics, and plumbing were all safe and in working order. He also wanted to repair the veranda outside each caravan and paint them all a more cheerful colour than the current black. Bea was bursting with ideas for improving the inside of the caravans, and mentioned that she was going to ask the designer who had worked on the house to come down from London and have a look.

Mim's pen paused in her hand. The house was gorgeous, there was no question of that. It was elegant and tasteful, and looked like it had cost a huge amount of money. Mim was worried about damaging something every time she came in. How would an ordinary family have a relaxing holiday if the caravans were fitted out like this?

'Did you make a note of that, Mim?' Bea said. 'I'll ring Althea this week to see when she can come and look at the caravans. She's in huge demand but I know she'll squeeze in a job for me.'

'Do we need her?' Mim asked. Everyone stared at her. 'I mean, she's done a great job with this house, don't get me wrong. It's beautiful. It suits you all. But I'm not sure it would suit a single mum with young children who just wants to have a rest and not worry about getting grass stains on the pale upholstery or sticky finger marks on the glass tables.'

Had she gone too far? No one spoke, which was a rare occurrence in this company. At last Mim received some support.

'Mim's right,' Ros said. 'I can be anxious taking the children to someone else's house. I even worry about them making a mess in here, and that's when I know you wouldn't be cross. Perhaps the caravans need to be practical rather than beautiful?'

'Mim? What do you suggest?' Bea asked.

Mim drank some beer and thought about what would work in the caravans. She wanted them to be cosy, comfortable, relaxing spaces and she knew the perfect example of that. She'd been there this morning. Karen's campervan, designed by her partner Susie, would make a perfect template with its rich colours, hard-wearing surfaces and clever use of space. It hadn't cost a fortune either. Karen had told her that Susie had used recycled fabric and remnants to create many of the soft furnishings. Susie would be the perfect person to advise them on refurbishing the caravans, if she felt well enough.

'There's no reason why they can't be practical and beautiful. Can I get back to you on that?' Mim said. 'I have an idea, but I need to check whether someone could help. Don't you think it would be good if any work was done by local people, though? It would make it seem more of a community project. Perhaps Bobby could help with fixing the verandas and doing any painting?'

From the corner of her eye, she saw Lia toss her hair over her shoulder. It couldn't do any harm if Bobby and Lia were thrown together on this project, could it? She smiled to herself and caught Corin giving her a curious look.

After the initial enthusiasm for setting the project up, Mim found that little thought had been given to the practical arrangements involved in running it day to day. She was met with blank faces when she asked about laundry, cleaning, taking bookings and all the other small details that would need to be sorted out before any visitors arrived. Bill tried his best.

'Bea and I will produce a set of directions,' he said, fingering the end of his moustache. 'How about that? It's not the easiest place to find, and as you showed us, we can't assume that everyone will have sat nav.'

'You can't assume everyone will have a car,' Mim pointed out. No one seemed to have thought of that.

'How will they get here without a car?' Lia asked.

'And what will they do when they're here? They can take the coastal path into the village, but Janet's deli won't keep them entertained for long.'

There was a path down to the village? Mim should have thought of that before. It would save petrol if she could walk to work, although the return journey wouldn't be much fun in the dark.

'We'll have to provide transport,' Corin said. He'd been quiet through much of the discussion so far. 'Train and taxi fares could be covered by the charity. Hannah will be glad of the work. She's the village taxi driver,' he explained to Mim. 'This is a fantastic stretch of coast. We could offer dozens of ideas of things to do.'

'Don't force them on one of your fossil walks.' Lia flopped against Mim and pretended to snore. She sat up and laughed. 'We're supposed to be brightening their lives, not boring them to death.'

'What's a fossil walk?' Mim asked.

'Oh darling, you will totally regret asking that,' Lia said. Corin ignored her.

'I run fossil hunting walks along the beach,' he said. 'This stretch of coast is famous for its fossils. Why don't you come along to one? Judge for yourself whether it would interest visitors.'

'Okay,' Mim said. Lia groaned at her side. 'I haven't a clue what it is but I'll give it a go. Let me know when your next walk is.'

There wasn't time to discuss much else. Ros and Jonty

needed to go home to relieve the babysitter, and Bill was snoozing in his chair. Mim pulled on her coat while Corin said goodbye to Ros and Jonty at the front door.

'Sure you don't want another beer?' he asked, as the car taillights faded in the distance.

'Better not.' Mim tried and failed to stifle a yawn. 'This dog's ready for her basket.'

Corin's laughter followed her down the lane.

Karen was thrilled when Mim asked whether Susie would be interested in helping to design the interior of the caravans.

'She'd love to,' she said, before Mim had even finished explaining the idea. 'In fact, she won't be satisfied with giving you some ideas. She'll want to make everything herself.'

'Is she well enough?' Mim asked. It was a brilliant idea, as far as she was concerned, but she didn't want to force a woman recovering from cancer to slave away over a sewing machine.

'She's feeling great. Bored, if anything. She's hated the lack of energy and having to rest so much. This is exactly what she needs.'

'We can pay her,' Mim said. 'For her time as well as all the materials.'

Bea had insisted that there was a decent budget for

renovating the caravans, but when Mim had asked where the money had come from, and how the charity was being funded, she'd declined to give an answer. Lia, usually so talkative, had been equally tight-lipped, telling Mim they had enough to start the work until they could properly fundraise for the charity.

'The money's not important,' Karen said now. 'Although we won't say no. She's looking for a change of lifestyle. A job she loves, not loathes. She's wondered about doing something creative like this. It will give her a chance to have a go and see if it would suit her. Besides,' she added, handing Mim a fresh cup of tea, 'this is a good thing you're doing. We'd all like to help.'

'Really?' Mim didn't know who 'all' was, but it sounded expensive. 'I'll have to ask. I'm not sure how much money there is.'

'We don't want money,' Heather said. 'And I doubt that we're skilled enough to deserve any, unlike Susie. But if enthusiasm can make up for talent, we can find you some helpers. The more we have, the faster the work will be done, won't it? I haven't seen the caravans, but Bobby's told me about them. We can give you a hand with the manual labour: stripping out the contents, painting, weeding. We'll give anything a go. A lot of people in this village have benefitted from a helping hand at the right moment. We'd love the chance to pay it forward.'

It sounded like a brilliant idea to Mim. If they could

find a team of volunteers who wouldn't need paying, that would leave more money for the people who needed it.

'I'll have to check with Bea and Bill,' she said, 'as it's their land, but it sounds perfect to me. There's something else you could help with,' she added to Heather. 'You said your cousin had been on a holiday like this before. Do you think she'd come here, when one of the caravans is ready, to test out what it's like? It could be a dummy run before real members of the public arrive.'

'I'm sure she'd love to. It will need to be in the school holidays, though. When are you hoping to have your first visitors?'

'There isn't a fixed date. It will depend on how long it takes to set up a charity, but it would be a shame if we weren't ready for summer.'

'You should aim for May half-term,' Karen said. 'So that would mean the trial would have to be at Easter.'

'Easter?' Mim repeated. 'That's early April this year, isn't it? We won't be ready by then.'

'Why not?' Karen smiled. 'It gives us at least eight weeks. How long do you need?'

Chapter Ten

C orin turned up at the pub on Sunday night, on his own this time. He approached Mim at the bar and ordered a pint for himself and a half for her.

'If only you had a mobile phone, I could have sent you a message instead of coming here,' he said, handing over his money. 'It would be better for my wallet and my liver.'

'You could always have come into the shop. You could have spoken to me for the price of a penny chew there.' Mim grinned. 'Is something the matter? Is it about the caravans?'

'No, it's about the fossil walk. I'm running a guided walk tomorrow and wondered if you'd still like to come.'

'What time? I'll be swimming in the morning.'

'I need to leave at ten thirty. Will that suit you?'

'Go on then. I'll miss out on the after-swimming cakes

just this once. I have to know whether this walk is as deadly dull as Lia says.'

Corin laughed.

'I'll pick you up in the morning.' He waved at a middle-aged couple who had just entered the pub and started towards them.

'Hang on,' Mim called. 'Do I need to bring anything?'

'Curiosity and an open mind,' Corin said. 'See you tomorrow.'

―――――――

Mim was ready and waiting the next morning when Corin pulled up in front of her caravan just before ten thirty. He was driving a 4x4, but a considerably older and scruffier one than the car that had let down Bill and Bea on the day Mim had first met them in Lancashire. Was that only a few weeks ago? It seemed much longer.

'I'm glad to see you're so keen,' Corin said, when Mim entered the car before he had the chance to switch off the engine. She didn't want to risk him coming into the caravan this time, as her knickers were drying over the kitchen sink. 'I brought you these.'

He waited until Mim had fastened her seatbelt then handed her a white cardboard box. There were four cakes inside: an iced finger smothered in yellow icing, a chocolate éclair, a doughnut oozing jam, and a scone sandwiched with jam and cream.

'I didn't know what you'd like, so I brought a selection,' he said.

'I like everything. Are these all for me?'

'Yes. I didn't want you to miss out on your after-swim cakes.'

'No offence to Heather and Karen, but the cakes we have don't come close to these. Thanks.'

Mim picked up the iced finger first and gave a soft moan of pleasure when she bit into it and discovered a delicious seam of lemon curd running through the centre.

'Good?' Corin asked. Mim nodded as she took another bite and he smiled.

There wasn't much conversation on the journey as Mim was busy eating – although she stopped at two cakes, deciding to save the scone and the doughnut for lunch. She was also engrossed in staring out of the window. They were travelling in a different direction than she'd taken when driving Bea to Exeter, and she was enjoying stretching the edges of her world. There was so much more time to observe as a passenger and she studied the villages that straddled each side of the main road, and the hills that rose and fell away on Corin's side, revealing snatched glimpses of the sea. She also noticed several caravan parks, filled with rows of mobiles homes facing out to sea.

'I didn't realise there were so many holiday parks here,' she said, gesturing towards another. 'We're not going to stir up trouble with the owners by offering free holidays at Vennhallow, are we?'

'Unlikely. It's a popular area – and can you wonder, with a view like that? Mum and Dad meant well, but their six caravans in a field with no sea view were never going to compete with the likes of these places.'

'Didn't you tell them that, before they dug up a field and spent their money?' Mim asked. 'There's no benefit in being wise after the event.'

'I wasn't here. It was too late to stop it by the time I heard about the plan.'

Too busy living the high life in London, Mim guessed. Wasn't that what posh people did? Hang about fancy restaurants and exclusive nightclubs? Attend society weddings and lavish parties? She'd seen it often enough in the tabloid newspapers and magazines they'd received in the hotel. Although it was hard to imagine the Corin sitting next to her in that environment, with his well-worn hiking boots and fleece. Sometimes she almost made the mistake of thinking that he was just an ordinary person like her.

Eventually they drove down a winding lane and turned into a car park overlooking the beach. A visitor centre, café, and toilet block fringed one side of the car park, and on the other side sat a row of picnic benches on a grassy ledge. Corin reversed into a space in front of the picnic benches.

'Tea?' he asked. Without waiting for a reply, he set off

across the car park to the café and soon returned with two polystyrene cups. He offered one to Mim.

'How much is it?' she asked. 'I'll pay for my own.'

'It was free.' He smiled when she pulled a sceptical face. 'Scout's honour. I promise I haven't done anything so ungenerous as buy you a plastic cup of weak tea.'

She wasn't sure whether to believe him or not but she wanted the tea so she took the cup he was offering. Corin went round to the back of the car and opened the boot. It was full of plastic boxes. The largest contained a pile of clipboards but there were lots of smaller boxes with lids whose contents Mim couldn't see. There was also a first aid kit – an alarming sight – and a couple of ring binders. Corin picked up a utility belt and fastened it round his waist.

'What's that for?' Mim asked, pointing at a hammer dangling off his belt. 'I thought we were here for fossils, not DIY.'

'Stop trying to jump ahead. You'll find out soon enough.' He uncovered a couple of folding chairs. 'Would you mind setting these up at the end of the table?'

It must have been a secret signal; as soon as Mim opened the chairs, a middle-aged couple sensibly dressed in boots and matching anoraks approached.

'Is this the fossil talk?' the woman asked. She looked at Corin and his car with a doubtful expression, as if she'd expected an altogether less scruffy business. 'Corin Howard?'

'That's right. I'm Corin. How lovely to meet you.' He held out his hand and the woman shook it, all reservations apparently swept away by a posh accent and a charming smile. She could hardly have looked more dazzled if he'd kissed her. Mim said hello and no one even seemed to notice.

Over the next ten minutes, more customers drifted over and took seats either at the picnic bench or on the folding chairs, until they were a group of nine in total. Corin asked them all to sign a disclaimer, which alarmed Mim as much as the first aid kit. How dangerous could fossil hunting be? More dangerous than she had expected, if Corin's safety talk was anything to go by. Apart from the inevitable risks of walking on an unstable and potentially slippery beach, he showed them photographs of recent rockfalls in the area and warned them not to go too close to the foot of the cliffs. Mim made a mental note to stay close to Corin. Better to be bored than crushed to death...

After the safety talk, Corin handed everyone a clipboard and sheet of paper to make notes while he gave a brief introduction to fossils and how to recognise them. He passed round a small plastic box and invited everyone to take out one item to study. Mim picked out a dark grey item in a spiral shape. It was beautiful but she had no idea what it was.

'These are ammonites,' Corin said. 'One of the most common fossils you'll find. Now, you need to train your eyes to find them. How would you describe them?'

'Dark-coloured,' someone suggested.

'Round?' called another. Mim ran her finger over the object in her hand.

'There are ridges around the spiral,' she said.

'Perfect,' Corin said, smiling at her. Mim felt as if she'd come top of the class. 'Remember those things as you walk along the beach. Look out for something dark and round with ridges.'

Everyone around the table obediently wrote a note and Corin passed round his next sample, which was a belemnite, a bullet-shaped fossil that he explained was part of the skeleton of a squid-like creature. He also showed them a piece of fossilised wood and an ichthyosaur vertebra, before ending with a lumpy black object.

'Who can guess what this might be?' he asked. Mim wracked her brains but it only looked like one thing to her and she didn't want to appear stupid by saying it.

'Children are usually better at guessing this one,' Corin said, after a few incorrect guesses. 'Can you imagine the reaction when I explain that this is coprolite – also known as dinosaur poo?'

Everyone laughed and Mim kicked herself for not saying that in the first place. Corin spoke for about forty-five minutes, but the time flew by. How could Lia say this was boring? Mim wished that she'd had a teacher like him at school: someone enthusiastic and motivational, someone patient and for whom no question was too stupid.

Corin allowed a ten-minute break for toilet visits and to buy hot drinks before they headed onto the beach. Mim helped him tidy up the boxes of samples and the chairs.

'I'm glad to see you haven't died of boredom yet,' he said, smiling at Mim. 'There are newspapers in the café if you've had enough and would rather wait in there.'

'No way,' Mim said. 'I'm not missing out on the fun bit. I can't believe such old things are lying about on the beach and not locked away in a museum. It's incredible.'

'We do have to hand it in if we find anything rare,' Corin said. 'It's unlikely, though. The serious fossil hunters will have searched the beach hours ago.'

'Really?' That was annoying. Mim had been hoping she might get lucky and find an ammonite. 'How do you know all this stuff, anyway?'

'From a degree in Geography, a master's in Geology, and an ill-spent youth combing the beaches for treasure.'

'Oh!' Mim looked at Corin with fresh eyes as he pulled down the boot and locked the car. 'I didn't realise you were clever.'

Corin laughed.

'I don't know how to take that. Did you think I was awarded a PhD simply for being posh?'

'Sounds about right.' Mim grinned. 'You have one of those too?'

'I do, but don't worry. I won't insist on you calling me Dr Howard.'

Mim dropped into a curtsey.

'You're too kind to us 'umble folk,' she said, putting on her thickest accent. She laughed and pointed towards the café where the customers were gathering. 'Better not keep your adoring fans waiting, doctor.'

Corin led the group down onto the beach. It was a grey day and drizzle hung in the air, but even so there were a fair number of people scattered up and down the beach, poring over the pebbles. They stopped a few hundred metres along the beach and everyone gathered round Corin. He showed them a couple of things he'd picked up on the short walk from the car park. The first was a small pebble, with thin ridged columns visible on the surface, which he told them were crinoids. The second looked like an ordinary grey stone, but there was a cream line running horizontally round the centre of it, which Corin explained meant there might be an ammonite inside. Everyone leaned close while he tapped it gently with his hammer and prised the stone open, and there was a collective sigh of disappointment when there was nothing of interest inside.

'See if you can do better,' Corin said and the group didn't need telling twice. Mim was amazed at how this group of mild-mannered, middle-aged people suddenly transformed into cut-throat fossil hunters, scrabbling for what they thought was the best place on the beach. She didn't know how Corin bore it with such patience; every couple of minutes, one or other of the group took him something to examine or a pebble to hammer, although the conversation usually ended with a regretful shake of the head. Even Mim was caught up in the competitive nature of the hunt and was determined to win more than a, 'Good try' from Corin.

After a couple of hours, Corin called the group together again as the guided walk had ended. Mim was frustrated to see that a few of the others had been quite successful and she admired a belemnite and a fragment of ammonite with a forced smile.

'Didn't you find anything?' Corin asked Mim, as they wandered back towards the car park.

'Nothing real,' she said. There had been plenty of false starts, including an embarrassing moment when she'd mistaken a piece of plastic for dinosaur poo. She kicked a pile of pebbles in frustration and then bent down, ignoring the throbbing in her toes. She picked up a smooth oval pebble with a clear seam running horizontally around the middle.

'Another dud, probably,' she said, and was about to toss it back on the beach when Corin took it from her.

'Let's try,' he said, and he tapped at certain points on the side of the pebble until it gently split in his hands. He held it out so that Mim could see. Inside the stone there was a clear imprint of an ammonite.

'This is the best find of the day,' he said. He smiled at Mim. 'In fact, the best find for a few days. You're a natural.'

'Can I keep this?'

'Yes. It's all yours.' He placed both halves of the stone in Mim's hands and she studied it, marvelling at this evidence of long ago life. 'What do you think?' Corin asked. 'Will this interest the guests?'

'What? Oh, the caravan guests.' It took Mim a moment to remember. This was supposed to have been a fact-finding mission for the charity, not a source of so much fun. Reluctantly, she put the pebble away in her pocket. 'I think it would be great, but perhaps I'm not the best person to judge. Everything down here is new to me. It's all exciting.'

'That makes you the perfect person to judge.' Several strands of Mim's hair had worked loose from her bobble in the wind, and Corin watched as she refastened it. 'It's easy to become jaded with what's on offer when you see it every day. You can breathe fresh enthusiasm into it. Into all of us.'

Lia didn't hang about. No sooner had Mim tentatively suggested a trial of the caravans at Easter than it was adopted as a plan, with a schedule of works drawn up to ensure everything was ready for that date. Bea and Bill had stepped back and allowed Lia to take charge of the scheme from the Howard side, and she had picked up the challenge with surprising efficiency and enthusiasm – so much so that Bill had rubbed his hands together with glee and declared that she 'was a chip off the old block after all'. Given what Mim had heard about Bill and his short-lived schemes, she didn't know if that was a good thing or not.

The first job, of making sure that the gas, electricity, and water supplies were safe and in working order, were already underway, including a check on Mim's caravan. The news wasn't good. All the caravans needed work to meet the current regulations and it would take a few days to complete the job.

'But it isn't all bad news,' Lia said, when she called in on Wednesday evening to update Mim. 'It means that you'll have to come and stay with us for a few nights.'

'There's no need for that. I'm sure I'll be fine here.'

'Darling, you can't mean that. All the services will be switched off. You won't have any lights or be able to flush the loo. Can you imagine how awful that would be?' She shuddered. 'You can't live like a savage.'

'It wouldn't be that bad,' Mim said. It would still be an improvement on sleeping in the car. At least the caravan had a bed. The surrounding field and trees would provide an adequate toilet, and she could fill a few bottles with water before it was turned off so she could brush her teeth and have a wash. There might even be a packet of wet wipes amongst her belongings for a more luxurious clean. 'I'm sure I can manage.'

Lia laughed.

'You are funny. You don't have to manage. Everything is arranged. Mummy has asked Mrs Dennis to prepare the spare room for you. It will be ready for you to move in tomorrow.'

'I can't move tomorrow. I'll be working, so I can't pack my things.'

'Yes, we know that, so we will move your things for you. I told you, it's all arranged. You don't have to do anything.'

Mim had to object, even though it did feel like she was kicking an adorable puppy. She realised Lia meant well but she wasn't comfortable with other people touching her things. It was a hangover from childhood that she'd not been able to shake off.

'I can't let you do that,' she said, as gently as she could. 'I'll pack my things in the morning and put them in the car until I've finished at the pub.' It wouldn't take long. Growing up the way she had, she was used to moving on at short notice. She never fully unpacked; even at the hotel, she'd kept an emergency box of her most important things, ready to grab and go if needed. 'It will only be for a couple of nights, won't it?'

'We'll see.' Lia grinned. 'You might not want to come back here once you've experienced life at Vennhallow.'

'I'll have to find somewhere else soon anyway,' Mim said. 'You'll need to do up this caravan for holidaymakers to use.' It was a timely reminder. She'd grown complacent here and hadn't even started looking for other accommodation. She'd need to find more work too if she was going to pay commercial rent. Three full days off was an indulgence, even if she was working over fifty hours on the other four days.

'We won't be using this caravan,' Lia said. 'Mummy was quite clear on that. We'll use the other five for now and see how it goes. Yours is safe.'

That was good news, although Mim felt a twinge of guilt at limiting the number of holidays available.

'What's the next step after the gas and electricity repairs?' Mim asked. 'Should we invite Susie to have a look now so she can start work?'

Susie had been thrilled to get involved with the project and had soon dismissed Mim's worries about whether she was well enough. They had spoken on Karen's phone, and Susie had told Mim in a forthright way that she'd beaten cancer and so had no concerns about knocking up a few pairs of curtains and cushions for five caravans. She sounded formidable and Mim was looking forward to meeting her. The Howards had happily agreed to her involvement.

'Absolutely,' Lia said, 'and I've arranged for Susie to

come round tomorrow morning before the workmen. Everything is slotting together, isn't it?'

'Tomorrow?' Mim repeated. Why did it all have to take place tomorrow? 'But that means I won't be here to meet Susie.'

'It's only the first meeting. You can join the next one. As long as you're free,' Lia added, laughing. 'I heard that Corin is arranging some more tourist activities for you to sample. Honestly, darling, you didn't need to be so polite about his fossil tour. He seems to think you enjoyed it. If he suggests one of his guided walks you must say no or he'll march you to Dorset and back before you know it.'

Chapter Eleven

The spare bedroom at Vennhallow was as elegant as the rest of the house. It was decorated in pale grey with a king-size bed and an en suite shower room that was almost as big as Mim's bedroom in the caravan. Lia had waited up to let Mim in after her shift at the pub and she sprawled on a chaise longue while Mim looked round.

'Didn't I tell you it was sumptuous?' Lia asked, as Mim stood at the window trying to work out what direction she was facing and if there would be a sea view or not. Not that it mattered, for two nights, but she was allowed to hope, wasn't she? 'You won't want to leave us once you've tasted this life.'

Mim flopped onto the bed and sank a few inches down, cocooned in the feathery softness of the bedding. It was total bliss.

'I don't think I'll ever want to leave this bed,' she said. 'Switch the light off when you go, won't you?'

Bea was equally keen to make Mim feel at home. When Mim eventually dragged herself out of bed the next morning, Bea was already in the kitchen, wearing an elegant silk robe and brewing a pot of tea.

'Good morning,' she said when Mim came in. 'How did you sleep, my dear? Were you warm enough?'

'Very.' So warm that she'd had to cast off the throw that covered the bed. This might be an old house, but the heating system was amazing.

'Your breakfast is ready,' Bea said, and she carried a tray over to the table and set it down. It was laden with a couple of boiled eggs, a rack of perfectly browned wholemeal toast, a dish of butter, and a steaming mug of tea.

'This is for me?' Mim asked, as Bea gestured for her to take a seat.

'Of course. You can't do a day's work without a good breakfast. I hope you like it. Boiled eggs are about my culinary limit. I always used to make some for the children before they went to school.'

She sounded so wistful that Mim didn't have the heart to tell her that she'd prefer a bowl of porridge.

'I've made your packed lunch too,' Bea carried on, lifting an insulated sandwich bag off the kitchen counter. 'Smoked salmon and cucumber sandwiches, and a slice of Mrs Dennis's finest carrot cake.'

'You really didn't need to do all this.' Mim sliced the top off an egg and dipped in a toast soldier. It was perfectly cooked and the yolk dribbled down the toast. 'I'm quite used to looking after myself.'

'You don't need to while you're with us. We all look out for each other.' Bea rested a hand briefly on Mim's shoulder. 'Besides, I'm buttering you up as I have a favour to ask.'

'Anything.'

'It isn't too horrendous. I wondered if you'd drive me to Honiton one day next week to collect my dress for the Valentine's event. Bill refuses to go near a lady's dress shop. I don't trust Lia's driving, and I'd prefer not to trouble Ros now she's expecting. What do you say?'

'I'd be happy to.' Mim smiled. 'As long as you give me directions as I haven't a clue where that place is.'

'Even better, we'll take Bill's car and then we can use the sat nav if we need to. No offence, my dear, but it will be a far more comfortable ride. Let me borrow your driving licence and I'll add you to the insurance.'

'Did I see you leaving Vennhallow this morning?' Corin asked, as Mim pulled him a pint in the Boat that evening. She didn't need to ask what he wanted anymore. He turned up at least two out of the four nights she worked there, usually with Dickens at his heels, and always had a pint of a local real ale with a half for her. If he was early, he would sit with Dickens and read a newspaper, but he was rarely on his own for long. He seemed to know everyone who came in and was happy to chat to them all.

'I can't answer that,' Mim said, placing his drink on the bar. 'I did leave the house this morning. If you were hanging about you might have seen me.'

'I was and I did.'

'There's a word for men who lurk in the bushes, spying.'

'There are two words. Dog owner. I was taking Dickens for his morning walk.' He bent down and scratched the top of the dog's head. 'Was there an emergency that you were there so early? Mum and Lia aren't usually awake at that time.'

'No emergency. I'm staying there for a couple of nights while work is done on the caravans.' She hesitated, his change clasped in her hand. She didn't want him to get the wrong idea – to think that she was *worming her way in*. That was one of the many accusations that Gordon's daughter had thrown at her while she was working at the hotel. She wasn't going through all that again. 'It wasn't my idea. I'd have been happy to stay in the caravan. But Bea and Lia insisted.'

'Insisted?' Corin smiled. 'I'm surprised that's all they did. I'm amazed they didn't simply move your things and present you with a fait accompli.'

Mim laughed but didn't reply. He wasn't far off the truth with that remark. She held out his change. He looked at it but didn't take it.

'Don't be afraid to stand your ground,' he said. 'My family have an annoying habit of taking over. Why let you do something yourself if they can do it for you?'

'I'm not afraid of anything.' Mim slapped his change down on the bar. 'Besides, I wouldn't call that annoying. Your family are kind and they care about each other. A lot of people would be glad to have a family like yours. It's all I ever wanted. And stop giving me that pitying look,' she added, as she turned away to attend to another customer. 'That really is annoying.'

By the time she'd pulled the next pint, Corin had taken his change and he and Dickens were talking to an old man at a table in front of the fire.

He was back at the bar an hour later with his empty glass.

'Another?' Mim asked.

'No, I'd better go.' Corin pulled some leaflets out of the inner pocket of his coat and put them on the bar. 'I only popped in to give you these. It's information about some of the tourist attractions in the area. Have a look and see if anything looks interesting. I have access to a minibus, so we could offer excursions if you think that would work.'

Mim flicked through some of the leaflets. There was a theme park, a donkey sanctuary, a swannery – whatever that was – and that was only from the first few on the pile.

'How can I choose?' she asked. 'They all look interesting to me.'

'No problem.' Corin smiled. 'I'll take you to check them out. Let me know when you're free.'

After missing out on the meeting with Susie, Mim was relieved that the first day of working on the caravans was fixed for a Wednesday. She knew that Heather and Karen would be coming up, and presumably Lia, but didn't have high hopes for a larger crowd on a midweek day. She was surprised to arrive back after swimming and find an additional half a dozen people ready to start work. Most were familiar faces from the pub or the shop, although she didn't know their names.

'Where have all these people come from?' she asked Heather, as they made their way over to the group.

'They're all villagers who want to support the charity,' she said. 'It's a popular idea. With most people anyway; there's inevitably a few who would install road blocks to keep the tourists out of Devon if they could. Bobby and Corin have been spreading the word for a couple of weeks.'

Corin wasn't here today; Mim had already noticed that.

'I didn't realise it would go down so well,' she said. Heather smiled.

'I didn't doubt it. We're a close-knit village, but not a wealthy one – with a few obvious exceptions. Many of us know what it's like to struggle for money. But we also know that we're lucky to live in such a gorgeous place, and being here enriches our lives more than a few pounds in the bank. Most of us are happy to share it with people who couldn't otherwise afford to come.'

Heather had put into words something that Mim had felt over the last few weeks. She'd been incredibly lucky to connect with the Howards, and with the rent-free caravan and her two jobs, she'd started saving money for the first time. It didn't mean that her worries were over. She could be kicked out of the caravan or be sacked at any moment. But there was something about this place – the view of the sea that changed every day, the rolling cliff tops, the salty breeze that blew in towards the shore – that gave her a sense of peace, and of optimism that somehow things would work out.

The group of volunteers gathered round Lia, who was dressed for the occasion in neon wellies and a trench coat, which seemed to be her idea of working clothes.

'Thank you so much for coming to lend us a hand,' Lia said. 'We're very grateful to you all for supporting our charity. We want As You Like It holidays to be the perfect retreat for anyone who needs a break. Mim – as it was your idea, why don't you explain how much it means?'

Had it been her idea? Mim didn't remember the original discussion going quite like that, but all eyes had now turned to her. She smiled.

'If you've spoken to me in the shop or the pub, you'll have gathered I'm not from round here,' she said. There were a few smiles of acknowledgement. 'I've spent all my life up north. I didn't have holidays when I was growing up, for various reasons. I'd never been to Devon, or seen the sea, until a few weeks ago. Already I've realised there's something special about this place, a peace and a beauty that creeps into your heart without you noticing and puts all the other worries of life into perspective. I'd love to be able to share that peace with families who need a break, and to help them spend time together with nothing to worry about other than having fun.'

She stopped, thinking that she'd said too much and been too sentimental, and was surprised when the volunteers burst into a quick round of applause.

'I hope that's inspired you all, because today's job isn't the most fun,' Lia said. 'Can we all divide up and start cleaning the exterior of the caravans? They are covered in so much grime that we can't see if there's any damage underneath.'

The group divided up into pairs. Heather and Karen teamed up, leaving Mim on her own, with Lia and Bobby also at a loose end. Neither of them looked at each other. Lia fiddled with the belt of her trench, her usual confidence seemingly vanished, and Bobby rubbed the side of his face.

'Why don't you two—'

'Perhaps—'

'I should—'

They all started to speak at once. Bobby was first to start again.

'I'll have a look at some of those verandas,' he said, addressing Mim. 'Make a note of any rotten posts and boards that need replacing.'

'Great idea,' Lia said, but he was already dashing away to the nearest caravan. Lia sighed. 'You see, Mim? He must think I'm far too silly to be in charge of a project like this. He's assigning his own tasks.'

'There's no point him cleaning,' Mim said. 'Anyone can do that. He's better off looking at the skilled jobs that need doing.'

Twenty minutes later, Mim was revising her opinion that anyone could do the cleaning. Lia had donned some rubber gloves, and had made a couple of sweeps with a sponge on the side of the caravan she was working on with Mim, but she wasn't exactly putting in hard graft. Not on the caravans, at least; she seemed extremely busy sorting out her social life. Her phone buzzed every couple of minutes and she gave Mim a running commentary on what was going on, and who would be pairing up for the Valentine dinner at the weekend. Apparently, Lia's date was a City banker called Algie, a friend of a friend who she had been told was totally hot. Mim didn't miss the glance across the field to Bobby when Lia said this.

Bea and Mrs Dennis arrived at lunchtime, carrying cool bags and wicker baskets full of food for the workers. Everyone squashed together on the steps leading to Mim's caravan to enjoy the food.

'Doesn't it look brighter already?' Bea said, gesturing across the field at the caravans, some of which were now looking clean again. 'It's a shame they are all that institutional cream colour. We were going for classic, neutral shades at the time we bought them, but something more cheerful would suit this project better.'

'You could always paint them,' Bobby said, picking a pork pie from a Tupperware box of treats.

'Could we?' Lia looked thrilled. 'I had wondered, but I wasn't sure what you could use on caravans.'

'It would have to be special paint,' Bobby said. 'You can get a metal topcoat that protects from UV light and weathering. I don't know what colours they do.'

Lia was looking at him as if he'd just discovered DNA.

'You're a genius,' she said. 'This is exactly what we need to make the site look more friendly and welcoming. We were thinking of a vintage look for the interior, so perhaps we can match that outside. What about cobalt blue, sea green, shell pink and maybe a yellow and a grey? Wouldn't that look brilliant?'

'Special paint sounds expensive,' Mim said, trying to rein Lia in before she got too carried away. 'The caravans will look okay once they're cleaned up, won't they?'

'Hush Mim,' Bea said. 'I don't want to hear another word about the expense. It will lift the spirits of our guests if they arrive and see some bright caravans waiting for them. We'll be painting yours too, so have a think about what colour you would like. Could you find us some paint charts, Bobby, there's a dear?'

The afternoon flew by as they finished cleaning the remaining caravans, and started work on the grounds. All the flowerpots were emptied of the dead plants and dry soil, and the worst of the weeds were cleared away. Bobby gave Mim a spray to use on the gravel drive to try to kill off the weeds poking up through the stones. Lia had given up all pretence of working by this point, and spent most of her time flitting from group to group, motivating the volunteers with a smile and some conversation.

'We need to keep the momentum going,' she said, when it was Mim's turn to enjoy her company again. 'I wonder if people will be happy to come back on Saturday? I'll be getting ready for the Valentine dinner, but Olly will be here by then and he and Corin could take our places, couldn't they?' She laughed. 'I know what you're thinking. They could do as much work in a couple of hours as I've done all day, couldn't they?'

'A couple of hours? I'm sure they'd only need thirty minutes.' Mim grinned. It was one of Lia's most endearing qualities that she didn't take herself too seriously. Unlike her eldest brother. 'Where is Corin today? I thought he would have come to help.'

'He wanted to, but he's working today.'

'A fossil walk?' Mim asked. 'How often does he do them?'

'Hmm?' The conversation was put on hold while Lia replied to a text message. 'No, it's one of his factory days today.'

Mim paused in her spraying.

'Corin works in a factory?' she asked. Lia laughed.

'Not on all the machinery, silly. It's Daddy's factory. He's teaching Corin how to run it, and the rest of the business.'

Bill owned a factory? Mim hadn't heard any mention of that so far. She hadn't really thought about where the Howard money came from. Some people were simply born rich, weren't they?

'What do they make in the factory?' she asked.

'Oh, I don't exactly know – some kind of industrial clip or fastening, I think. I've never really paid all that much attention to be honest, darling. Daddy was terribly clever and invented it when he was younger than me, and now it's used all over the world. It was definitely one of his better ideas.'

'And Corin's going to take over?' Mim asked. It seemed a waste of all those Geography and Geology qualifications he'd told her about.

'Someone has to when Daddy retires, don't they? It's the family business and pays for us all,' Lia said. 'Corin's the first-born son and heir, so why shouldn't it be him?'

'Because daughters and younger sons could run a factory too?' Mim suggested.

'Of course we could,' Lia said, with a disarming smile. 'But none of us want to.'

'Does Corin want to? What about his fossil walks?'

'That's only a hobby – and an awfully dull one as you now know. I expect he'll be glad to have something better to do.'

Would he? When Mim had joined Corin on the fossil hunt, she'd seen his passion for the subject, and his enthusiasm for sharing it with others. She'd thought that was genuine – a glimpse of the real man behind the riches. But what did she know? Perhaps the lure of making money was even more appealing. She pumped the weed killer over the drive, trying to ignore the twist of disappointment. There was no point giving it another thought. She would never understand the ways of rich people, and whatever Corin chose to do with his life was no concern of hers.

The Valentine dinner was in a league so far beyond Mim's comprehension that she felt she'd strayed into a different world. The event was being held at a local golf club, where a large function room had been transformed into a romantic paradise. Clouds of shimmering fabric draped the ceilings and walls, lit by flickering lights spaced out along the sides of the room. There were fresh flowers everywhere, and a beautiful display of rosebuds formed the centrepiece of each table. Everything shone and glittered and sparkled, but not in a tacky way. Elegance and expense were evident in every aspect.

As for the guests, Mim could only watch in wide-eyed, open-mouthed wonder as they started to drift into the room. Most of the men were wearing black tie – the first time she'd ever seen it in real life, and she wasn't immune to how attractive it was – and the ladies were dressed in exquisite gowns that shimmered as they moved and jewels that sparkled in the light. She wasn't the jealous type, but as a woman about her own age floated past in a sheath of powder-blue silk, looking and smelling heavenly, she did feel a pang of wistfulness that she would never have the chance to dress up like that. And then she pushed it firmly away, picked up her tray of Champagne glasses and got on with her job.

None of the Howards were seated at the tables she served with dinner, but she noticed them as she made her way to and from the kitchen. They weren't sitting together as a family, which surprised Mim. Bill and Bea were with couples of a similar age, and seemed to be leading the laughter and conversation at their table. Ros and Jonty were at a table nearby, and Lia and Olly had joined forces with a group of other young people. It took longer to spot Corin, partly because he was at the opposite side of the room to the rest of the family, and partly because he didn't look like the Corin she knew. Despite the obvious dress code, she'd been looking for the scruffy man with sticking-out hair and a woolly jumper. Her gaze must have passed over him four or five times before she realised that the handsome man in crisp black-tie was the one she had been searching for. Mim glanced at his companions – well-groomed men and shiny women who looked like they'd never scrubbed a toilet in their life – and whisked invisibly back to the kitchen with her arms full of dirty plates.

Once the dinner was over, Mim moved to work a shift behind the bar, although there wasn't much call for normal drinks as two mixologists were making cocktails at the other end of the bar. Their popularity left her plenty of time to people watch. A live band was playing and some couples were dancing – proper dancing, like she'd only seen on television before. It was mesmerising.

'Mim darling, please pour me a glass of Champagne or I'll literally die of thirst.' Lia interrupted Mim's observations. 'You're going to be so proud of me when I tell you what I've been doing tonight. I've been working incredibly hard.'

'Have you?' Mim poured the Champagne, unable to hide her smile. From what she'd seen, Lia had been eating, drinking, and flirting all night. Nice work if you could get it.

'Don't be naughty. You shouldn't laugh at me. This has all been for a good cause.' Lia waggled her glass at Mim. 'I've been telling everyone about As You Like It holidays. We've had some incredible pledges of support, and not just money. I remembered what you said about the practical issues, and so I targeted Charlie Heatherington. His family owns a contract laundry business and he's offered to service all the laundry from the caravans, without charging us at all. Isn't he a darling?'

'That's brilliant news.' A relief too. Mim had been worried that the day-to-day issues, such as who would clean the caravans between guests and launder the sheets, had been forgotten in the excitement of logos and social media sites. She had expected the job to fall to her and Mrs Dennis. 'I hope you've not neglected your date though. Is he as hot as you expected?'

'Urgh.' Lia slumped against the bar. 'Don't mention him. Remind me never to accept a blind date again. I mean, have you seen him? I was promised a cute face and fantastic muscles, but frankly, I've seen a cuter face on Dickens. Dickens isn't such a messy eater either. I don't know what Bella was thinking of, trying to fix us up. I'm not happy with her at all.'

'Why don't you just enjoy being single for a while?' Mim asked. 'It suits me.'

'Oh, I'm a much shallower creature than you, darling. I grow bored of my own company after five minutes.'

'You could get yourself a Dickens.'

Lia laughed and wandered off to rejoin a lively group who were skirting the edge of the dancefloor.

It must have been an hour later when Mim was interrupted by a Howard again. She turned away from watching the mixologists juggle their shakers to find Corin leaning against the bar, his back to her as he observed the crowd in the room. His hair had begun to stick out again at the nape of his neck, and his bow tie hung loose so he seemed a curious hybrid version of Corin, neither the scruffy nor the smart man. It was still the familiar smile he gave her when he turned to face her.

'Don't you wish you were back in the Boat?' he asked. 'I'd give anything to be nursing a pint in front of the fire with Dickens.'

'I'm getting paid more to be here.' Mim smiled. 'I can help with the pint, though. It's not your usual, but there is real ale on pump.'

'You're a lifesaver.' He watched while she poured his pint and passed it over. He drank deeply. 'Do you mind having to work tonight? It's not the most romantic way to spend the Valentine weekend.'

'I'm not bothered about all that romantic stuff. Last year, Valentine's Day consisted of three pints and half an hour rolling around in a single bed with a man who never called me again. The most exciting part of the night was when I fell out and sprained my wrist.' Mim grinned. 'I'm better off working.'

Corin stared at her and then laughed.

'What do you make of all this?' he asked, nodding towards the crowd.

'I love it. It's like something from a film.'

'Really?' Corin leaned his elbow on the bar. He was close enough that she could smell his aftershave, warm and spicy, as it filled her head. 'I was sure you'd disapprove. The money spent on this event could have gone a long way to help those in need.'

'But all the profit is going to a mental health charity, isn't it? I don't see why you shouldn't have fun and raise money at the same time,' Mim said. 'Anyway, you didn't have to be here. You could have gone to the Boat if you wanted.'

'Ah, you still underestimate the influence of my family.'

'They couldn't force you to come.'

'No. But the trouble with a family like mine is that they don't need to force you to do anything. They simply love you so much that it becomes impossible to disappoint them.'

He sounded again like the man that Mim had first met under the trees on New Year's Eve. But how could that be right? That man had sounded dissatisfied with his life. She couldn't understand why Corin should be dissatisfied with his. He had everything she had ever dreamed of growing up, on those dark nights hiding under her duvet when she had felt most alone.

'That doesn't sound like much trouble to me,' she said. They looked at each other and though physically there was barely half a bar's width between them, Mim felt like they may as well have been a million miles apart.

Corin downed his pint in one go and held up the empty glass.

'No. I'm an ungrateful devil, aren't I? I must be more Mim and be thankful to have a glass.'

'Are you involved in this caravan business, then?' Janet asked Mim one Thursday morning when she arrived for her shift in the deli. 'What's it all about?'

'Haven't you heard? I didn't think there was anyone left who hadn't been given all the details by Lia. We're renovating the caravans to provide holidays for people who need a break and can't afford one.'

It was early March now, and in the couple of weeks since work had first started on the caravans, they had made great progress. Bobby had cut the grass all through the field on his ride-on mower, which had instantly transformed the site. The weeds had gone from the gravel road, and all the planters had been cleaned up and filled with small plants and bulbs. They had chosen the paint colours for the exterior of the caravans and were waiting for a break in the weather to make a start on that job. It was all going remarkably well, and Lia was proving a better project leader than anyone had expected.

'I can't afford to take a break. Do I qualify?'

Mim laughed, although she wasn't sure if Janet was joking or not.

'No, it's not for people who already live here. It's for those who don't know where the next meal is coming from, and can't even dream of taking a holiday. Or for people who have had a tough time through illness or caring for others. We can't change their lives, but we can give them some time away from the worry of ordinary life.'

She took off her coat and hung it on the peg in the corridor at the back of the shop. She'd wondered about approaching Janet about the charity before but hadn't found the right time. Now seemed the perfect moment, as she had already shown an interest. She pulled her apron over her head.

'Would you be willing to help?' she asked. 'We'll need to supply the basics – you know, toilet roll, washing-up liquid, cooking oil, pasta, and rice. All those sorts of things. The butcher has offered to provide sausages and bacon, and the Sandcatcher Café will bake a cake for each set of guests. Lots of local businesses are happy to help.'

'More fool them.' Janet pushed past Mim to turn the shop sign to 'open'. 'I've not worked hard for the last fifty years to give away my profits. It's not going to help my holiday cottage business, having free caravans available, is it? My business is my pension. It's a bit rich that those Howards expect us all to contribute to their latest scheme. They're worth more than this entire village several times over and don't need to worry about the future. No, charity begins at home in my book, and that means right here.' She pointed upwards to her flat above the shop. 'Don't let me catch you promoting this idea on my time. I'll be keeping an eye on you.'

'I'd offer to boycott the place,' Karen said, when Mim repeated Janet's words at the next swimming meeting, 'but I never go in. I can't afford it. Three pounds for a loaf of bread. Who pays that sort of money?'

'You'd be surprised.' It had amazed Mim that the shop had a good trade, despite the prices. Many of the customers were old people from the village who didn't have a car; there was no bus service and they had no choice but to buy their groceries from Janet. It frustrated Mim to see them being overcharged, and she slipped an extra potato or slice of cooked meat into their order as often as she thought she could get away with it. Now that March was rolling on and the weather was turning milder, more tourists had started to visit the shop too, apparently prepared to pay any price for something with a 'local produce' label.

'I did warn you that some people would be against

the scheme,' Heather said, pulling off the baggy trousers she was wearing over her wetsuit. 'Littlemead is relatively unchanged by the tourist trade, and they'd prefer it to stay that way. I'm surprised Janet is one of them, as her business relies on tourists. What a misery. I don't know how you can stand to work for her. I'd probably have walked out within an hour.'

'I can't afford to have principles. I need the money. It's not too bad now she leaves me alone most of the day, and I like working in the Boat.'

'How long are you going to stay there?' Heather asked. 'Are you looking to move on? I thought your experience was in hotels.'

'My experience is, but I don't have any qualifications to back it up. Or a reference. I can't see Janet giving me one any time soon. I've plummeted in her estimation again now because of my involvement with the charity.' Mim laughed. 'Although I might be flattering myself that I'd ever risen.'

'Howie might provide a reference,' Karen said. 'He's a good sort. Paula would too, now you've worked for her a couple of times. There's no harm in looking for something else, is there? You don't have to be stuck with Janet forever.'

Mim mulled it over as she swam. The sea was rough this morning, and it tossed her around so much that it took a huge effort to move forward at all. It was tempting to stop fighting and drift wherever the waves carried her.

Was that what she was doing with her life? She'd done it for the last ten years with Gordon; after years of struggling, it had been a relief to be able to drift. He'd given her the stability she craved, and the security of knowing she could get out of bed in the morning and return to the same bed that night. No one else could understand how precious those things had been to her. He had changed her life. Perhaps it was time to stop drifting and change her own life now?

A dry spell of weather was forecast and Bobby decided that it was a good time to work on the exterior of the caravans. It wasn't a straightforward job, as he explained when a group of volunteers met up on Monday morning. There would be a lot of preparation work first, including smoothing the surface of the caravan walls and applying masking tape around the edges and windows. They would have to be patient before they could move on to the fun part of painting and seeing the caravans transformed.

There were some changes to the group of volunteers this time. One of the previous couples was on holiday, but three new women had arrived in their place, thanks to Heather promoting the project with her book group. Karen had started a different shift pattern at work so couldn't make it, and Lia was inexplicably absent too.

The plan was to paint one caravan first, as a test run, and so everyone set to work on the caravan closest to Mim's, dividing into teams to cover each side. It was harder graft than Mim had expected, as she buffed the exterior wall to remove cracked and peeling paint, old stickers and uneven ridges. How could the walls be so huge when the interiors were compact? After a couple of hours, her arms ached more than after the most gruelling swimming session.

She was perched on a ladder to reach the top of the wall and she paused to roll her shoulders back and ease some of the tension. She hadn't realised that the others had stopped work. Most of the volunteers were sitting on rugs on the grass – the book-club ladies had come well prepared – and only Mim and Bobby were still hard at it.

'I can't believe they've all buggered off,' Mim said to him. She laughed and pointed down to the rest of the group. 'We're mugs still being up here. It's obviously tea-break time.'

Bobby checked his watch.

'It's well past that. I reckon it's lunchtime.' He knelt up on the roof of the caravan and looked across the field. 'There's a car coming this way from the house. Perhaps Mrs Dennis has made sandwiches again.'

'Enough to fill a car? Sounds about right. I'm starving.'

Mim scrambled down the ladder, followed by Bobby, and they met the car when it pulled to a stop at a strange angle half on, half off the gravel road. Lia jumped out of the driver's seat, followed at a more sedate pace by Bea from the passenger side.

'Happy birthday!' Lia called, and before Mim could wonder at the coincidence of someone else also having a birthday that day, Lia dashed over and kissed her on both cheeks. 'Isn't this the best surprise, darling? Mrs Dennis has made a special picnic and we even have birthday cake. I picked it up from the cake shop this morning and they've done an amazing job. You'll love it.'

'But who told you it was my birthday?' Mim asked. She was sure she hadn't mentioned it.

'Not you, which is very naughty of you.' Bea took Mim's hands and squeezed them. 'Happy birthday, dear Mim. I saw the date when I borrowed your driving licence to arrange the car insurance. I hope you weren't planning to celebrate without us.'

'I wasn't planning to celebrate at all.'

'Oh, come now.' Bea smiled. 'You're only thirty-four. You needn't despair at the passing years just yet.'

Mim didn't feel despair. She loved birthdays, and Gordon had always made a fuss of her, forbidding her from work and sharing a bottle of wine while they watched an old film on the TV. This year was different; she was still a relative stranger here and she'd been resigned to having no one to celebrate with. But as she looked around at the smiling faces of Lia and Bea, Bobby and Heather, and realised why the picnic rugs and other paraphernalia had appeared today, she felt a glow of warmth at how wrong she had been. She had friends, perhaps for the first time in her life; real friends who liked her for who she was, despite everything that had happened in her past. She couldn't remember ever feeling so happy. It was the best gift she could have wished for.

Bea took two folding chairs from the boot of the car and insisted that Mim sat on one. Mim felt like the Queen as baskets of delicacies were brought forward for her delight: sandwiches, quiche, mini-pasties, fruit… Mrs Dennis had excelled herself, as Bea was first to admit. There was even a bottle of Champagne to wash it all down. Mim lolled in her chair, feeling pleasantly drowsy after the food and drink, breathing in the sea air, and she thanked all of her lucky stars for bringing her here.

'Time for cake,' Lia said, clapping her hands and waking everyone up after the feast. She dashed to the car and came back carrying a large white cake box. She grinned at Mim. 'Are you ready for this? Ta da!'

She pulled away the lid and the sides of the box, and Mim laughed. It was the best cake she'd ever seen. It had been decorated with blue-green icing, rising in peaks to look like waves, and in the centre, there was a figure of a mermaid with coils of auburn hair spreading across the cake.

'You do love it, don't you?' Lia asked.

'It's perfect.' Mim leant across and gave Lia a hug – a

tentative, awkward one, because she still wasn't used to positive gestures like that, but it felt absolutely the right thing to do.

'Let me light the candles and you can make a wish.' Lia produced a box of matches. 'Are you ready? You'll need to be quick before the wind blows the candles out for you.'

Mim nodded. 'I'm ready.'

Lia lit the candles and Mim took a deep breath and blew them all out. Her wish hadn't needed any thought at all. She had somewhere to live, a job, and a group of friends. What more could she possibly want? Her only wish was that her present situation would last forever.

The cake was delicious, but it wasn't the last surprise of the day. While Bea poured out tea, Lia went to the car again and came back with two gift-wrapped parcels.

'It's time for presents,' she said. 'I'm so sorry there are only two. I suggested lots of other ideas but Mummy said you were too stubborn to accept them.'

'Oh Lia,' Bea said, shaking her head. 'You weren't supposed to repeat that.' She smiled at Mim. 'It was meant in the kindest way, my dear. It's true, though, isn't it?'

'Yes it is, and I'm not sure I should even accept these. You really shouldn't have.'

'Oh pooh, never mind that nonsense. You'll soon see it isn't much, and is more for our benefit than yours.' Mim knew better than to believe that. Bea's idea of 'not much' was very different to hers. 'Open the small one first. That's a joint present from all of us.'

Bea passed over a rectangular shaped parcel. Mim pulled off the bows, ribbons and foil wrapping paper to reveal a box containing a mobile telephone. Bea held up her hand to silence Mim.

'I won't hear a word of objection, so don't even contemplate it,' Bea said. 'We were frugal and didn't buy the top of the range model. The phone is registered to you and all the charges are taken care of for the next twelve months while you get yourself back on your feet.'

'You really shouldn't have,' Mim said again, but already she was opening the box and feeling the weight of the phone in her hand. She hadn't realised how much she'd missed having one over the last few months. She felt normal again, like she'd taken a step towards civilisation and away from being the homeless woman in the car. 'Thank you. I don't see how this benefits you, though.'

'Now we can get in touch with you whenever we like. It's highly inconvenient having to trail down here if we need you, or risk life and limb leaping in front of your car.'

'You never need me,' Mim protested. 'You're not keeping up your end of the bargain at all.'

'That will change now, and you can begin by driving me back to the house once you've opened Corin's present. He sends his apologies for missing the day, but he's leading a Duke of Edinburgh expedition this week and couldn't get away.'

Bea held out the other parcel. It was also rectangular, but larger and looked as if it had been wrapped in a hurry. There were no bows and ribbons, and bits of Sellotape were peeling off. It definitely had a Corin look about it.

'Do you think Dickens wrapped it for him?' Lia asked, inspecting the parcel critically. 'It's hard to imagine he could have done a worse job.'

'I thought the phone was from all of you?' Mim said. 'I didn't need a second present as well.'

'Oh, the phone wasn't from Corin.' Bea smiled. 'He likes to go his own way.' She sighed as Mim pulled off the wrapping paper. 'Not always the most appropriate way. I wish he'd asked me. I expect you'd have preferred a juicy novel, wouldn't you?'

Mim looked at the two brand new books in her hand: one a hardback, the other a paperback, both promising gripping accounts of feats of bravery and endurance. She'd rather have these than a novel any day. She folded the paper over them again to keep them clean.

'People often ask me why he's thirty-five and still single,' Lia said. She pointed at the parcel that Mim was still clutching in her hands. 'We don't need any further explanation, do we?' She picked up the mobile phone that had fallen off Mim's knee. 'Do you need any help with this? I could help you set it up and show you how to use it.'

'You're all right, thanks,' Mim said, grinning. 'I'm thirty-four, not ninety-four. I've had a phone before.'

Lia stayed behind to check on progress with the caravans while Mim drove the car back to the house. She helped Bea carry the picnic baskets into the kitchen.

'Shall I load the dishwasher?' Mim asked.

'No, dear, Mrs Dennis can… Actually, Mim, why not? We can have a chat while you're doing it, as there's something I've been meaning to discuss.'

That sounded ominous. Mim emptied the plates into the bin and started to fill the dishwasher, waiting for Bea to continue.

'Now, I think you said you'd worked in the hotel for ten years, is that right?' Bea asked.

'Yes.' Mim looked up. She hadn't been expecting that question. 'It would have been eleven in May if it had stayed open.' And if Gordon had still been alive. It was impossible not to miss him today, even with the surprise birthday celebrations.

'And you were busy there?'

'The occupancy rate varied but we were trying to get it up.'

'No, I mean *you*, not the hotel,' Bea corrected herself. 'You had a full-time job, with a decent wage?'

'Well, yes…' Mim filled the sink with hot water so she could wash the Champagne glasses.

'Only, I'm struggling to understand,' Bea pressed on. 'You had a good job for ten years and you're the least extravagant person I know. So how did you come out of it with no savings and no assets other than a battered old car? Not even a mobile phone! Surely you were entitled to a redundancy payment when your employment ended?'

Mim rinsed the glass she was washing and set it down on the draining board. She turned to Bea, soap suds dripping from her hands.

'I wasn't entitled to a payment because I never actually had an employment contract.' She wiped her hands on her jeans. 'Most of the money I should have received as a wage was ploughed back into the business.'

It sounded stupid when she gave the facts like that, baldly and without any context; she knew that even before seeing the shocked expression on Bea's face.

'Oh Mim.' Bea came over and studied her face. 'How did that happen? This man – Gordon, did you say? – did he take advantage of you?'

'No!' Mim was appalled. Gordon had taken nothing and given her everything. 'He was the dearest, kindest man I've ever met. He saved me. That hotel was the closest thing to a home I've known, and I was glad to give every penny and every minute I had to keep it going.'

And now the tears that she'd bottled up for so long poured out of her. She hadn't cried when Gordon died because she'd had to carry on and put on a front for the guests. She hadn't cried when she'd locked the door of the hotel for the last time because she wouldn't give his daughter the satisfaction of seeing her pain. But now her grief wouldn't be silenced and when Bea gathered her in her arms, Mim sobbed until she was exhausted.

Chapter Thirteen

Bea didn't waste any time in proving how useful it was for Mim to have a phone. The day after Mim's birthday, she sent her a text, booking Mim to take her and Bill to Exeter airport the following week.

'It's a last-minute break for our wedding anniversary,' Bea explained, when Mim called in at Vennhallow to find out the details. 'Thirty-nine years. Can you believe I've put up with the old devil for so long?' She squeezed Bill's hand, with obvious devotion. 'We weren't going to bother, but it hasn't been the easiest year and at least we don't have to worry about what Lia will get up to, now you and Corin are here to look after her.'

'Me? I don't know what I can do about Lia,' Mim said. She didn't mind doing the airport run, but babysitting a twenty-five-year-old seemed unnecessary.

She couldn't imagine anyone stopping Lia once she set her mind on something.

'Hmm, it will be tricky with you in the caravan,' Bill said, stroking his moustache. 'I've had an idea. Why don't you stay here at the house while we're away? You two girls could keep each other company. That's more like it, eh?'

Mim gave him a suspicious look. He wasn't going to win an Oscar for his acting skills.

'Are you still trying to persuade me to move in here?' she asked. 'I really am happy in the caravan. It's not as bad as you all think. And now the weather is improving, it's hardly cold at all,' she added, before Bea could use that argument against her again.

'Of course you want to stay in the caravan,' Bea said. 'It's your space.' She sighed. 'But it would put our mind at rest if you could move in with Lia just while we're away. It would give Bill one less thing to worry about.'

How could Mim refuse when Bea pulled the health card? And really, it would be as good as a holiday for her to be staying in that gorgeous spare room again.

So, after driving them to the airport the following week, Mim moved her things into Vennhallow.

Any illusion that she was in charge of looking after Lia vanished within an hour. Lia had plans and Mim had no choice but to go along with them. During the day, they continued to work on the caravans, and it was exciting to see the coloured paint being applied to the first one. Bobby showed them what to do, and they all took a turn at spraying the top coat until the old caravan was transformed into a glossy, shell-pink home. In the evening, Lia cooked surprisingly delicious meals, and then they settled down to some pampering. Mim had never experienced anything like it. Her face was scrubbed, polished, and stretched with a mask, her hair was given a deep conditioning treatment, and Lia painted her nails – against Mim's better judgement, having seen what a mess she had made with the spray paint. Mim had never had the money for indulgences like this and loved every minute of it.

Wednesday would be Mim's final free evening at the house with Lia before she had to return to work at the Boat. Lia announced that they were having a pyjama party, which was a new concept to Mim but apparently involved the pair of them lying on the sofa wearing pyjamas and watching a film. Wine and chocolate were also mentioned. What was there to dislike about that? Lia lit the fire – to Mim's horror, as she was terrified the house would burn down on her watch – and brought Mim a fluffy cardigan and slipper boots to compensate for her thin pyjamas. Then they snuggled into the sofa, wrapped in blankets, and watched the film Lia had chosen.

The romantic story wasn't Mim's cup of tea, but by the time an hour had passed, and she'd drunk a couple of glasses, she was warming to the story, so it was irritating when the door opened and Corin walked in, followed by Dickens. Lia shrieked and slopped wine all over her blanket.

'You are such an idiot!' she said, jumping up and tripping over the blanket, so she landed on her knees on the floor. 'I thought I was literally going to die of a massive heart attack. What are you doing here? I locked the door. Or I think I did.'

'You did.' Corin held out his hand and yanked her back onto her feet. 'But it doesn't tend to stop someone who also has a key.'

'You had no right—' Lia stopped, and Mim noticed for the first time that Bobby was standing behind Corin. Lia smoothed down her hair. 'You could have rung the bell.'

'We did. There was no answer. You were obviously too engrossed in whatever's going on here.'

'It's a pyjama party,' Mim said, deciding that Lia could do with some support. 'Isn't it obvious? You've not made much effort, have you?'

Corin was wearing his usual outfit of old jeans and a jumper. He looked Mim up and down, his eyes lingering on her hair, which for once was falling loosely around her shoulders. He smiled.

'My invitation must have gone missing. We'll have to stick to our plan to spend the evening in the Boat.' He put some papers on the coffee table. 'Olly has sent over the paperwork for the charity. I thought we could all sign it while Bobby's here to act as a witness.'

Lia signed where he indicated and Corin held out his pen to Mim.

'Your turn.'

'To be a witness?' Mim asked. 'I thought you said Bobby was doing that.'

'No, you're signing as trustee of the charity.' Corin looked from Mim to Lia. 'Didn't you know? Lia was supposed to have asked you.'

'Sorry, darling.' Lia grimaced at Mim. 'I was caught up in the work at the caravans and forgot about the boring legal bit. You, me, and Corin are the trustees. That's okay, isn't it?'

Was it okay? Mim had no idea what it involved and wasn't keen to sign anything official without being clear what she was committing to. Corin must have sensed her hesitation.

'Sorry, I thought you'd already agreed,' he said. 'We won't spring this on you. I'll print out some information for you about what it involves. We need to carry out the police check as well.'

'Police check?' Mim stood up and glared at him. 'What are you suggesting? I've never been in trouble with the police. Just because I was brought up in care—'

Corin shook his head.

'We all need police checks. It's a legal requirement, not an accusation. There's a declaration to complete too.'

He stopped talking but didn't move, other than to rub the back of his neck with his finger, making the ends of his hair stick out even more. Mim watched him suspiciously, wondering what was coming next.

'Is that everything?' Lia asked. 'We're trying to watch a film.'

'While we're here, would you mind looking for the guarantee documents for the ride-on mower for Bobby?' Corin replied. 'They should be in the filing cabinet in the study.'

'Do you need them right this minute?'

'Tomorrow will be okay,' Bobby said.

'Why not now?' Corin said. 'Go on. It will only take a minute. Bobby will come with you to check it's the right thing.'

'Because I can't be trusted to read a piece of paper,' Lia grumbled, but she headed out of the room, Bobby trailing behind.

'You need to brush up your acting skills,' Mim said, when she was alone with Corin. She smiled, relieved that his obvious discomfort was only about this and nothing to do with her. 'That was the most obvious piece of matchmaking I've ever seen.'

'Matchmaking? Between Bobby and Lia?' He looked astonished at the suggestion. 'I really don't think so.'

'Why not? Is he not good enough for her?'

If anything, Corin looked even more astonished.

'Quite the opposite. I wouldn't wish her on him.

She'd talk him to death. Literally,' he added with a smile, which Mim couldn't help returning. 'I did send them away on purpose, though. Mum has asked me to speak to you.'

'Has she?' Mim sat down again, disturbing Dickens who had settled down on her blanket. 'Should I be worried? Have I done something wrong?'

'It's nothing like that.' Corin prowled round the room. 'That would have been an easier conversation.' He stopped and perched on the arm of a sofa on the other side of the fireplace to Mim. 'It's about the hotel you used to work at.'

'What's happened?' Mim leant forward in her seat. 'Is it bad news? Has it been knocked down? I thought the building was just being converted.'

She dreaded the answer; it would be devastating to hear that the closest thing to a home she'd known no longer existed. Corin shook his head.

'Nothing like that. That would have been an easier conversation too.' He picked at a loose thread on the sofa, not looking at Mim while he spoke. 'You told Mum that you'd contributed towards the running of the hotel, but you didn't inherit a share on Gordon's death. Mum asked Olly to look into whether you could challenge that.'

Mim didn't say anything. She couldn't. She was too dumbfounded. Why had Bea done that, without even discussing it with her? What if Gordon's daughter,

Yvonne, found out, and started her accusations again? If she thought Mim was challenging the will, it would prove all the horrible things she'd said about her over the last ten years.

Corin ploughed on, rushing through the words as if he couldn't wait to get rid of them.

'Apparently, if you can say you were living as husband and wife with Gordon for at least two years, you might be able to contest the will.'

Mim stood up so quickly that Dickens rolled off the sofa.

'You want me to lie?' she said, her voice wobbling. She had thought these people were her friends; how could they so wholly misjudge her? 'Do you all think so badly of me? That I'd do anything for money?'

'No.' Corin stood up and walked towards her. 'No one suggested you should lie. Look, we're not making any judgement. Your relationships are your own concern. But Mum described how devastated you were the other day talking about Gordon … and it's not normal to put money into a business that isn't yours unless there's a good reason…'

'My life hasn't exactly been normal, or not by your standards.' Mim brushed a tear off her cheek, frustrated with herself for letting her emotion show. She didn't want pity. 'There was a good reason and it wasn't the one you seem to think. You're as bad as Gordon's daughter with your dirty minds and grubby insinuations. Yes, I loved him, but we weren't lovers. He was thirty years older than me! He was my saviour, my mentor, and my friend. He gave me a chance when I had no one else to turn to. He gave me security. Helping save the business was the only way I could repay him. It is possible to have a relationship with someone that isn't about sex!'

It was unfortunate timing that Lia walked back into the room as Mim uttered this last sentence. Corin was standing only a metre away from Mim, reaching out his hand in a tentative gesture of apology. Lia took one look between them and her eyes widened.

'What are you doing?' she asked, crossing the room and punching her brother on the arm. 'Are you trying to take advantage of Mim?'

'Don't be ridiculous.' Corin stepped back with what Mim thought, perversely, was an unflattering degree of speed. 'Blame our mother. She can do her own dirty work next time. Dirty-minded work,' he added, as he looked at Mim. He offered her a hesitant smile. 'I'm sorry.'

'I think you boys should go away now and let us carry on with our film,' Lia said. 'We were having a perfectly lovely evening until you came in and ruined it.'

'Fine. We're going.' Corin whistled at Dickens, who immediately ran to his side. He walked towards the door and then looked back at Mim. 'For what it's worth, I've never thought badly of you. And yes, I believe in the relationships you mean. I hope we're friends, aren't we?'

Karen peered round the door to the shop, spotted Mim on her own behind the counter, and came in. Heather was close behind.

'What's going on?' Mim asked. They both had wet hair, so could only recently have finished their Friday swim. 'Have you forgotten the cakes? That's an expensive mistake if you have to buy some from here.'

'Look what we've found,' Karen said. 'It was pinned to the notice board on the car park.'

She put a crumpled A4 sheet of paper on the counter. The corners had been torn off, presumably where it had been stuck down. The centre of the poster was filled with a few words in lurid orange capitals.

'No scum in our bay!' Mim read out loud. And then she gasped, because this wasn't a protest about sea pollution, as she had initially thought. It was clear from the rest of the poster that this was a protest against the caravans – about the Vennhallow caravans, and the whole idea of the As You Like It charity.

'It's not the only one,' Heather said, when Mim looked up in dismay. 'They're spread through the village. This one was stuck to the post box. I'm not even sure that's legal.'

She held up another poster, this one bearing the central message, 'No louts in Littlemead!'

'This is awful,' Mim said. 'Who would do this? Have

you read what it says? I can't believe the words they've used. Scum ... delinquents ... hooligans. They are misrepresenting what the charity's about. All we're trying to do is help people who need a holiday. What's so bad about that?'

'Nothing,' Karen said. 'Whoever wrote these posters is scum as far as I'm concerned.'

'I can't see who in the village would do it, though,' Heather said. 'Even the traditionalists who don't like tourists wouldn't be malicious like this. Do you think this is personal? Something to do with the Howards rather than the charity?'

'But who could hold a grudge against them?' Mim asked. She pushed aside the fact that she'd been feeling resentful towards them for a couple of days, after Bea's interference and Corin's intrusive questions. Their intentions were always kind, even if they didn't think before they acted. It had touched her more than she cared to admit that Corin had called her a friend. Gordon had been the only friend she'd known before she came to Devon. She'd thought that having normal friendships, with people more her own age, of both sexes, was a path in life that was closed to her. Now she knew better.

She suddenly had an awful thought. What if it wasn't a grudge against the Howards but against *her*? What if Yvonne really had heard about the idea of her challenging Gordon's will and had tracked her down to Littlemead? She could easily imagine Yvonne calling her scum; it wasn't far off some of the insults she'd used in the past. Might she be trying to scupper Mim's new life by causing trouble for the charity? Surely it was too far-fetched an idea?

'What are we going to do?' Mim asked, gesturing at the posters.

'We'll walk up and down the village and take down any posters we see,' Heather replied.

'We carry on,' Karen said. 'Working on these caravans has revitalised Susie. I'm not having her brought down again by a narrow-minded so-and-so. Just wait until I get my hands on whoever is behind this. I'll tell them exactly where they can shove their posters...'

Bea and Bill's flight was due to land in the early hours of Monday morning so Mim was spared the job of collecting them from the airport. She'd assumed they would sleep in and was surprised to find Bea in the kitchen when she came down for breakfast before her swim. Bea was sitting on the sofa beside the floor-to-ceiling windows, drinking tea and looking out at the view.

'Good morning, dear Mim,' Bea said, turning to smile as Mim approached. 'It's trite to say there's no place like home, but on a morning such as this I can't wish to be anywhere else.'

'It's stunning.' Mim stood in front of the window, gazing out. It was a beautiful day, one of the best since she had arrived in Devon. The early spring sunshine made the dew sparkle across the lawn and, in the distance, a strip of calm sea glistened like a mirror. She didn't wish to be anywhere else either. This place had crept into her heart, maybe into her soul. And that was exactly why she had to move on.

Mim had spent a lot of time thinking since the conversation with Corin about Gordon's will. Her initial anger hadn't lasted long. Yes, Bea had gone too far and interfered where she shouldn't have, but she'd been motivated by kindness. She was looking out for Mim, in the same way she would have looked out for one of her own children. But Mim wasn't part of this family, however much she might wish it; she couldn't get used to being looked after by them. She'd established her independence over long, hard years and now it was in danger of slipping away, as she'd realised she relished being part of a team rather than going it alone. She couldn't let that happen. It was all about self-preservation. Who knew when she might be on her own again? The novelty of her arrival would wear off one day, if it hadn't already, and the Howards would be caught up in other weddings, other dinners, other family occasions in which Mim had no part. These past months had been precious, perhaps the most precious she'd known; she didn't want to follow them with awkwardness and embarrassment if she outstayed her welcome. She had to leave, had to believe it was the right decision. Better to go on her own terms with happy memories intact. But her heart hurt; it would be the most agonising thing she'd ever done.

She turned her back on the view and smiled at Bea.

'I'm glad you're up,' she said, and she was relieved to hear her voice sound so calm, so normal. 'I would have hated to leave without saying goodbye. And thank you. You've been amazing.'

Bea laughed.

'You're only going down the track to your caravan. I don't think we need sentimental goodbyes, do we? It's us that should be thanking you for holding the fort here. I think it's done Bill the world of good to have a break.'

'I meant that I was leaving here,' Mim explained. 'Littlemead. Vennhallow. The caravan.'

'Leaving Vennhallow?' Bea stared at her. 'What are you talking about? I don't understand. I thought you were happy here.'

'I am. But it was only ever a temporary solution, wasn't it, staying in the caravan? I should have sorted myself out and gone weeks ago, not let myself get so comfortable.' Mim willed Bea to understand, not to drag this out a moment longer when every part of her wanted to hold back the words and stay. 'You've been more than patient. I'm embarrassed to have scrounged off you for so long. It's no wonder you wanted me to inherit some money so I could stand on my own two feet at last and move on.'

Bea reached out and grasped Mim's hand.

'This is because of the business with Gordon's will, isn't it?' she said. 'Forgive me. That was none of my concern. Corin did warn me not to interfere and I was mortified when he told me how upset you were by it. You both have every right to be cross with me. But it has nothing to do with wanting you to move on. Far from it.' Bea glanced behind her, and picked up her cardigan from the sofa. 'Come with me.'

'What?' Mim said. 'Where?'

'To the caravans. We were going to show you later but it can't wait.'

'What can't?'

'Mim, would you stop asking questions and come along?'

Mim had never seen Bea look so fierce. Without another word, she followed her out of the house and down the track towards the caravan field until they turned through the gate and Mim stopped short at the sight in front of her. She hadn't been near the field for a few days, as she'd been working and staying at Vennhallow overnight. The caravan that she'd helped to paint was now completely finished, with all the masking tape removed and it looked amazing: the shell-pink colour reminded her of the early morning light that she'd sometimes seen from her window. Work had now started on a second caravan and it had already been covered with the base coat.

'Well, what do you think?' Bea asked.

She was facing towards a third caravan – Mim's caravan. When Mim had left it on Wednesday, it had looked as it always had, with bland cream walls streaked with dirt that no amount of elbow grease could clean off. Now it was transformed. The exterior walls were painted in a soft sea-green and shone in the morning light. The steps and veranda had been repaired and painted chalky white, and the flowerpots that previously harboured weeds now were filled with bright flowers. It looked gorgeous, better than Mim could ever have imagined.

'Come and look inside,' Bea said, nudging her arm. Mim climbed up the steps, unlocked the door, and stepped in. It was hard to believe it was the same caravan she'd left only five days before. The drab, damp interior had gone, and the place glowed with light and colour that co-ordinated with the exterior paint. The sofa that ran round the wall had been reupholstered with rich, green fabric and scattered with cushions that looked perfect to sink into. The curtains had been replaced with thick drapes that would keep out the winter draughts and a large, fluffy rug covered the floor. The mixture of fabrics, colours and textures blended perfectly to create a relaxed, cosy atmosphere. It was warm and welcoming. It felt like a home.

'It's perfect,' Mim said. She forced herself to smile.

This was what she'd hoped for, wasn't it, for As You Like It holidays? This would offer the ideal retreat for those people that the charity wanted to help. She just hadn't realised that her caravan was being used after all. 'The people who stay here will love it.'

'The people who stay here?' Bea repeated. 'For goodness' sake, Mim, will you stop being so difficult? No one will be staying here except you. This is your caravan, for as long as you want it.'

'So why have you decorated it?'

'For you, my dear. Did you really think we would renovate the others and leave you in the damp and the cold? None of us want you to go. You're one of us; don't you remember me saying that on the day we met? But we know you like your independence. We did this as a surprise, so that you had a proper place of your own and to stop you having any thoughts of leaving.'

Mim sank down onto the sofa and nestled into one of the cushions. It was every bit as comfortable as she'd anticipated. The whole caravan looked amazing. It was hard to take in that it was for her. So many people must have worked long hours over the last week to get this ready, and all for her. All so that she would stay. She really wasn't in the way, or outstaying her welcome. She didn't have to leave. She couldn't speak; it was too overwhelming.

Bea sat down beside her and gently took her hand.

'We lost a child, Mim,' she said, unexpectedly. 'It was

a late miscarriage, a couple of years after Ros was born. That's why there was such a gap before Olly. We were too scared to try again for a long time. It was another girl, and I still think of her as my number two-point-five. Can you guess what we were going to call her?' Mim thought she could, despite her limited knowledge of Shakespeare. 'Miranda,' Bea continued. 'She was our Miranda. And now you'll think me foolish, but that day we met in Lancashire, it felt as if she had sent you to our rescue. As it turned out, perhaps she had sent us to your rescue too.'

Bea brushed tears from her cheeks. Mim's cheeks were wet too. She acted on impulse. She leaned forward and put her arms round Bea, the gesture feeling at once unfamiliar and completely natural.

'So why all the questions about Gordon?' Mim asked, when they eventually broke apart. 'He really was a friend, nothing more. Looking back, perhaps I should have had a contract and a formal wage, but it didn't seem important at the time. The arrangement worked for us. I was used to living one day at a time and not dwelling on the future. I didn't expect to inherit anything from him.'

'I hoped you might have some money of your own, to give you opportunities,' Bea explained. 'You're a bright young woman. You could do better than selling bananas in Janet's shop. You must have had some ambitions when you were growing up.'

'My ambitions were to have a safe place to live, an

honest job, and to survive each day.' Mim smiled. 'Don't knock selling bananas. I think my teenage self would be impressed.'

'But don't you wish for more?' Bea pressed.

'Oh, if we're talking about wishes…' Mim laughed. Of course she'd nursed wishes over the years. A home of her own, however modest. A family of her own, however small. A stable job, where she might have money left over at the end of the week for the occasional treat, maybe even a holiday. Wishing was the easy part. 'If Bill can invent a way to make wishes come true, be sure to send him my way.'

'And where will he find you?' Bea asked. 'Will you still be here?'

Mim smiled and gestured around.

'Look how gorgeous this place is. I'd be daft not to stay, wouldn't I? I think you're going to be stuck with me for a bit longer.'

Chapter Fourteen

At last the Easter weekend arrived. The weather was forecast to be dry and mild for the entire four days, and Mim couldn't resist comparing the weather in Lancashire and feeling smug that she was missing out on heavy rain and winds. She didn't think the novelty of going outside without a coat in early April would ever wear thin.

They had made good progress on the caravans. Four were now fully painted on the outside, with a powder-blue and pale-yellow added to the collection; the group of caravans reminded Mim of the lines of colourful beach huts she'd seen on the postcards in the deli. Three of the interiors had been renovated, including Mim's. She supposed she should feel guilty that the charity's work had slowed down for her, but she was far too snug in her cosy caravan to let it bother her for long.

Heather's cousin was due to arrive at lunchtime on Friday and would stay for three nights to test out one of the caravans and to identify any problems before the charity was officially launched on the last Saturday in April. Mim was gutted that she would miss out on the fun, as she would be working through the weekend as usual. She had asked Janet for one day off but had been told that if she took time off over the busiest weekend of the year, she needn't come back at all. It might have been a bluff but Mim couldn't afford the risk.

She popped into the yellow caravan early on Friday morning to check that everything was ready. This was familiar territory; she'd done this with each hotel room before guests arrived and knew the importance of first impressions. She'd made the beds herself on Wednesday and the bedrooms needed nothing more than a last-minute flick with a duster. She plumped a cushion in the living area, tweaked a curtain so that the folds were even, and then stood back to survey the room with an objective eye. It all looked perfect.

Lia had offered to be in charge of preparing a welcome basket; the caravans would be self-catered, but they had agreed it would be a thoughtful touch to leave some basic provisions to start the holidaymakers off. The white wicker basket sat on the dining table bearing a hand-painted 'welcome' sign. It looked perfect, but when Mim checked the contents her heart sank. A jar of olives, walnut and seed crackers, green tomato chutney, dark chocolate truffles… Where was the pasta, the cooking oil, the bread, the eggs? There wasn't even any milk in the fridge, only what looked like an expensive bottle of wine. Lia had clearly meant well, but perhaps she hadn't been the ideal choice to supply basic provisions rather than luxury treats.

How was Mim going to fix this quickly, in the few minutes left before she started work? There was one obvious person who might be able to help, if he was free. She toyed with her phone. She hadn't seen as much of Corin since their conversation about her relationship with Gordon. Their few meetings had been awkward, and it felt as if their newly established friendship was scuffed and dented already. She was hesitant about asking a favour but he wouldn't mind if it was for the charity, would he? There was no time to debate. She tapped out a quick text to see if he could do an emergency shop.

She could have saved the cost of a text. The man himself was standing at the gate posts that led out to the public road when she drove through a few minutes later. He had a scrubbing brush in his hand and a bucket of soapy water at his feet.

She wound down the window and called out to him.

'You're keen. I don't think the guests will mind if the gate posts are dirty.'

Corin didn't return her smile.

'It's not just dirt,' he said. Mim got out of the car and

went to have a look. The posts had been sprayed with bright red paint. The word 'GO' was written on the left hand post, while 'AWAY' was written on the right hand one; the first A was only just visible as Corin had scrubbed most of it off.

'Is this aimed at the charity's guests? This is a step further than the posters,' Mim said, looking at the gate posts with dismay. She remembered her earlier suspicions that Gordon's daughter, Yvonne, might have tracked her down; nasty posters were one thing but it seemed unlikely she would go this far. 'This is criminal damage, isn't it? Who could feel so strongly?'

'I don't know. Was it there when you came back from the Boat last night?'

'No. I'd have noticed it.'

'They must have done it in the early hours of this morning.' Corin looked down at Dickens. 'Some guard dog you are.'

'Do you think it's a rival holiday park?' Mim asked. 'Worried that we'll take away some business?'

'I doubt it. Our guests wouldn't have booked a holiday themselves so there's no loss. Besides, we know many of the park owners. They're decent people and wouldn't do this. The nearest park is owned by Henry Burrows and it certainly isn't his style. He's rich enough not to worry about five rival caravans.'

'You should have called me.'

'I almost did,' Corin said. He dipped his brush in the

soapy water again, so he wasn't looking at Mim. 'I wasn't sure you'd want me to.'

'Of course I would. I could have shown off my expertise this time. If they gave PhDs for use of a scrubbing brush, I'd have two.' Corin laughed and Mim felt the lingering awkwardness between them melt away. She glanced at her watch. 'I wish I could help now but I don't have time. I'm almost late for work.'

'Don't worry, Bobby is on his way with a stronger cleaner. We'll make sure there's no trace of this by the time the guests arrive, even without your expertise.' He smiled. 'They'll also have milk, coffee, and tea bags.'

'Thanks.'

Mim was about to drive away when Corin knocked on her side window. She stopped and wound it down again.

'You won't be working on Monday, will you?' he asked. Mim shook her head. 'There's an open sea swim taking place at Beremouth. It's a regular Easter Monday event. Some people take it seriously, others wear fancy dress. It's quite a spectacle. Would you like to come?'

It sounded fun, especially as her regular swimming date with Heather and Karen was off because of the Bank Holiday. But would it be weird to go with Corin? This wasn't anything to do with the charity; this would be the two of them, going out as friends. She hesitated.

'The standard swim is 4k, but there's a 2k version if

that's too much,' he added. That comment was enough to make Mim's decision.

'It's not too much. I can manage that.' She laughed when Corin grinned. 'You only said that to persuade me, didn't you? You knew I wouldn't resist a challenge.'

'I wouldn't stoop to such tricks.' He stepped back from the car, still smiling. 'Have a good day.'

It was frustrating being stuck in the shop when As You Like It holidays welcomed their first guests. Mim was reliant on her phone for news about what was happening. Corin sent her a photo of a well-stocked fridge, and Lia sent a picture of herself perched on the veranda steps, waiting to greet the arrivals, but Mim still felt like she was missing out. She was determined not to miss out on the official launch of the charity at the end of April, but when she asked Janet for the Saturday off that weekend, she was met with an abrupt refusal.

'You can see how busy we are during the holiday season,' Janet said. It was true, unfortunately; they'd been so busy that Janet had come down from her flat to help out. 'I can't manage these crowds single-handed.'

Crowds was an exaggeration – Mim had never seen more than six people in the shop at once.

'Could whoever works here on Monday to Wednesday cover an extra day?' Mim asked.

'Maybe,' Janet replied. 'And maybe they'll get a taste for Saturday working and want to keep it up. Do you want to risk that?' Mim shook her head. 'And don't be claiming a sickie, either. I've made a note of that date now, so don't try to fool me. You need to be worrying more about your own job and less about this charity business. You have to look out for yourself in this world.'

By Monday, Mim was exhausted, grumpy, and very glad that she'd agreed to join in with the swim in Beremouth so she could release her tension in the water. It was the best day of the weekend, with a clear blue sky and a gentle breeze, and she wandered across the fields to Corin's lodge.

'Hello,' he said, looking surprised when he opened the door. 'Didn't I say I'd pick you up?'

'I thought I'd save you the bother.' Mim looked at him. He was dressed in his usual style, adapted for the warmer weather – jeans and a well-worn shirt instead of the previous scruffy jumpers. 'What fancy dress outfit is this? Lord of the manor?'

'No. I'd have put on my top hat and tails for that.' Mim wasn't sure if he was joking until he laughed. 'The people in fancy dress usually only dip in and out of the sea. I don't think I could swim 4k dressed as a teddy bear.'

This time she did think he was joking until they arrived in Beremouth and joined a throng of people heading down towards the promenade. Corin hadn't been wrong in promising a spectacle. Mim couldn't see a teddy bear, but she did spot a couple of giant Easter bunnies, a handful of chicks, an army of superheroes, and an assortment of people wearing random outfits including nightdresses, ballgowns, and nurses' uniforms – and that was just the men.

She found a space and stripped off down to her wetsuit, stuffing her clothes in a bag.

'Give them here,' Corin said. 'A friend has come to watch and will look after the bags and Dickens.'

He seemed to have no shortage of friends here. They climbed down the steps from the promenade to the beach, shuffled through the gathering swimmers to find a good spot, and every few metres someone stopped him to give him a slap on the back, or a hug, or even a head wrestle. They finally came to a stop next to a trio of sleek-haired, long-legged women who were all wearing tiny white bikinis with a fluffy tail attached to the bottom and a headband with bunny ears. Was it a coincidence they'd stopped here, Mim wondered, eyeing them up suspiciously? Apparently not. They threw themselves at Corin with squeals of delight that astonished her. Why was he generating such excitement? She glanced at him from the corner of her eye. He was the same old Corin as far as she could see – chestnut hair sticking out at angles, a wide smile on his face, and a red lipstick mark on his cheek. Although, she had to admit, as her gaze went lower, he did fill out his wetsuit extraordinarily well... She tore her gaze away and started talking to a giant octopus on her other side.

The event was due to start at 11a.m., by which time the beach was packed several rows deep with at least a hundred people. The promenade was equally crowded with spectators. A klaxon sounded and the first rows of swimmers raced across the pebbles into the sea, whooping and squealing as they splashed into the waves.

'This way,' Corin shouted, and Mim followed him as he sprinted forwards, dodging the people who were already dashing back to dry land in their wet fancy dress costumes. She waded through the shallows and watched as Corin dived in ahead of her, taking huge, powerful strokes to slice through the water. Mim soon lost him in the crowd of swimmers; she was a strong swimmer but there was no way she could match his pace. It didn't matter. He'd pointed out the route they would take, swimming right along the coast until they reached a lifeboat, which they would circle and head back left towards another boat. The loop could be completed once for 2km or twice for 4km.

The conditions were perfect for the swim. The sea was calm, and only the occasional gentle wave lifted the swimmers as they made their way round the circuit. This was a totally different experience to the swims she carried out with Karen and Heather. When Mim looked up, all she could see were slick bodies sliding forwards, united in this activity, at one with each other and with nature. It was the most exhilarating thing she'd ever done.

She completed the 4k and waded out of the sea reluctantly, at the same time as another swimmer. She looked at them to share a smile of satisfaction and was surprised to see it was Corin. His wetsuit glistened in the sun and seemed to cling to him even more snugly now it was wet. He looked as happy as Mim felt.

'What are you doing here?' she asked. 'I thought you'd have finished ages ago.'

'I wasn't going to leave you behind.' He smiled. 'How was it for you?'

'Bloody fantastic!' She grinned. 'I could have done at least another loop.'

He laughed.

'See how you feel tomorrow before you make rash promises like that. There are some 6k events held over the summer.'

'I'd better start training then.'

'Really? Did you enjoy it that much?'

'I loved it.' Mim grinned. 'Who needs money? Doesn't this go to show that the most fun things in life are free?'

'I've known that since I was sixteen.'

226

He bent over and rubbed his hands through his hair, shaking the water out. The smile on his face left Mim in no doubt that he wasn't thinking about swimming. Despite the goose bumps that were rising on her skin, she felt unexpectedly hot.

They collected their bags and Dickens. Mim pulled out a towel, shivering as the adrenalin of the swim faded. Corin was holding a strange garment that seemed to be a coat with a towel lining. Some of the other swimmers along the promenade were already wearing them.

'Don't you have one of these?' he asked.

'Hmm, let me think, do I have an expensive towel coat?' Mim smiled and pretended to rummage in her bag. 'No. Not in here. Obviously, I have dozens of them in a range of colours, but left them all back at the caravan. Silly me.'

'Here, let's swap.' Corin passed her the coat and took her towel. He stripped off the top half of his wet suit so that it dangled from his waist, and started drying himself. He was clearly a regular swimmer, as he had the typical physique of muscular shoulders and arms. Not that she was studying his physique. Not much. She turned away and met Dickens's sceptical gaze.

'I'm starving,' Corin said, when they were both as dry as they could be, and Mim was snugly cocooned inside his coat. 'How about lunch? My treat, before you become angsty about the cost.'

Angsty? Mim turned to object to that but was

confronted by his bare chest and the words died on her tongue.

'I don't think we're dressed for it,' she said instead. Or dressed at all, in his case. She hoped he was going to put his shirt back on soon. She might have no interest in a relationship but she wasn't blind. Who knew that all this had been hiding under the woolly jumpers?

'Never mind that.' At last he pulled on a T-shirt. 'I know the perfect place.'

He set off along the promenade, then ducked left up a narrow street. There was a fish and chip takeaway on the corner, with a small queue outside. Mim's mouth watered at the delicious smell wafting out of the door.

'The best fish and chips in town,' Corin said. 'Will this do?'

She nodded and he left her with Dickens and their bags as he joined the queue. A couple of women near the front gave him an appreciative glance as he passed. Mim studied him curiously. How did she reconcile this half-dressed man queuing at the chippy with the dinner-suited version drinking Champagne and rubbing shoulders with the well-to-do at the Valentine dinner? This man here could pass as part of her world; the other one was miles outside it. She had no idea who the real Corin Howard was at all.

They took their steaming parcels of food back to the sea front and sat on the edge of the promenade, dangling their feet towards the beach. Corin hadn't exaggerated about the food. Fish and chips had never tasted so good.

'The caravan trial seems to have gone well this weekend,' he said, when they had satisfied the initial pangs of hunger. 'Everything ran like clockwork as far as I can tell. I've never seen Lia apply so much effort. I suspect that's partly down to you.'

'Hardly at all. You shouldn't underestimate her. Anyway, we'll find out the verdict later. I left a feedback form in the caravan.'

Corin waved at someone down on the beach.

'How come you were treated with such delight when you turned up this morning?' Mim asked. 'You've lived away for a while, haven't you? How long were you gone for?'

'Almost nine years,' he said, spearing a chip with his plastic fork.

'Nine years? Wow.' She hadn't expected that. 'That was quite a holiday.'

'I wasn't on holiday.' He looked puzzled. 'It was my job. I spent a few years working for conservation charities in Peru and Ecuador, and then moved to Africa to work on humanitarian projects. Who said it was a holiday?'

No one had, Mim realised, thinking back. She'd assumed it, because he was rich and had a posh accent and presumably didn't need to work for a living like normal people. She really must stop making these assumptions. She hated it when people judged her for her background, so how could she justify doing it to him?

'But to be away for nine years?' Mim said. 'I don't know how you could bear to be away from your family for so long.'

'Really?' He smiled. 'You have met them, haven't you? The talkative, interfering bunch that live in the big house?'

'That's not fair. I know you must have done amazing things in Africa, but if I had a family like yours – a loving, supportive family – I can't imagine anything would be powerful enough to make me leave them.'

Corin balled up his empty food wrapper and stared out to sea.

'Perhaps you can have too much of a good thing,' he said at last. 'I've had it hanging over me for my whole life that I'm Bill and Bea's son – the number one – the son and heir. I studied the subject I loved but when I finished my PhD, I was expected to start work in the family business. I was twenty-six and my whole future was mapped out, from taking over the business from Dad to passing it to my own child one day. I wasn't ready.' He rubbed Dickens's head. 'On an impulse, I took three months out to volunteer on a sustainable farming project in the Amazon rainforest. It changed everything. I could make a difference. I didn't come home after the three months because out there I could achieve something on my own merits, and not have it handed to me on a plate.'

Mim put down her chip wrapper and picked up the cup of tea that Corin had also bought. It was lukewarm now but she still gulped it down. She didn't know how to react to what he'd told her. He hadn't opened up like this before, and it touched her that he'd chosen to do it now. It was a step forward in their friendship and that meant a lot. But she could never understand his frustration. Family would always have come first for her, whatever her own wishes.

'You're lucky,' she said eventually. 'Most people would be glad to have a solid future handed to them on a plate. You wouldn't find someone with my background complaining about it.'

'Even if that future isn't the one you want?' he asked softly.

'Only the obscenely rich think they're entitled to get what they want. The rest of us make do with whatever we're given.'

'Do you disapprove of me so much?' There was no trace of Corin's smile now. The breeze teased the hair round his face as it dried and he frowned as he looked at Mim. 'None of us choose our background. I can't help my family's wealth, or the size of the house they live in, or that they choose exotic holidays and expensive clothes. None of that is me. All I ever wanted was a roof over my head and a job I loved. A quiet, contented life. I thought you might understand.'

'Surely Bea and Bill wouldn't have forced you to work in the business if you didn't want to?' Mim replied. 'They're good people. They love you.'

'I know.' He smiled, but it wasn't the dazzling smile that Mim was used to. 'And I love them. That's the problem. A loving family brings responsibilities as well as rewards.' He tugged Dickens's lead to bring the dog back to him. 'We reached a compromise. I'd follow my path until I was forty and then come back to join the business. The plan had to change last year when Dad was ill. But you're right. It was my choice to come back early. No one forced me.' He stood up, and the look he gave Mim seemed laced with regret. 'Enough of this. You're the last person I should ever complain to. I'm not doing much to dispel your image of the spoilt rich, am I? Just … don't be too quick to judge, okay?'

Chapter Fifteen

The caravans were ready. The weather forecast was predicting a gorgeous weekend with clear blue skies and temperatures in the low twenties. Lia and Ros had exploited all of their social contacts and organised a launch party for As You Like It holidays to take place on the last Saturday of April. Mim was gutted to be missing it, but when she went to bed on Wednesday night, with two days to go, she was satisfied that she'd done everything she could to make the event a success. The beds were made up with crisp white linen, every piece of crockery, cutlery, and glassware shone, and the bathrooms gleamed. Based on the feedback from the trial at Easter, she'd added some finishing touches, and now a shelf of paperback books graced each living room, together with a box of board games and jigsaws and a folder of tourist information leaflets and local information. It all looked perfect and she couldn't have been prouder of what they had achieved.

She fell into an exhausted sleep easily enough, but tossed and turned as her mind went through the details again, looking for anything they might have missed. She sat up to make a note on the pad of paper beside her bed and as she did, a light flickered across her bedroom window. She watched but it didn't happen again. She waited, straining to hear any noise and then it came – the quiet rumble of a voice. There was someone outside.

She picked up her phone and switched on the torch function; she'd never been so grateful for Bea's birthday gift. She picked her way to the front door, stepped outside, and shouted, 'Stop! Don't anyone move.'

She had no idea why she shouted that; it was the first thing that came into her head. It was what the police shouted on TV shows, wasn't it? No matter. It had an effect. She saw three tall figures beside the nearest caravan, and as she moved towards them, they grabbed their torches from the ground and ran away through the gate in the direction of the coastal path. They were fast. Mim would have no chance of catching them up.

She dashed back into the bedroom and threw on some clothes and shoes with growing fury. Had they been trying to burgle the caravans? There was nothing in them of particular value except the televisions, but it was the principle of the thing; who would steal from a charity? She didn't think they could have taken much as she hadn't spotted them carrying anything, but if they'd messed up her pristine caravans she'd be livid.

It was only when she stepped outside and turned back to close her caravan door that she noticed. The slim light from her phone lit up the side of the caravan and illuminated a squiggle of bright red paint that ran the entire length of the wall. She followed the veranda and found that all four walls had been daubed in the same way.

For a moment, despair threatened to overwhelm her. A burglary would have been bad but televisions were easy enough to replace. This was devastating. This had undone hours of painstaking work. A huge number of potential donors were coming to the launch on Saturday, as well as the local press, and were expecting to see an attractive holiday park, ready to welcome families in need. What would they think now?

She took a deep breath. There was no time for despair. They had two days and two nights to fix this. She didn't know if it was possible, but she wasn't going to give up without trying. Never mind the fact that it had taken them weeks to reach this stage. She wouldn't lose hope until the first guests started to arrive on Saturday.

She went back inside the caravan and dialled Corin's number. She didn't think he was going to answer until finally the call connected and she heard a scuffle as if he'd dropped the phone and a soft expletive.

'Mim?' His voice was husky with sleep, gravel in the usual smooth tone as he said her name. 'What's wrong?'

'The spray painters have been back. They've attacked my caravan.'

'Stay inside and lock the door. I'll be right over.'

She switched the torch back on and headed across the field to the caravan opposite hers. The glossy blue exterior was now decorated with a wiggly orange stripe that ran round all four sides, covering walls and windows. Something crunched under her foot and she noticed that the flowerpots had been smashed, and flowers and soil spread across the veranda. It was heartbreaking to see.

She carried on exploring and found some relief. The yellow, grey, and lavender caravans were all untouched. The pink one nearest to hers, where she'd seen the intruders, had been sprayed in one corner but she must have interrupted the vandals before they could do more. A couple of aerosol cans had been abandoned on the ground.

She turned as a wide beam of light fell on her.

'What the hell are you doing?' Corin said. 'I told you to lock yourself inside. You don't know what might have been out here.'

'I've faced a lot worse than three kids with aerosol sprays,' she said, kicking the cans with her foot. 'Do you think bored teenagers have been behind all the trouble? Have there been problems with local kids before?'

'How do you know they were kids?'

'I saw them when they were running away. They were tall and lanky, and fast. Too fast for me to catch them,' she added with regret.

'Did you confront them?' Anger laced his words. 'You should have phoned me as soon as you heard a noise. You could have been hurt.'

'I've looked after myself for years. I don't need you to start doing it for me.'

Briefly, a strange tension seemed to hum in the darkness and the silence of the night, and then Corin sighed, as if letting go of whatever he had intended to say.

'You are infuriatingly independent,' he said. Mim laughed.

'Sorry to disappoint you. I know you're used to squealing women throwing themselves at you, but I'm a different sort of woman and come from a different world. I don't need a hero.' She shone her torch on the damaged area of the caravan. 'I won't refuse your help to fix this, though. This caravan isn't too bad, but mine and the blue one have paint on all sides. Instead of fussing about me, let's worry about how we're going to sort this out in two days...'

After a couple of hours' sleep, Mim was up at five the next morning to start work on cleaning the caravans. Some brief internet research the night before had revealed that the sooner they set to work the better, and certainly within the first twenty-four hours before the paint dried. The forecasted warm, sunny weather was now unwelcome, as it would speed up the drying time. Every minute was crucial. Mim had been prepared to work through the night until Corin had pointed out with infuriating sense that they risked spreading the paint if they couldn't see what they were doing.

The sun hadn't risen yet, but it was light enough to see and Mim inspected the caravans more carefully now. She didn't know if it was better or worse than she'd anticipated. The garish graffiti paint made a glaring contrast with the soft pastel shades chosen for the caravans, like a streak of fresh blood on pale skin. The good news was that there was only a wavy line along each side, not a full drawing. The vandals who had done this were no graffiti artists.

She was returning to her own caravan when Corin drove through the gates and parked on the drive. Mim wasn't surprised to see him. They hadn't arranged to meet but she'd expected him to turn up at some point.

'You're lucky I'm not still in bed,' she said, as he got out of the car.

'I know you better than that,' he said, smiling. 'Although I did wonder if you'd have worked through the night. Have you actually listened to my advice for once?'

'Don't let it go to your head. This was too important to get wrong.' She followed him round to the boot of the car. 'What have you brought?'

'Anything that the internet suggested might prove useful. Buckets, towels, sponges.' He began to empty the boot. 'Microfibre cloths, cooking oil, baby oil. Mrs Dennis is going to be furious as I raided her supplies and took most of the spare towels from the house. The only thing I don't have is nail varnish remover. I don't suppose you have any?'

'No.' She held up her hands. 'These hands are made for work, not decoration.' She grabbed a bucket. 'Shall we start with soap and water?'

They filled up two buckets and agreed to start work on the back of Mim's caravan, which was the least conspicuous place. Mim dipped the corner of the towel in the water and gingerly rubbed at a patch of the paint. Nothing happened. She tried again, rubbing harder. There was some evidence of colour transferring to the towel but no noticeable difference on the caravan wall. She tried a third time, with a fresh patch of towel.

'Does that look any different?' she asked Corin, pointing to the patch she was working on. He bent down beside her to peer where she was pointing. She caught a sudden whiff of fruity shampoo; his hair was damp from the shower and beginning to curl out from the nape of his neck as it dried. He tilted his head to look at her.

'A little.' He smiled. 'Shall we try the baby oil next?'

Mim was temporarily robbed of words by the unexpected image that flashed into her head as Corin continued to smile at her. She jumped up in relief when she heard another car approaching and peered round the side of the caravan.

'It's Bobby,' she said. 'Did you call him?'

'I knew he wouldn't mind an early start. We can call on the others when it's a more civilised hour.'

'This is going to take forever, isn't it?' she said, doubt creeping in. 'We'd need an army to have any chance of fixing it.'

'Then we'll have to find an army.'

All very well for him to say but Mim was conscious that she wouldn't be much use. She didn't know anyone to call on other than Karen and Heather, and that would depend on Karen's work shifts. Speaking of work... Mim checked her watch and groaned. She was due at the shop in a couple of hours. Would Janet give her some time off, as it was an emergency? She would have to ask, however unlikely it seemed. Janet wasn't heartless, underneath the gruff surface. She'd understand the urgency, wouldn't she?

She was a couple of minutes late when she finally arrived at the shop. She ran across the street from the beach car park and saw a cross-faced Janet in the doorway, changing the sign to 'open'. By the time Mim entered, she could hear Janet's heavy tread clomping up the stairs. She followed her up and caught her settling down at her desk in the office.

'You shouldn't be up here,' Janet said, swivelling in her chair as Mim burst in. 'You're already late. I'll have to dock your pay. I hope you haven't left the shop door unlocked.'

Mim had, but didn't think admitting it would help her cause.

'I'm sorry I'm late,' she said, 'but there's an emergency at Vennhallow. The caravans have been vandalised overnight. Some kids have sprayed paint all over them. Can you believe they'd do that?' Mim looked for a flicker of sympathy but Janet's face was impassive as usual. 'We have to clean them before the charity launches on Saturday. We need as many people as we can find to help.'

'I hope you're not expecting me to help. I can't do it with my legs the way they are.'

'No.' Mim smiled. She could imagine the reaction if she sent back Janet instead of returning herself. 'I hoped you might let me have the day off and possibly tomorrow too if we need it. I could take it as holiday or work different days to make it up.'

'It's too short notice for time off. Who will cover the shop if you go? I've a busy day ahead.'

'What about the morning then?' Mim asked. It wasn't

ideal but it would be better than nothing. 'I'll come back at one and work the afternoon.'

'That's not convenient.' Janet swivelled from side to side in her chair. 'You need to sort out your priorities. What's more important, your job or this charity nonsense?'

'Nonsense?' Mim repeated, surprised at Janet's reaction. 'It's not nonsense to want to help people who are having a rough time in life. You can't make me choose between earning a living and being kind.'

'I'm your boss. I can do exactly that.'

Janet spun her chair away from Mim, ending the conversation. As she did, she knocked the edge of her desk, and the screensaver vanished from the computer screen, revealing the document she was working on. It was a poster and the central message in large, red capitals read, 'COAST LINE NOT KNIFE CRIME'. Mim gasped. Surely not...

'It was you?' she said. She couldn't believe it. 'You're behind the attempts to sabotage the charity?'

'What if I am? I'm not ashamed of it.' Janet stared at Mim. She wasn't embarrassed or defiant; there was no emotion in her face at all. 'This is a good village for decent people. I've worked hard all my life to build up my business as a nest egg for retirement and I won't have it ruined by this scheme. We don't want layabouts coming here from those sink estates in the city, peddling drugs and flashing their knives around. It will drive the tourists away. I watch the news. I know what goes on.'

'Those aren't the people we're going to help,' Mim said. She was probably wasting her breath but she had to try. 'This charity is for the people who work hard but who can still barely afford to eat, let alone take a holiday. It's for the people who have had bad luck and lost their job, or who can't work because of illness or through caring for an ill or disabled relative. There are all sorts of reasons why people might need a holiday.'

'If they can't afford a holiday then they need to work harder. I run three businesses to make ends meet and I've never had to beg for handouts. I don't know what the Howards were thinking, setting this up in our village. They could afford to send these people anywhere on holiday. Why do we have to have them in our backyard?'

Mim was too incensed to hold her tongue.

'These people?' she repeated. 'These people are *my* people. I know what it's like to work multiple jobs, to be so tired that you can barely stand up, and still worry about where the next meal is coming from or whether you'll have a roof over your head the next night. I know what it's like to have people judge you unfairly for things that aren't your fault. When I was living in care—'

'In care?' Janet heaved herself on to her feet. 'So that's your story, is it? No wonder you didn't have references. What was Corin Howard thinking of, vouching for you?' She gave a scornful laugh. 'What was he thinking with, more like! Hooked by a pretty face, was he? Hankered for something rough? Don't get your hopes up for anything more. You'll never be good enough for him.'

'You're a nasty old witch!' Mim said. 'You can stick your job. I wouldn't work another second for you if you paid a million pounds an hour!'

'You can't quit. You're fired,' Janet shouted, but Mim was already halfway down the stairs, desperate to get away from the poisonous air of Janet's flat.

It wasn't quite an army, but a platoon of volunteers had arrived at the caravan field by the time Mim returned. She could see many familiar faces, including Bill and Bea, Lia and Bobby, Ros, Howie, Paula... She stood by the gate, taking in the sight with mixed feelings. It was brilliant that all these people were here and after Janet's words, it was reassuring to be reminded of all the good people in the world. But there was a shaft of sadness too. She'd thought of nothing else all the way back. She loved it here but now she had thrown away her job, how could she afford to stay?

'Mim!' Corin was standing on the veranda of her caravan, talking to Bill. She joined them and he smiled. 'I knew you could handle Janet. Have you worked a miracle and persuaded her to give you the day off?' His smile wavered. 'Mim? Is something wrong?'

Where to start? She took the easiest option.

'It's Janet,' she said. 'She was behind all this – the posters and the vandalism.'

'Are you sure?' Corin frowned. 'I know she can be grumpy but I wouldn't have expected her to be malicious. I thought you said the vandals were young people.'

'She must have persuaded or paid them to do it. There's no doubt. I caught her preparing another poster. She wasn't bothered about being found out. She wasn't ashamed at all.' Mim had never come across anyone so blinkered. Janet hadn't even been willing to listen to what Mim said. She'd made her mind up and, as far as she was concerned, everyone else was wrong. 'She doesn't want penniless scum polluting her village and driving down the value of her business.'

'*Her* village?' Bill repeated. 'Well, I'll be blowed. Who the devil does she think she is? What did you say to that, love?'

Mim grimaced.

'Probably the wrong thing. I lost my temper and refused to work for her anymore. So now I'm unemployed and without a reference again.'

'Good for you,' Bill said unexpectedly. 'We'd have been disappointed if you'd done anything else. I'm only sorry we persuaded you to take the job in the first place. Let me have a word with Bea and see what we can do.'

He beetled off.

'Janet said something else, didn't she?' Corin asked. 'Come on, Mim. It's not like you to hold back.'

Mim couldn't meet his eye. She had no intention of repeating what else Janet had said. It was far too embarrassing. She didn't want to dwell on that part of the conversation or examine the fact that she'd only quit her job *after* Janet had said those things about Corin, not before. She shrugged and tried a smile.

'Oh, you know. Just a load of stuff implying that people with no money have no morals. It's not very nice to be reminded of how worthless you are.'

'Don't say that. You're worth a thousand of Janet.' He reached out and touched her hand briefly, so that she looked up at him. His eyes were full of warmth, not the pity she'd expected. 'A thousand times more than most people I know. Come on. Where's the Mim who less than twelve hours ago was chasing away vandals and who was raring to fix these caravans? We only have forty-eight hours to go. We need her back.'

'You're good at this.' Mim laughed, and the tension of the last hour drained away. 'Don't tell me. You were head boy at your posh school, weren't you?'

'There was no such thing at the sixth form college I attended.' Mim looked at him, not sure whether to believe him. With his money and accent, he must have gone to a private school, mustn't he? Corin smiled at her. 'Don't judge, Mim.'

It was a long, hard day. They had decided to work on the damaged blue caravan first and even with several people working on each wall it was slow progress. After a process of trial and error, they had discovered that Lia's nail varnish remover and some strange butter wax that Bill had found in his workshop were most successful in removing the paint, but it was tiring work rubbing at the damaged area without spreading it to the rest of the bodywork. Mim's arm ached, and she was sure the muscles in her right arm would be twice the size of those in her left by nightfall.

Reinforcements came and went during the day. Someone must have spread the word about the nail varnish remover, as a group of women turned up after the school run carrying half full bottles, although Ros had been sent on a mission to buy as much as she could. Parcels of sandwiches were passed round, but no one wanted to stop to take a proper break. By five o'clock, only Mim, Corin, and Bobby were still on site, and they worked on for another couple of hours until one caravan looked relatively clean.

Corin threw his sponge into a bucket and stood back to take a look.

'That looks passable, doesn't it?' he asked, appealing to Mim and Bobby.

'It's much better,' Mim said, inspecting the caravan

wall. 'Is there still a shadow where the paint was, or am I imagining it?'

'It's definitely in your imagination.' Corin came alongside her. 'I think we're only conscious of it because we've focused on the paint all day. No one who attends the launch on Saturday will be scrutinising the bodywork like this.' He stepped back. 'I say we need beer and food. Who wants to come round to my house? Bobby?'

'Sorry, I'm meeting a mate tonight,' Bobby replied. Corin looked at Mim.

'It's just you, me, and Dickens then,' he said to her. 'What do you say to seafood risotto?'

'Is it one of Mrs Dennis's specialities?'

'Certainly not. I can actually throw a meal together. Are you brave enough to try it?'

A meal on her own with Corin? Mim wavered. She would have agreed yesterday, glad of this sign of friendship, but now Janet's insinuations echoed in her ears. Did everyone else think she was setting her sights on Corin? She didn't want to fuel gossip for either of them, especially when it was so far from the truth. Before she could answer him, her phone rang.

'You're late for work,' Howie said, when she answered the call. 'Are you on your way?'

'No. I quit this morning. And Janet sacked me,' she added, compelled to tell the truth. 'I thought you knew.'

'Aye, Bill mentioned it. You quit the shop, not the Boat. As long as my name's above the door as landlord,

I'll decide who works here. Janet owns the building, not the business, whatever she might think. You're a good worker and popular with the customers. In fact, now you're free of the shop, what do you say to working more nights and all day Saturday? After the caravan launch. I know you won't want to miss that.'

'I'd love to.' Mim grinned. 'I'll be there in ten minutes.'

'I gather you're turning me down?' Corin said as she put away her phone. 'Have you received a better offer?'

'I have. Sorry.' Mim smiled. It was the best offer possible. Now she would be earning again; now she could afford to stay here in Littlemead, in her gorgeous caravan. 'Howie has offered me my job back at the Boat, and extra shifts too.'

'That's great news.' Corin looked genuinely pleased for her. He started to tidy away the cleaning equipment as Mim dashed up the steps and into her caravan. He called after her. 'We'll have to do dinner another time.'

Chapter Sixteen

'I'm really not sure about this,' Mim said, studying her reflection in the mirror. 'I don't look like me.'

'Oh darling, you look gorgeous,' Lia replied, circling round Mim. 'Like an even better version of you. This is how you should always look.'

'It wouldn't be very practical for scrubbing the bathrooms in the caravans, would it?'

It was Saturday morning, launch day for As You Like It holidays, and initially Mim had been pleased that she could attend. It was the one bright part of losing her job in the shop. Or it was, until Lia had told her that as a trustee of the charity, Mim was expected to be a visible face, selling their story and talking to the press, not just serving the drinks. That bombshell had led on to the suggestion that she might like to wear something more attractive than her everyday work clothes. And on Mim

251

admitting that she didn't have anything more attractive, Lia had roped in Ros, and here they all were, getting ready together.

It had been fun. This was a new experience for Mim – the laughter, the camaraderie, the mutual support of being with other women and getting ready for an event together. Except, to her dismay, it had soon become all about Mim. Lia had blow-dried her hair, and worked a miracle in arranging it into a half-up half-down style, so that soft waves rather than messy curls framed her face. Ros had skilfully applied make-up so that her eyes seemed twice as big and her face glowed like a film star. They'd even solved the clothes issue by bringing a selection of dresses that Ros could no longer fit in for Mim to borrow. The result was little short of a total transformation.

She cast another glance at her reflection. She'd eventually chosen a soft green dress decorated with tiny white daisies, fitted round the bodice and then falling to calf length in a full skirt. It wasn't like anything she'd ever worn before. She swayed from side to side, enjoying the way the silk fabric swirled around her legs. She didn't look like Mim Brown. She looked like Miranda, as if she'd been born to this life. She smiled. She was going to enjoy it while it lasted.

She wasn't the only one dressed to impress. They had worked hard on the caravan site this morning and it looked magnificent. The three caravans that had been damaged by spray paint had cleaned up well, after another day of hard graft on Friday; they weren't perfect, and Mim could still see a shadow, but she didn't think the guests would notice. Susie had made some long strips of bunting which they had draped between the caravans, and it fluttered prettily in the gentle breeze coming in off the sea. Bobby had refilled the plant pots, and now an abundance of vivid coloured flowers brightened each veranda. He had also created a games area in one corner of the field, by cutting short a square of grass, and now giant outdoor games were set out, waiting to be played. Everything was perfect, from the blue sky and warm sunshine to the delicious smell of the barbecue wafting across the field. Mim looked around and felt a surge of pride that she'd been able to contribute to this project. This could bring some pleasure to those who really needed it. Whatever it took, it had to be a success.

Lia and Ros had been in charge of the guest list for the launch party. Ros had worked in modelling and promotion before she married and had a huge list of useful contacts, many of whom she had persuaded down to Devon for the weekend. Lia had focused on social media and had drawn in an impressive selection of bloggers and influencers as well as the local press. Villagers and local businesses had been invited too, to emphasise that the community was behind this scheme – with the obvious exception of one business. The aim of the party was simple: to obtain as much publicity as they could, and to spread the word that the charity existed in the hope of securing donations and filling up the caravans for the summer.

The five guest caravans were all open for viewing, and Mim enjoyed showing groups round. It was easy to be enthusiastic about the interiors when Susie had made them look so beautiful. Each had a different colour scheme, which co-ordinated with the exterior of the caravan, but they all brought the same feeling of cosy warmth with the textured cushions, snuggly blankets, and fluffy rugs.

'You're doing a great job selling the place,' one of the visitors said, after Mim had shown him and a couple of bloggers around the blue caravan. 'I love what you've done with these caravans. I haven't seen anything like them before. It's unusual to have created a premium product for holidays you're giving away.'

'We were lucky. A local lady designed all the interiors and she's done a gorgeous job, hasn't she? She's here today if you'd like to meet her.' Mim had no idea who this man was but if he had a blog perhaps he could give Susie a push? Although, he didn't look like a blogger. He was casually dressed in jeans and a shirt but he had that indefinable whiff of money about him that she'd come to recognise since meeting the Howards. Perhaps he was one of Lia's friends; he was more Mim's age, but he was handsome enough to be part of Lia's set.

'Anyway,' she said, as the other members of the group wandered away. 'I don't think premium products should be reserved for rich people. Everyone deserves some luxury in life.'

'And what's your luxury?' he asked.

'That.' Mim smiled and pointed at her caravan. 'I live there. So you see, I know what I'm talking about when I say it would be a treat to stay here. I love it, and I know that everyone we can offer a holiday to will love it too.'

'Do you think your guests might be bored?' the man asked. 'You can't compete with the larger parks along the coast that can offer swimming pools and leisure facilities.'

'True. But our caravans aren't crammed in cheek by jowl, and we offer personal services such as collection from the railway station and transport to activities and tourist attractions. We're not trying to compete. Our holidays are free, and they'll allow families to have quality time together and create memories that no amount of money can buy.'

The man smiled. It was a good smile but not dazzling.

'I should make a confession,' he said. 'We haven't been introduced yet. I'm Henry Burrows. I own several of the holiday parks along the coast. The ones where the caravans are cheek by jowl.'

Mim recognised the name; Corin had mentioned him before. She grinned.

'Sorry. If I'd known who you were...'

'You wouldn't have been so honest?'

'Oh, I would. But I might have thought of a fancier way of putting it.'

Henry laughed.

'I like what you said before. We provide holidays. You want to create memories. I think you're doing a great thing here and I'd like to help. Our nearest park is only three miles away. There's a swimming pool and mini golf, and a fantastic adventure play area. What if we offered all your guests free use of the park facilities?'

'Do you mean it? That would be brilliant.' More than brilliant – Mim couldn't believe her luck. She'd discussed with Lia in the past whether they could provide membership to the nearby leisure club for guests who came to stay, but it had proved too complicated. This would be even better.

'Why don't you come and have a look at what we offer?' Henry's arm brushed her back as he guided her towards the other caravans. 'Let's make it a date and we can work through all the details.'

Mim was taking a five-minute break in the shade behind her caravan when Corin joined her. She'd only seen him from a distance during the afternoon, and every time he'd had a group of women around him, hanging off his every word and lapping up his charm. He'd made an effort today, abandoning the scruffy clothes for a pair of linen trousers and an open-necked shirt that clung over those swimmer's shoulders. He looked like rich Corin again, not the one she'd come to think of as a friend. She still couldn't work out which one he really was.

'I thought you might welcome one of these,' he said. He held out two bottles of beer, and Mim grinned and took one. There was a true sign of friendship. She closed her eyes in pleasure as the cool liquid slipped down her throat. When she opened her eyes again, he was watching her.

'That's exactly what I needed,' she said. 'Thanks. It's going well out there, isn't it?' She gestured back towards the centre of the field, where the guests continued to enjoy the food, drink, and sunshine. Corin nodded, still watching her.

'You look different,' he said.

'Thanks.' Mim laughed. 'The compliment every woman wants to hear. Thank your sister. Ros has great taste in dresses.' She spun round in a circle so the silk skirt flared around her legs. 'I'm enjoying a taste of the high life before crashing back to reality tomorrow.'

'Like Cinderella,' he murmured, and smiled the full, dazzling Corin smile. Mim was transported back to that first time she'd met him, remembered the spark of connection she'd felt with the stranger under the trees on New Year's Eve. Here they were again, hiding away together, sharing a sneaky drink, and she marvelled at how things had changed over the last few months; the connection had grown and blossomed into a friendship she valued more than she could ever have imagined on that winter's night. Then she noticed his gaze stray to her left arm and reality crashed back in sooner than she'd expected. The short sleeves of the dress exposed a stretch of puckered, shiny skin that ran down her inner arm towards her wrist.

'What happened?' he asked.

'My family happened. I never had a problem with mine loving me too much.' She drank more beer. She'd lived with the burn scar since she was eight, but something about Corin's scrutiny made her more conscious of it than she had been for years. Was he judging her for her flaw and for the squalid history that it represented? The idea gave her an unexpected twist of pain and made her defensive. 'Ugly, isn't it? You can say it. I doubt you can come up with anything worse than the insults I used to hear at school. Can you imagine? Ginger and a freak…' She smiled but couldn't look at him, wary of what truth she would see on his face. 'But I don't see why I should cover it up. I'm not ashamed. It wasn't my fault.'

'Mim…' The word was husky, like a caress, and Corin took a step towards her. She looked up. The expression on his face puzzled her – it was more like anger than anything else but that made no sense. Why should he care what names she had been called at school?

'What are you two doing, skulking back here?' Lia's arrival broke the moment. 'Mim darling, I need you to come with me. The press photographer wants a picture to go with the article and you absolutely must be in it.'

'Must I?' Mim grimaced. 'Why me?'

'You're one of the trustees. Besides, you're looking gorgeous today and we absolutely have to exploit that.'

Today? Did that mean she looked a hideous troll every other day? Mim spotted Corin stifling a laugh at Lia's comment and didn't see why he should get out of it.

'What about Corin?' she said, sending him a look of mischief, glad that the strange atmosphere of a few moments ago had been replaced with their usual laughter. 'He's a trustee too. Shouldn't he be in the photo?'

'Perhaps it will look better with the three of us.' Lia smiled. 'I suppose he might help attract attention. Some people do seem to think he's handsome, though it's totally bizarre to me. Leave your beer behind, darlings; we don't want to appear uncouth.'

The afternoon couldn't have gone better. Everyone Mim spoke to loved the caravans and the idea of the charity, and promised support in whatever way they could, whether through financial donations or publicity. It had been lovely to see some of the local children chasing across the field and playing with the outdoor games, demonstrating what a safe, fun place it could be. Bill had surprised everyone, even Bea, by announcing that he would allow the charity guests access to his model railway, under his supervision. It was his pride and joy, built over many years, and Mim had never seen anything like it. It filled one of the workshops and had several tracks that ran through countryside and along a coastline not dissimilar to the one on their doorstep in Littlemead. The attention to detail was amazing with animals grazing in the fields, deckchairs on the promenade, and washing hanging on a line outside a row of cottages. It was a hit with everyone, young and old, and its unveiling was the perfect way to end the day.

Howie had allowed Mim the afternoon off work but she was expected in the Boat by seven. She thought that would give her time to help clear up once the launch party ended but Bea had other ideas. Having failed to persuade Mim to miss work and join the family for a celebratory dinner, she frogmarched her over to the house for what she described as a debrief but which turned out to be an excuse to drink Champagne. Not that the Howards needed much excuse, Mim reflected, as she joined Ros in having a cup of tea instead.

She couldn't deny that there was much to celebrate. Everyone had a story to tell about a generous donation they had won or a connection they had made. Corin had charmed the headteacher of the nearest school, who had agreed to spread news of the charity within her headteachers' association, so they could refer any families they thought would benefit from the scheme. Olly had walked away with the largest individual donation of the day. Lia had persuaded a local business to sponsor one of the caravans for a year, in return for choosing a name; for the next twelve months, the yellow caravan would be called Rosie after the owner's wife, and Lia had already drawn up a shortlist of businesses who might like to sponsor the others.

'And let's not forget Mim's achievement,' Lia said, after everyone had toasted her success. 'Did you all hear? She's persuaded Henry Burrows to allow our guests free use of the facilities at the Happy Days holiday park. Isn't that fabulous? It's a double celebration because he's asked her out on a date as well. To darling Mim!' Lia raised her glass and winked at Mim, who laughed and shook her head; she should have known that Lia would exaggerate a perfectly innocent meeting. She was looking at the Happy Days park with Henry on behalf of the charity, nothing more. He'd hardly be interested in dating her. Just as well, as she wasn't interested in dating him. 'Wouldn't it be the most wonderful piece of publicity if we could claim an As You Like It wedding?'

'Surely that would be a case of all's well that ends well?' Bill said and everyone laughed except Bea, who was looking at Mim with a puzzled expression, and

Corin, who was rubbing Dickens's tummy and didn't seem to be listening.

Mim's own clothes were still upstairs in Lia's room and she reluctantly left the celebration to change before work. She'd made it as far as the foot of the stairs when she heard Corin's voice behind her.

'So you're going on a date with Henry Burrows,' he said. 'I didn't think he would be your type.'

Mim turned round. Corin was standing in the middle of the hall, a bottle of beer in his hand. The evening sun beamed through the windows and lit him up like an angel.

'Not my type?' Mim repeated. Her dress swished against her legs and she smiled, waiting for the punchline. 'Go on, why not?'

'He's obscenely rich and comes from a posh family, for a start.'

'I see.' His words brought her crashing back down to earth after the happy fantasy of the last few hours. He wasn't teasing or making a joke. He was serious, and Janet's barbed words from a few days ago came rushing back to the surface from where she'd tried to bury them. Despite the borrowed clothes, the make-up, the fancy hairdo, she was still a bit of rough – not *one of them*. How could she have been stupid enough to believe anything else? The scar on her arm, that he had studied only a few hours ago, branded her forever with the troubles of her past. He had judged her on it, just as she had feared.

Now she had the answer to her question about whether he was the rich man or her friend.

'Are you actually saying I'm not his type, being obscenely poor and coming from a common family?' she asked.

'That's not what I meant at all.'

'Isn't it? Really? Don't worry,' Mim said, trying to steady her voice so he didn't guess how hurt she was. It was one thing hearing it from Janet, but from him… Why did it feel like she'd been punched in the chest? 'I know my place. Lia was making a joke. It's a meeting, not a date. I may have no money and no class, but I have enough pride to refuse to be any rich man's bit of rough.'

'Mim.' In a few quick strides he had crossed the hall. 'Listen.'

'I've heard more than enough, thanks.' She climbed a couple of stairs, creating a gap between them. She took a deep breath and looked him square in the eyes. 'You're right. Stuck-up, snobbish, rich men aren't my type at all. Thanks for reminding me.'

At first it seemed that all of their hard work had failed. There were a few encouraging tweets about the charity over the weekend but not the rush of publicity they had hoped for. Only Lia's confidence was undented as she cautioned them to hold their nerve and she was proved right. During the course of Tuesday, three bloggers posted features about As You Like It holidays. Traffic to the website they had set up grew and email enquiries finally trickled in.

The story featured in the local newspaper on Wednesday and Lia brought a copy to show Mim. It filled the whole of page five, with a large photo of Mim, Lia, and Corin, a smaller shot of the caravan site, and a half-page article. Mim studied the photo of the three of them. It was a good picture. Lia was unsurprisingly photogenic. Corin's smile dazzled even from a static image. Mim stood between them, looking happier than she could ever remember. She looked like she belonged. It was amazing what a few borrowed clothes could do.

'The photos are the wrong way round,' she said to Lia, dragging her gaze away from the image and ignoring the wistful feeling that was hovering round her heart. 'The picture of the caravan site should have been the prominent one.'

'I agree, darling, but what can we do? The article has taken a different angle than we'd planned, but all publicity is good, isn't it?'

Mim skimmed through the story. It should have been about the charity and what they were hoping to achieve, but although that was mentioned, it wasn't the focus of the article. It was all about *her*, going back to the day when she had given Bill and Bea a lift to Devon and explaining how she had been the inspiration for offering the caravans for free holidays.

'This isn't true,' Mim said. 'It was all your idea.'

'But you were the inspiration and it was your idea to make the holidays free.' Lia smiled. 'I guess a story of a rich girl helping the poor doesn't have the same appeal.'

'Can't you put them straight?'

'We both can. I've just had the most exciting phone call. We've been invited to appear on BBC local radio to talk about it. What do you say?'

'Me? On the radio?' Mim was struggling to share Lia's excitement. 'No way. I'll sound thick.'

'Of course you won't, darling. You'll sound very natural.'

Mim suspected that 'natural' was the posh way of saying 'thick', but appreciated Lia's attempt to be tactful.

'When is it?' she asked.

'Friday evening.'

'I'll be working in the Boat,' Mim said, with ill-disguised relief. 'And no, I can't take time off. It's the busiest night and good tips. You'll have to do it yourself. Just concentrate on the charity and how people can be referred for a holiday. That's the only story we're offering.'

Karen produced a box of homemade chocolate brownies for their post-swim treat on the following Monday morning.

'I thought I'd up my game now we have a celebrity in our midst,' she said. 'I wasn't even sure you'd come today.'

Mim laughed.

'Because of that story in the local newspaper? That's old news now and I came on Friday, didn't I?'

Another perk of not working in the deli was that Mim was now free to join Heather and Karen for the Friday morning swim. Even better, now the mornings were light, she could walk down into Littlemead along the coastal path. It was a steep climb back up but worth it to save on petrol money, and the view from the path was spectacular and lifted her spirits whatever the weather.

'Not the local paper,' Karen said. 'The tabloid. You did see it yesterday, didn't you?'

'I haven't seen anything. I try to avoid all the gloom in the papers. What tabloid? You mean the details of the charity have made it into a national paper? That's brilliant.'

Karen opened a drawer and took out a copy of a national Sunday newspaper. She opened it and passed it over to Mim. "The Kindness of Strangers" ran the headline over the familiar photograph of Mim, Corin, and Lia. Mim read on, her heart thumping and her initial enthusiasm about the publicity quickly disappearing.

This wasn't brilliant at all. This was worse than the local newspaper, far worse. The charity was barely mentioned; the feature was entirely about Mim. They knew every detail: that she'd been brought up in care; that she'd lost her job and been sleeping in her car when she met Bill and Bea; that she'd offered them a lift across the country, and in return they had offered her a home and welcomed her to their family as she had none of her own; how they had combined forces to spread kindness to other people in need through the As You Like It charity. It was a powerful story; Mim could see that objectively. But it was a story about *her* and she hadn't agreed to it being told.

'It's all over the internet,' Heather added. 'It's one of the BBC's most read stories on their news page. There's so much bad news around at the moment that people have latched on to this as a feel-good story. You've gone viral.'

Heather showed Mim her phone. The story was everywhere and had inspired lots of other people to share examples of random acts of kindness and paying it forward. Some people had even started using the hashtag *#BeMoreMiranda*. Mim swiped from page to page, hardly believing what she was seeing.

'Great publicity for the charity,' Karen said. 'I wonder if Susie could benefit? She should start promoting that she designed the caravan interiors. She might get some work out of it.'

'Were you really sleeping in your car?' Heather asked,

looking at Mim with sympathy. 'You didn't tell us things had been so bad.'

She hadn't told anyone. Only the Howards knew. Only they could have passed on this information to the press. And though she might once have been glad to see Bea's 'one of us' claim confirmed in black and white, now it felt that they had cut her loose and exposed her to the curious gaze of the world. It hurt more than Mim could say. Did her feelings not matter to them at all?

She walked back up the cliff path, dumped her wet swimming clothes at the caravan, and carried on up the track to Vennhallow. Bea and Lia were outside the house, debating whether to lower the roof on Lia's convertible. Everything seemed surprisingly normal. Bea waved when she saw Mim.

'Perfect timing, Mim dear. Are you free to drive me into Exeter later? I'm meeting friends for lunch but Lia can only take me now and it's far too early.'

'I saw the story in the Sunday paper,' Mim said. Lia smiled.

'Hasn't it gone well?' she said. 'Mim, darling, you are the heroine of the internet at the moment. Aren't you thrilled?'

'No! We agreed that the focus would be on the charity, not me.'

'I know but a good story needs a hook, darling, and it soon became obvious that you were it.'

'You don't mind, do you?' Bea asked, smiling at Mim

over the top of the car. 'It's gone better than we could have hoped. The reaction has been entirely positive. I wouldn't be surprised if you were invited on to daytime television soon. Wouldn't that be exciting? We could all have an outing to London.'

'But all those things about me living in care and sleeping in the car were private,' Mim said. They didn't seem to get it at all. They had ridden roughshod over her own wishes, thinking they knew best. An uncomfortable memory flashed up of Corin warning her about this and of her dismissing him. She hadn't understood his frustration until now. 'It should have been my decision who to tell.'

'You've always said you weren't ashamed of your past. Nor should you be.' Bea walked round the car to stand in front of Mim. 'Have we done wrong, Mim dear? I'm mortified if we've upset you. We thought we were acting for the best.' She squeezed Mim's arm. 'Wait until you see the impact the publicity has had already. The inbox is full of messages offering donations and support, and referring families for holidays. A holiday park in Yorkshire has offered one of their caravans for two weeks in the summer holidays for anyone who can't travel down here. This is going to make a difference to so many families and it's all thanks to you. You have made this charity a success. Surely you can't be unhappy about that. Isn't it exactly what we wanted?'

Chapter Seventeen

Bea spent the next few days apologising to Mim, even though she'd insisted it wasn't necessary. She'd been hurt at first, but she couldn't regret the publicity for long, whatever it had cost her, when she saw the result. Emails and donations to the charity were pouring in. It broke her heart to see pensioners offering the few pounds they could afford and to read some of the stories of the people who were nominated for holidays. Hadn't she vowed to do whatever it took to make the charity a success? And it was, beyond her wildest dreams. So what if her history had been bandied round the internet for a couple of days? Bea had been right; she wasn't ashamed of it. All that mattered was what she did with her life now, and being involved with this charity was the best thing she'd ever done.

She received a text from Bea on Saturday morning

saying that there was a surprise waiting for her at Vennhallow. She wandered up the track, enjoying the warm sunshine on her face, and speculating what the surprise might be. It wasn't the first one Bea had arranged, although it was hard to imagine anything beating the Chinese takeaway she'd been invited to share at the house earlier in the week.

Bea answered the door looking very pleased with herself and Mim's hopes rose. Had Mrs Dennis made one of her delicious lemon drizzle cakes? Bea laughed when Mim asked the question.

'She made coffee cake this week, but the surprise is even better than that.' Bea led Mim towards the drawing room and paused dramatically at the door. 'You have a visitor.'

'Do I?' Mim couldn't think who it might be. The friends she'd made in Littlemead would come to the caravan, not disturb Bea. She had an awful thought. 'It's not another journalist, is it?'

'No, nothing like that. I've learnt my lesson there. No, this is a surprise you'll like. A friend from the hotel has come to see you. Isn't that wonderful? It's all because of the article in the newspaper. I'm thrilled that something good has come out of it for you. You can't still be cross with me after this.'

A friend from the hotel? Mim's mind spun with images of Robbie the chef and Beryl the cleaner, before Bea swung the door open and ushered Mim inside. And there, sitting on the sofa in front of a tray of tea and cake, was Gordon's daughter, Yvonne, absolutely the last person that Mim could wish to see. A friend? It wasn't the word Mim would have used.

Yvonne regarded Mim, a satisfied smirk on her face.

'What are you doing here?' Mim asked. She couldn't believe it. Was this a joke? A journalist would have been a thousand times better than this.

'Tracked you down, haven't I?' Yvonne replied. 'Shouldn't have sold your story to the press and splashed your face across the papers if you were trying to hide.'

'I'm not hiding.' Mim looked at Yvonne with a growing feeling of unease. What was she doing here? She wasn't about to offer a donation to the charity, that much was clear.

'Mim dear, who is this?' Bea asked. She couldn't have missed the frosty atmosphere in the room. 'Is she not a friend of yours?'

'Absolutely not. This is Yvonne, Gordon's daughter.'

'The one who threw you out onto the streets without so much as a reference?' Bea marched over to Yvonne and whisked the cup and saucer from her hand. She picked up the tray of cakes and carried it to the opposite side of the room. Mim could have hugged her for the gesture.

'How dare you infiltrate my house under false pretences,' Bea said. She had never sounded so posh.

'It's this one you want to watch in your house,'

Yvonne said, pointing at Mim. 'Don't believe whatever sob story she's told you. She wormed her way in with my dad, a man twice her age, in the hope of inheriting our hotel. And now she's had the nerve to tell the press that *I* treated *her* badly by getting rid of her! She probably has her eye on this place now. Don't trust her if you have a husband or son.'

It shouldn't still hurt to hear such things, but it did. Yvonne lived in Bristol and had rarely visited Gordon at the hotel. Mim had been happily installed there for over a year before Yvonne had discovered her existence and, jealous of her relationship with Gordon, had accused her of sleeping with him to obtain the hotel. Gordon had set her straight but the suspicion had never gone away and, if anything, had worsened when it was Mim who had been with Gordon when he died. Yvonne had inherited everything so why was she pursuing her vendetta? There could be no benefit now, nothing in it for Yvonne but the satisfaction of seeing Mim upset. Did she really hate her so much?

'I think it's high time you left my house,' Bea said. She held the door open, waiting.

'I'm going nowhere until I've got what I came for,' Yvonne said. 'I couldn't believe it when I read in the paper about her sleeping in her car. *Her* car! That car belonged to my father and now it belongs to me.'

'It's worth next to nothing,' Mim said. She knew; she'd had it valued when she'd lost her job, but it hadn't been worth selling. 'You've can't have come all this way for that?'

'Not just for the car. I want the watch too.' Yvonne looked at Bea. 'My dad had a gold Rolex watch that meant the world to him. He always wore it.' Her voice shook. 'I want it to remember him by. I scoured the hotel from top to bottom and it wasn't there. She must have stolen it. It's worth at least ten grand.'

'You silly woman,' Bea said. 'Why would she be living in poverty if she had an expensive watch in her possession?'

'All part of the act, isn't it? Perhaps she's not had time to sell it yet. I want the police to be called.'

Bea glanced at Mim, picked up her phone and left the room. Yvonne smiled. Mim gazed out of the window, seeing nothing. Was Bea actually calling the police? How could Bea think her capable of this?

Bea didn't return for almost ten minutes and when she did, Corin was at her side. Mim hadn't seen him since the day of the charity launch. She'd tried to find him, to apologise for overreacting during their conversation about Henry Burrows, but Lia had said he was away helping on another school expedition. He looked at her now and didn't smile. That hurt even more than Bea's reaction. She'd thought they were friends, that they had a connection, despite their silly argument. He couldn't believe this, could he?

'Is he police?' Yvonne asked.

'He's my son,' Bea said.

'Ha!' Yvonne laughed. 'That answers the question of whose bed she shares in this house. Didn't I tell you what she was like?'

'I think we've heard enough from you.' Mim had never heard Corin sound so angry. It did the trick. Yvonne fell silent at last. 'Let's sort this out now. Mim, do you know anything about a gold watch?'

'Yes.' Three faces turned to her, one triumphant and two surprised. 'Gordon did have a Rolex watch. It was the most valuable thing he owned, apart from the hotel.'

'You see?' Yvonne stood up. 'When she didn't get the hotel, she took the watch. Have you called the police?'

'No.' Corin shut her down with a look. 'Did you take the watch, Mim?'

'Yes,' she said. Yvonne's snort of triumph echoed round the room. Corin's gaze didn't falter. Mim looked straight back at him. 'I took it to the pawn shop two years ago, at Gordon's request, and I haven't seen it since.'

'There you go. The case is closed.' Corin gestured at the door. 'Perhaps now you would care to leave us alone and take your squalid accusations with you.'

He believed her, just like that? Mim could have kissed him – in a strictly platonic way. Unfortunately, Yvonne wasn't so easily convinced.

'We only have her word for it,' she said, but she didn't sound as confident as she had done.

'I have proof in the caravan.'

'Do run along and fetch it, Mim dear, then this ghastly woman might finally go,' Bea said. 'I'm tempted to call the police after all and report her for squatting.'

'You're letting her leave?' Yvonne said. 'She might run away.'

'Where would she run to? This is her home.' Bea sighed. 'Corin, will you go with Mim and make sure she comes back? Heaven knows no one could blame her if she didn't.'

'And who's to say they won't run away together?'

'Don't be so ridiculous.' Corin didn't wait to hear anything further but marched out of the room, swiftly followed by Mim. He was halfway down the track before he slowed his pace and she was able to catch up.

'Now I see why you weren't daunted by Janet,' he said. 'You've encountered far worse. Where did that God-awful woman spring up from?'

Mim laughed, and it felt like such a relief after the tension of the last half hour.

'They're not all like her up north,' she said. 'There are good people too.'

'I know.' He looked at her and smiled.

'She saw the story in the newspaper and tracked me down.'

'Ah. Something else we owe you an apology for then. I'd no idea they were going to do that. I was away or I'd have stopped them,' he said. 'Mum and Lia had the best intentions. They always do. It doesn't always help though, does it?'

'No.' They reached the gate and walked towards Mim's caravan. She stopped at the bottom of the steps.

'Thanks for believing me,' she said.

'Why wouldn't I? You're the most honest person I know. It's one of the things…' He stopped and put his hand on the banister rail. 'I'm sorry about that conversation on the launch day. I only meant that I thought you disapproved of the idle rich. It wasn't a criticism of you. You know that, don't you?'

'Yes.' It was true. She'd spoken in the heat of the moment on the day of the charity launch and had regretted it since. She'd seen Corin in all sorts of company – with working-class men in the Boat and with the upper-class people at the Valentine dinner – and he treated everyone with the same easy friendship. And that was the way he treated her too. She hadn't realised the value of it until she thought she'd thrown it away.

'But Henry isn't really the idle rich,' Corin continued. He rubbed his hand over the banister rail. 'He isn't stuck-up or snobby either. Don't let my clumsy words put you off, if you like him.'

Mim unlocked the caravan and he followed her in.

'Wait there a minute,' she said. She went into the bedroom and reached under the bed to pull out a battered old shoe box. The cardboard sides had softened over the years and it was now held together with a couple of elastic bands. She took them off and removed the lid, moving a few items onto the bed while she searched for what she wanted.

'What's that?' Corin was in the doorway, watching her. Mim sighed.

'I don't think I invited you into my bedroom,' she said. She smiled. 'You don't own the place yet, son and heir.'

He ignored her and wandered in.

'I came to see if you needed a hand.' He gestured at the box. 'What is all this?'

'It's my emergency box.' She shrugged. 'I was moved around a lot, sometimes at short notice. It was easier to keep in one box the things I couldn't be without. I could grab it and go if I needed to.'

'But you haven't unpacked it here.'

'No.' It was hard to explain. She hadn't unpacked it at the hotel either, even after ten years – and that had proved to be the right decision, hadn't it? She'd been evicted from there at short notice too. But she wasn't giving up hope. 'Maybe one day I'll find a home – not just a place to stay – where I feel safe,' she said, 'and then I might unpack it. If not, I'll be needing a new box. This one's on its last legs, isn't it?'

Corin stared down at the assortment of items spread across the bed and visible in the box. On the top lay a photo of Mim as a tiny baby with her mum and dad, barely more than children themselves, from a time she couldn't remember but had always thought must have been the happiest moment of her childhood; it was the only memento of her dad she had. There were her birth and exam certificates, a medal she had won in a maths competition at school, a photo of Gordon behind the bar at the hotel, the pebble containing the ammonite that she had found on the beach, the local newspaper article with the picture of her, Lia, and Corin… She wished she could scoop it all up in her arms and hide it from his gaze, so he couldn't see how little there was to her life. She picked out a memory stick and the car registration document from the bottom of the box and piled everything else back in, stowing it away again under the bed.

'If any of these treasures are stolen now, I'll be pointing my finger at you,' she said, trying to make a joke of it. He didn't smile. 'Don't be giving me that pity face again. Did no one ever tell you that if the wind changes you might be stuck like that? Imagine the disappointment among the single women of Devon.'

She weasled a smile out of him at that and they returned to the house with the memory stick. Corin brought in a laptop from the study.

'Here's the car registration document,' Mim said, passing it to Yvonne while the computer switched on. 'The car is in my name. You can't argue with that.'

Yvonne looked like she might try but Corin whisked the paper out of her hand. Mim opened the contents of the memory stick. It was all here, all the documents relating to the business: accounts, occupancy statistics, bar sales, receipts, all neatly organised and filed away. It wouldn't have suited everyone, but she had loved doing all this, had savoured the solidity and reliability of working with numbers. You knew where you were with numbers. They didn't judge or behave differently for different people.

'Here's the receipt from the pawn shop,' she said, bringing up a copy that she had scanned and saved. 'And just in case you were about to make more accusations, on the next tab you'll find the bank statement confirming the money was paid into the business account on the same day.'

Corin took the laptop and showed it to Yvonne.

'You shouldn't have all this,' Yvonne said, peering at the screen. 'This is confidential hotel business.'

'Okay, I'll hold up my hands to that one,' Mim said. 'Perhaps I shouldn't have copied it. But it was my insurance and I was right to think I might need it, wasn't I?' She stood in front of Yvonne. Should she say more? Yvonne had treated Mim badly for years, but it was Yvonne's behaviour towards Gordon that angered Mim most. She had to stand up for him one last time. 'It's a bit late to get sentimental about Gordon's watch. If you'd bothered to visit when he was alive, you would have had real memories to treasure. If I'd had a dad like yours, I'd never have abandoned him like you did. My family would have come before anything. And now I really do think it's time for you to go.'

'After you've apologised,' Corin added, removing the laptop from Yvonne's grasp.

'I'd sooner cut my tongue out.'

'Gracious me, I can't bear this foul-mouthed woman a moment longer.' Bea stood up and opened her arms wide as if she were herding animals. 'Come along. Out. Out you go.'

She was magnificent. Without another word, she steered Yvonne out of the room, leaving Mim alone with Corin. Mim retrieved the laptop and closed down the folders she'd opened.

'Are you okay?' Corin asked, perching on the arm of the chair beside her. He touched her shoulder – a tentative touch, but it was enough to drive away Mim's lingering tension.

'Fine.' She smiled. 'I've dealt with far worse than Yvonne and lived to tell the tale.'

'You deserve better.'

'If life worked like that, and gave people what they deserve, I'd be living in a palace, waited on hand and foot, I expect.' She laughed. 'As it doesn't, I'll make do with my caravan. As long as Bea lets me stay after today's mess. She won't want to risk any repeat of this, will she?'

'You have to stay.' He spoke quickly. Mim looked up and caught an odd expression on his face, as if he'd surprised himself with his words. He smiled. 'For purely selfish reasons. Now I've seen what you can do with accounts, I hope you might take pity and help me with mine.'

'Out of pity?' Mim grinned. 'I'll never make it to my palace on those terms.'

'I'll pay you in hard cash and with as much cake and disgustingly milky tea as you like.'

He knew how she liked her tea? It was a little thing but it felt significant, as if a root was winding down into the earth and anchoring her here. She felt she belonged here more than anywhere else she'd stayed and had a real connection to the place and the people. She didn't want to leave.

'You've got a deal,' she said.

'This is your filing system?' Mim asked, when she went round to Corin's house the next day to look at his accounts. 'It's not very impressive, is it?'

'Don't be rude. That's a top quality padded envelope,' Corin said.

'It isn't even a new envelope.'

'I'm a keen recycler.'

Mim laughed and tipped the contents of the envelope onto Corin's desk. An assortment of papers fell out: receipts, handwritten notes, printed pages, and one paper napkin with a telephone number on it. Corin grabbed that, screwed it up and dropped it in the wastepaper basket. Mim sifted through the rest.

'Most of the outgoings are in there,' Corin said. 'You'll have to access the bank statements for the rest and for the income.'

Mim pulled a face.

'It seems a bit nosy going through your bank statements. Are you sure you want me to? Don't you have accountants for the business who could do this for you properly?'

'Don't worry. You won't find any embarrassing standing orders in there.' Corin smiled. 'And if you'd ever met the family accountants, you'd understand why I'd much rather have you in my house than them. They bore me to sleep with complicated words.'

Mim didn't object. She was lucky to have a whole caravan to herself, but nothing compared to being in a house with solid walls and a firm roof, as she'd discovered on a few stormy nights when it had felt as if the wind might lift the caravan off its base, or the pounding rain might penetrate the metal above her head. And there was something cosy and comfortable about Corin's house, even today when the sun streamed in and the windows were wide open, letting in the sea air. It wasn't as fancy as Vennhallow and was a fraction of the size, but it had everything it needed to make it a home. She could understand why Corin preferred to live here.

While Mim tried to make sense of the accounts, Corin carried out jobs around the house, ironing a pile of sheets and then cooking something that smelled delicious and made Mim's mouth water.

'You're quite the domestic goddess, aren't you?' she said, when he brought her another mug of tea and a chocolate brownie.

'I like to be self-sufficient. I'm making lasagne – is that okay?'

'Do what you like. You're not bothering me.'

Corin laughed.

'I meant, is it okay for you? Do you like it? I should have checked first, I suppose.'

'You're making it for me?'

'Not just for you. I was planning to eat some too. At the same time and in the same place, in case you were going to ask that next. I'm beginning to think doing the accounts is easier than inviting you for dinner.'

'You know I'm working at the Boat tonight?'

'I do. The meal will be ready in plenty of time.'

'Great. I could…' Mim stopped. She'd been about to say she could get used to this, but luckily her brain had put a brake on her mouth for once. She didn't want him to think she was making herself too comfortable here, or reading anything into the invitation other than one friend offering to share a meal with another. 'Can I ask a quick question about the bank statements while you're loitering here? There are some payments in and out and I can't tell if they're to do with the business or not.'

Corin leaned over her shoulder to look at the computer screen while Mim pointed out a couple of the entries she was querying. Each week a huge sum of money – in her eyes – was paid in, and the majority of it was paid out again almost immediately.

'That's nothing to do with work.' Corin straightened up. He scratched the back of his neck. 'That's a payment from a trust fund my grandparents set up.'

'Oh.' There wasn't much more Mim could say. She had no experience of trust funds or grandparents. And the sort of figures she was seeing here... She'd known Corin was rich, but this was beyond anything she might have imagined. What was a man with this sort of money doing making tea for her? 'You must really love wearing jumpers full of holes. You could buy dozens of new ones.'

'I know how it must look. Further proof that I'm part of the elite, snobby rich. But I meant what I said before, in Beremouth. I may have been born into it, but it's not what I choose to be.' Corin studied Mim for a moment and then opened the drawer of the desk. There was a photograph album in it and he opened it on a specific page. 'This is a school I sponsor in Rwanda. I worked there for a year and it was the most amazing and humbling experience of my life. The children are incredible and so keen to learn. My clothes don't matter.

Their education does. Giving these children a better future matters.' He found another photograph of a girl aged about ten. Her gorgeous smile filled the picture. 'This is Benite. She wants to be a doctor and save lives. I'd wear rags if it would help her achieve that.'

The passion in his voice was unmistakable. His gaze was steady on hers, as if he was willing her to look beyond the surface and see who he really was. She broke eye contact, telling herself not to be so fanciful.

'You give your money away?' she asked.

'Most of it. Olly set up a charity for me.' He smiled and Mim realised why he had been so knowledgeable about setting up the As You Like It charity. Why hadn't she spotted that before? 'It's not really mine, is it?' Corin continued. 'I didn't earn it. I doubt my grandparents would have approved but I can't think of a better way to spend it.'

He wandered over to the kitchen and Mim stared after him, as if she hadn't really seen him until now. Forget the accent and the privileged upbringing, the family estate, and the trust fund. They didn't define him or make him who he was, any more than her past defined her. When all else was stripped away, he was a kind, hardworking man, doing his best to make a difference where he could. How had she, of all people, judged him on the external trappings? Soul to soul, heart to heart, mind to mind, they were more similar than she could have imagined.

By the end of the afternoon, Mim had prepared a basic spreadsheet of his income and outgoings.

'It should be straightforward now if you keep on top of it,' she said. 'You can easily extract the information you need for your tax return when it's due.'

'You're a star.' Corin crouched next to Mim as he looked at what she had done. 'This is worth more than a brownie and lasagne.'

'Don't forget the cups of tea,' she said. She shifted in her chair, unsettled by his proximity in a way she had never been before, newly conscious of him on a fundamental level, as a man, not as the son and heir of Vennhallow.

'It's worth more than all that.'

'Don't go overboard. This is basic stuff. Someone with bookkeeping or accountancy skills could have done a more sophisticated job.'

Corin stood up.

'Why don't you get more qualifications? You clearly have a flair for numbers. Or what about hotel management, using your experience?'

'I've tried formal education,' Mim said, relaxing now that he had moved away. 'It didn't go well. I must be a bit thick.'

'That's not true. You haven't had any support before. You have us now. You're not on your own. Why not think about it?'

Mim did think about it; it was in the back of her mind

all through the meal later, despite the interesting stories that Corin told her about his time abroad. Perhaps she wasn't really thick, but it had been hard to focus on studying when she'd moved from school to school so often and no one had cared whether she did her homework or revised for exams. Why shouldn't she try again now and see what she could achieve?

The time to leave for the Boat came round too soon.

'I'm seeing Henry Burrows tomorrow night,' Corin said, as Mim picked up her bag and reluctantly headed for the door. 'How did the meeting with him go? Is there anything you need me to follow up?'

'No, it was great. He showed me round the site and we agreed that the charity guests could have a special pass to use the facilities there.' Mim paused in the hallway. 'He also showed me pictures of his house in France.'

'Did he?' Corin's face was hard to read. 'I didn't know he had one. Was it impressive?'

'Incredible. It was enormous – more like a palace than a house. It even made Vennhallow look small.'

'A palace?' Corin held the door open for her. A warm breeze blew in, heady with the tang of the sea air. 'Exactly where you said you deserve to be. When are you going?'

'I don't think I will.' Henry had misjudged if he'd thought a fancy house would impress her. How many schools could he have sponsored with the money he'd spent buying that place? She looked at Corin. 'Don't let it go to your head but you were right. He's not my type.'

Corin smiled that special smile of his that radiated warmth and was impossible to resist.

'I'm pleased to hear it,' he said.

Chapter Eighteen

L ia had worked wonders and found sponsors for the remaining four caravans. She'd decided to hand paint name-plates to attach to the veranda of each one, but had refused to let Mim see them until they were finished. Mim was sitting on her caravan steps with a cup of tea one morning when Lia and Bobby entered the field. Bobby was laden down with a tool bag and a stack of name plates.

'Darling, you look like a beautiful statue sitting there so serenely,' Lia said, kissing Mim's cheeks. Mim had grown used to these public displays now, and it no longer felt odd when someone tried to give her a hug or squeezed her hand. It felt normal, and she didn't think she would ever tire of that; normal was a condition she'd been longing to achieve for years. 'You must let me paint you soon. I have the most wonderful idea for it.'

'As long as it's not a nude picture. I don't think either of us are ready for that.' Mim grinned. 'Are these the name plates? Can I see them at last?'

'Only if you promise to be kind about them. I had to finish them more quickly than I'd have liked so they're ready for when the guests arrive.'

The first guests were booked in for the half-term break at the end of May, only a couple of weeks away now. It was both a thrill and a relief that the idea of As You Like It holidays had taken off, but it was terrifying too. Their guests might not have enjoyed a holiday for years, if ever. It was a huge responsibility to get this right and make it an occasion they would treasure.

Lia showed Mim the name-plates one by one. They were incredible: each name had been painted in fancy script and was surrounded by tiny images that either linked with the name or the seaside location. Mim knew nothing about art but these seemed quite exceptional to her.

Bobby was still holding one board after Mim had inspected them all.

'Now, you won't be cross with me, will you, when I show you this?' Lia said. 'I made it as a surprise, darling. We couldn't have one caravan without a name.'

Bobby handed the final board to Lia and she held it up so that Mim could see the image. The words in the centre read, 'Mim's caravan'. The pictures round the edge showed a series of red-headed mermaids in different poses, both in and out of the water. It was perfect. She couldn't believe that Lia had done this for her.

'Oh darling, do tell me that those are happy tears and not because you loathe it.'

'I love it. Thank you.' Mim gave Lia a hug, something that would have been unthinkable five months ago.

'Well, I still wish you would come and stay in the house and keep me company, but as you won't be tempted we're going to make this place as cosy as can be for you. I suppose it isn't too bad when the weather's like this. Perhaps you could live here in the summer and hibernate in the house with us over winter?'

Mim hadn't thought ahead to next winter. Would she still be here? She hoped so. The Howards were the next best thing to a family of her own; Bea and Bill certainly fussed around as she imagined that parents would, Lia behaved as if Mim were another sister, and Corin... That line of thought shuddered to a halt. Corin was a friend and one she would be sorry to lose if she had to move on. But why should she go? She could stay here, save her money, resume her education, and work towards a better future. Maybe even one day she could have a real home of her own. She wasn't drifting anymore.

Bobby attached Mim's name-plate first and then he and Lia wandered off to the next caravan, just as Bea approached. She was carrying a pile of envelopes.

'I thought I'd bring your post round, Mim dear, as it

looks most intriguing. Shall we sit at the table and have a look? I think my days of perching on steps are long gone.'

Without waiting for a reply, she headed over to one of the picnic benches that had been donated by a garden centre and dropped the post on the top.

'Are you going back to college?' she asked. 'You simply must let me help. I've steered four children through education of one sort or another, from boarding school to sixth-form college, so I'm sure I can offer some advice.'

Mim explained about Corin's suggestion that she could continue her education. She'd looked it up on her mobile phone as best she could, and had discovered that there were courses she could do even with her limited qualifications to date. She'd applied for a few prospectuses to have a better look.

'I think it sounds like a wonderful idea,' Bea said, tearing the wrapper off a prospectus for a college in Exeter. 'Good for Corin for persuading you. He's always loved a cause.'

Mim ran her hand over the glossy surface of the prospectus. Is that how Corin saw her? As a cause, like Benite in Rwanda? The idea made her feel curiously flat. She looked out over the field, watching Lia and Bobby as they attached the signs to the other verandas. They were laughing and joking and it was remarkable to see the change in Lia, and how confident she appeared around Bobby now.

'Have I missed a development in Lia's love life?' Bea asked. She was looking in the same direction as Mim. There was no clue in her expression or her tone as to what she was thinking. Would she disapprove of a relationship between Lia and their handyman? Mim answered cautiously.

'I think they've become closer while working on the caravans,' she said. 'But only as friends.'

'Just good friends?' Bea laughed. 'That tells me everything I need to know. Lia never takes her time over a relationship. This one must be serious.'

'Would you disapprove if it was?' Mim asked.

'Disapprove of Bobby? Why would I do that?' Bea closed the prospectus she was flicking through. 'I don't think I've ever told you how Bill and I became a couple, have I?' Mim shook her head. 'I was brought up with my brother down near the Cornish border, on a glorious estate with land running down to the water's edge. It was a charmed life, and an idle one, I admit. I had nothing to do but attend parties and make myself look beautiful so that a suitable young man would come along and choose me as his wife. My parents took it all very seriously and invited a parade of men they thought would be just the job.'

'I thought that sort of thing had stopped years ago,' Mim said, pulling a face. 'It's a bit sexist, isn't it?'

'It sounds it now, but my parents married late in life and they still liked to do things the old-fashioned way. They were keen to ensure their money would one day pass to an appropriate custodian, one selected by them.' Bea's disapproval was obvious. 'Then, when I was nineteen, my brother brought home a friend of his from Oxford. His name was William Howard and he was quite the most handsome man I'd ever seen. Not only handsome – he was clever, kind, and his head was full of ideas and inventions. He wasn't like any of the other men of my acquaintance. I was totally bowled over.'

'And so you married him?' Mim asked. She loved hearing this story. It was clear that Bea was still as bowled over now as she had been from the start.

'I wish it could have been so simple,' Bea replied. 'He was the perfect man in my eyes but my parents didn't agree. He had many fine qualities but he didn't have the necessary breeding and he was poor as a church mouse, and that was enough to rule him out as a potential son-in-law. Bill asked for my hand in marriage and my father refused.'

'That's awful,' Mim said. 'I hope you ran away and did it anyway.'

'Not straight away, I'm ashamed to say. I'd been brought up to respect my parents and old habits die hard. I carried on seeing Bill in secret and tried to persuade them to change their minds. But they found out about our meetings and were furious. They said that if I didn't stop seeing him, they would cut off my allowance and my inheritance.'

Mim leaned forward across the picnic table, engrossed. 'What did you do?'

Bea laughed.

'*Then* I married him. It was simple, in the end. I found I could live without money but I couldn't live without Bill. I've never regretted it for a moment. Don't settle for anything less in a relationship, my dear. Look for that person who is the most important piece of your world.'

Mim had no experience of that kind of relationship. It hadn't been a feature of her childhood and it wasn't anything she'd ever really thought of for herself. But why should her future be limited by her past? She wasn't unhappy on her own but she could be happier. Seeing the relationship between Bea and Bill had made her long for more and dream of possibilities. What if there was a missing piece of her world out there, waiting for her to find him? Although, it seemed unlikely he was waiting in Littlemead. Most of the men she encountered in the Boat were over fifty, or were already attached. Or saw her as a *cause*.

'Did your parents change their minds?' Mim asked, turning away from that thought. She gestured around. 'You have all this now.'

'They never gave me a penny,' Bea said. 'We're not as different as you might think, my dear Mim. I was cut off by my family and so I made my own instead. Eventually, my parents softened and divided my inheritance into trust funds for each of the children. I wish I could see their reaction to how Corin spends his!' She laughed. 'Everything we have now is down to Bill and all the more precious because of that. He promised when we married that he would make up for what I lost and though I assured him it didn't matter, he did it anyway. He made our fortune with his invention and the business that flowed from it, and he bought this beautiful house for us to live in. I have the best life I could wish for. And so you see, my dear, I would never disapprove of my children following their hearts. I'd disapprove in the strongest terms of them doing anything else.' She reached across the table and took Mim's hand. 'And to be absolutely clear, that applies to them all, not just Lia. Whoever they choose to love we would welcome as one of us.'

'There was a bloke in here earlier, asking after you,' Howie said, squeezing past Mim as she pulled a pint for Corin later that night.

'It wasn't Henry Burrows again, was it?' Corin asked, leaning forward. 'Is he still pestering you?'

'Who said he was pestering me?' Mim replied. 'A man like that wouldn't chase after someone like me.'

'I don't see why not.'

'Then this clearly isn't your first pint of the evening.' Mim handed Corin his drink and turned to Howie. 'Who was it?'

'No idea. I'd not seen him in here before. Here's an odd thing, though. He called you Miranda. It wasn't until he'd gone that I made the connection. I've not heard Miranda since I filled out the paperwork when you started.' Howie let out a rumbling laugh. 'Not in trouble with the law, are you?'

'No,' Mim said. Corin was still standing at the bar. Dickens was sitting on a stool next to him. They were both watching Mim. 'What?' she said to them. 'I thought we'd established that I wasn't a dodgy criminal.'

'We have, but do you think Yvonne was satisfied? Does she have a partner?' Corin asked. He called over to Howie, who had moved along the bar. 'What did this man look like?'

'Barely a man at all, actually. He was young, lanky, sandy-haired. I'm no good with faces. There was nothing remarkable about him. He was one of you, though.'

'One of me?' Mim repeated.

'You know, a northerner.'

Mim looked at Corin.

'You don't really think Yvonne would have another go, do you?' she asked.

'I don't know. Is there anyone else who might be looking for you?' Corin scratched the top of Dickens's head. 'An old boyfriend, perhaps?'

'No one ever hung around long enough to earn the title of boyfriend. The men I knew rarely thought I was worth visiting at the hotel, never mind at the opposite end of the country.' Mim laughed. 'And don't even think of dragging out the pity face. I wasn't interested in a boyfriend then. I got what I needed and that was fine by me.'

'Then?' Corin looked up. 'So you are interested now?'

'I might be up for it. The trouble is, now I'm stuck in a land of southerners and I'm not sure I'm up for that...'

Corin laughed and Mim went over to serve another customer. He was still at the bar when she'd finished.

'So what changed your mind?' he asked when she joined him again. 'I thought you didn't believe in all the hearts and flowers.'

'I didn't, but then Bea told me about her history with Bill.' She'd thought about it a lot over the last few days and how it might tie in with what she wanted in her own life. 'It's a good story. Perhaps there's something in this romantic stuff after all.'

'Perhaps there is.' He smiled. 'Dad has set the bar high. He built a business and made a fortune to show Mum he loved her. How do you follow that?'

'Not everyone wants grand gestures,' Mim said. 'It's the thought behind it that matters, isn't it? He understood what she needed and provided it.' She passed him a bowl of water for Dickens. 'Are you worried about taking over? Because it means so much to them?'

'Yes. The business is Dad's Taj Mahal – it was built as a symbol of love. I can't let it fail.' Corin spun his glass round on the bar. 'It's not just the personal connection. We employ over a hundred people in the factory. We pay above average wages and offer good benefits. Our employees are happy. We have a responsibility to them to keep the business running.'

'You don't have any vacancies going, do you?' Mim grinned, but Corin's words had reminded her of the awful day when the hotel had closed and she'd had to tell the staff that they were out of work. It hadn't been her decision but she'd still felt guilty and had hated being responsible for ruining Christmas for the families involved. How much worse would it be for Corin, having the fate of a hundred families in his hands? Especially when it wasn't the career he'd chosen for himself. No wonder the rest of the family didn't want to take it on. It would be easier to employ someone to run the business and sit back and enjoy the money but that wasn't Corin's way.

'Don't forget that you need to be happy too,' Mim said. 'Is there no room for compromise? Can you work in the business part time so you can carry on with the fossil tours and the educational work? You know what else Bea said? She wants you all to follow your hearts.'

Another customer came up to the bar and Mim started to move away.

'She said that?' Corin smiled at her. 'Perhaps on this occasion I should follow her advice.'

Over the next few days, Mim had the odd sensation that she was being watched but when she turned round there was no one there. She told herself she was imagining it, but when it happened a fourth time she mentioned it to Karen and Heather after their next swim. It was now warm enough for them to sit outside the campervan for their tea and cake, on deckchairs provided by Heather.

'There is someone looking for you,' Karen said. 'I was going to tell you. I was in the shop yesterday—'

'Janet's shop?' Mim interrupted. 'How could you go in there after what she did?' There had been no further activity against As You Like It holidays but Mim was still nursing a grudge.

'I know, I have tried to boycott it,' Karen said, holding up her hands as if to ward off any further criticism. 'But Susie wanted brownies and I'd run out of cocoa powder. I don't hear you complaining now,' she added, pointing to the half-eaten brownie in Mim's hand. Mim grinned.

'Tell me who was looking for me,' she said. 'Someone's been in the Boat as well. A young bloke according to Howie.'

'Could be the same person,' Karen said. 'This was a young lad, early twenties I'd say. Tall and gangly, gingery hair. A bit anxious-looking but he was talking to Janet so that might account for it. You can imagine how helpful she was.'

'Did you hear what he wanted?'

'A little. He asked if she knew Miranda Brown and Janet said she didn't and that she was running a shop not an information service. Then he showed her a newspaper clipping. It was about the charity launch – you know, the one with the photo of you with Lia and Corin.'

Mim knew the one. It was the photo she kept in her emergency box – that, embarrassingly, Corin must have seen. It was also the photo that had brought Yvonne to Vennhallow. Her heart sank. What trouble was it causing now?

'He pointed at your picture,' Karen continued, 'and asked Janet if she recognised you.' She smiled. 'I won't repeat Janet's exact words. She made it clear that if he was another of your sort he wasn't welcome in the shop.'

Mim was beginning to feel sorry for whoever this man was. She could imagine that Janet wouldn't have minced her words.

'Did he say what he wanted?' she asked.

'No. He was persistent. He asked if you lived in Littlemead but Janet refused to tell him anything.'

'Quite right,' Heather said. 'She can't be giving your address out to strange men.'

'I think she refused out of bloody-mindedness rather than for Mim's protection. But you're right. That's why I didn't speak to him. He carried on up the hill towards the café but I didn't see him again after that.' Karen passed the box of brownies to Mim. 'Have you no idea who he is?'

'None at all. But it's not likely to be good news, is it?' Mim picked out the largest brownie she could find, deciding to console herself with chocolate. 'Hopefully Janet will have scared him away.'

Mim was taking a break in a quiet corner of the Boat the next night, reading one of the books that Corin had given her for her birthday when a shadow fell over her table. She looked up. There was a young man standing at the side of her table – tall, skinny, early twenties, exactly as Karen had described him. He was wearing jeans and a T-shirt and had a rucksack on his back, which wasn't unusual around here. The Boat was a regular stop-off for ramblers walking the South West Coast Path. He didn't look much like a walker though. One gust of wind might blow him off the cliff top.

'Are you Miranda Brown?' he asked, in a definite northern accent. 'Mim?'

'Who wants to know?' she asked. She put down her

book. 'What's going on? Have you been asking around the village about me over the last few days?'

He nodded. Colour rose in his cheeks, making him look even younger.

'I've been trying to find you for months,' he said.

'Why?' Mim asked. 'Who are you?'

He smiled – a nervous but determined smile.

'I'm your brother.'

Chapter Nineteen

It was the last thing Mim had expected to hear.

'I don't have a brother.' She pushed back her chair and stood up. 'If this is a joke, I don't think it's very funny.'

'It's not a joke.' The young man slipped his rucksack off his back, opened it, and took out an envelope. He pulled out a sheet of paper and gave it to Mim. 'This is my birth certificate. Have a look at my dad. He's your dad too, isn't he?'

'I never met my dad.' Mim sank back down into her chair and studied the paper. It confirmed that a boy called Lucas Hamer had been born twenty-four years ago. His mother was a Carol Hamer – the name meant nothing to Mim. His father was a plasterer called Martin Hamer. She stared at the name with a jolt of surprise and confusion. She recognised it. It was the only information she'd ever had about her father, along with the photo she kept in her emergency box.

'That was my dad's name,' she said. 'Or so I was told.' She looked at Lucas. 'Surely it's just a coincidence – two men with the same name. It's not an unusual one, is it?'

'It's no coincidence. Dad told me about you and asked me to find you. I've been looking for a year. I've contacted loads of Miranda Browns but none of them were the right one. Then I saw this in the paper.' Lucas waved the now crumpled cutting at Mim. 'It said you'd come from Lancashire. You look like Dad. I had to come and see.'

Mim studied his face. Could this be true? Did she have a dad and a brother, a loving family of her own? She wanted to believe it more than she'd ever wanted anything in her life. But she mustn't let hope become proof. She had a thousand questions first.

'Everything okay, Mim?' Howie paused by her table. 'Not having any bother, are you?'

'No. It's fine. Better than fine. Howie, is there any chance I could take some time off? I need to talk to Lucas.'

'Well, there's only the two of us on tonight and it might get busy later. Can you do your talking here and come back behind the bar if you're needed?'

Mim nodded and Lucas sat down at the table with her. He tipped a few more things out of his rucksack.

'I've brought some ID so you can check who I am,' he said. 'Here's my driving licence and passport, and my old student card.'

It hadn't crossed Mim's mind to check his identification. She picked up each item in turn, absorbing the details. He had a passport, so he'd travelled abroad at some point. He'd studied at the university in Keele and his driving licence gave his address in Blackpool. Even these three basic items painted a history of his life that was vastly different to hers.

'I have these too.' Lucas opened an envelope and took out a photograph and a piece of plastic. Mim picked up the plastic. It was like a tiny bracelet, cut open at one end, and her name and birth date were written on it. She rubbed her thumb along the letters, feeling dazed, wondering if something so small could really hold such huge significance.

'It was your baby name tag from the hospital,' Lucas explained. 'Dad kept it.'

She looked at the photograph next but it only needed a glance. It showed a pair of teenagers with a baby. She knew every detail of it already because she had an identical copy. She made an odd noise, half gasp, half sob. Was it too soon to believe this was real? Should she wait, insist on some kind of test, some actual, scientific proof? But she didn't need science when every instinct told her it was true. It wasn't too soon. It was years later than it should have been. But not too late. It could never be too late.

She looked up at Lucas.

'Is our dad here with you?'

She knew the answer before he spoke and she slumped back in her seat. It *was* too late. The grief was still fresh on his face.

'He died last summer,' Lucas said. 'He had a tumour. There were only two weeks between the doctors finding it and him going. It was horrible.'

His shoulders shook and he bit his lip, trying not to cry. He looked so young and lost that there was only one thing Mim could do. She went round the table and hugged him, and as he hugged her back the truth sank in. She was a sister. She had someone to look out for, like the Howards looked out for each other. She had a role and a purpose that had been missing until now. She had someone to love. As Lucas's tears dampened her shoulder, she made a silent vow. She was going to be the best sister possible, whatever it took, whatever the cost. It felt like she'd found the missing piece of her world that Bea had talked about – not romantic love, but sisterly love. Nothing else mattered.

Over Lucas's shoulder, she saw Corin walk into the pub, Dickens trotting at his heel. She watched as he scanned the bar and then spotted her in the corner. He hesitated, his smile wavering, and then wandered over to speak to Howie, who shrugged in response to whatever Corin said. Mim turned away and resumed her seat.

'Tell me everything,' she said to Lucas. 'I want to know all about you.'

She was thrilled to hear what a happy, conventional life he had led: brought up by the sea in Blackpool with married parents who clearly adored him, especially when no other children followed. He'd had grandparents from both sides and his maternal grandmother was still alive. There were aunts, uncles, and cousins on his mother's side, and they'd enjoyed holidays and Christmases together. He'd been average at school and had obtained a degree in Biology but was now training to be a plumber. He lived at home with his mum, and yes, he had a girlfriend but it was early days, he admitted with red cheeks when Mim asked what she thought would be an obvious big-sister question. And she learnt as much from what he didn't say as what he did. He was quietly spoken, shy, and clearly didn't enjoy talking about himself. He loved his family and had no desire to move away from them or from Blackpool. Mim liked him, genuinely liked him.

'What about you?' Lucas asked at last. 'It said in the paper that you'd been sleeping in your car. That's not right, is it? What about your mum?' He flushed. 'Sorry. Has she died too?'

'I don't know.' Mim shrugged. The story of her life sounded even more tawdry after hearing about Lucas's upbringing, but she wasn't going to shrink from it now any more than she had in the past. It wasn't her fault. Gordon had instilled that belief in her and it was the best inheritance he could have given her. 'She had problems and had a habit of picking the wrong men. I was taken into care when I was eight. I moved in and out of foster homes for a while, because she kept promising to sort herself out. But she didn't and I ended up in a care home. We didn't have any contact after that.'

There were many gaps in the story and she noticed Lucas's gaze flick to her arm, where the scarring was clearly visible below the sleeve of her T-shirt. Perhaps one day they would build a relationship and she could tell him everything. Or perhaps not. He looked so young, so innocent. Perhaps it was the role of a big sister to protect him from some truths.

'You must hate me,' Lucas said. 'I've had such an easy life. Dad can't have known what was happening to you. He was a good dad.'

'I'm glad.' She would never wish her childhood on anyone else. She was happy for Lucas, not jealous of him. But Lucas had said he'd been looking for her for a year. Where had her dad been for the thirty-three years before that? 'Did he never mention me?' she asked. Lucas shook his head.

'Not until the end. He told me and Mum, when he knew he wasn't going to live. She hadn't known about you either. She was furious with him.'

'I'm not surprised. It's a pretty big secret to keep from your wife.'

'Yeah, it wasn't that. She wasn't furious with him for herself. It was for you, because he'd never made an effort to find you.'

'And what does she think about you trying to find me now?' Mim asked.

'She's been helping me. Dad asked us to do it. It was all he was bothered about in those last two weeks.' Lucas looked tearful again. 'And anyway, she wanted to find you as much as I do. You're family. You're one of us.'

The next few days were strange and wonderful. In between shifts at the pub, occasional work for Paula, and dealing with emails and admin for As You Like It, Mim spent as much time as she could with Lucas. He was staying in a B&B nearby, and each day he would cycle over to Littlemead and they would walk along the coastal path or sit in the caravan if it rained, trying to fill in the separation of the past and build a foundation for the future.

For the first time, she had to turn down a request from Bea to drive her on an errand.

'Would tomorrow morning be too late?' Mim asked. 'Lucas is coming over this afternoon.'

'Lucas?' Bea repeated. 'Do you have a boyfriend, Mim

dear? Corin said he'd seen you with a young man in the Boat. It wasn't anyone he knew.'

'He's not my boyfriend. He's my brother.' Mim grinned. It was still an amazing thing to say those words. She told Bea the whole story about Lucas seeing the article in the newspaper and tracking her down.

'And so now you have your own family. I can't tell you how pleased I am for you.' Although Mim didn't think she looked entirely pleased. Was there a trace of sadness in Bea's expression? It soon passed. 'Of course the errand can wait, or I'll risk Lia's driving. Family must always come first.' She smiled. 'Why don't you bring him to dinner so we can all meet him? I'll ask Mrs Dennis to make something special.'

Mim couldn't imagine Lucas coping with a room full of noisy Howards.

'Thanks, but he's quite shy and I'll be working at the Boat every night. I'm sure you might bump into him soon though. He cycles here most days.'

Corin hadn't been in the Boat since the night Lucas had introduced himself. Mim thought he must have gone away on one of his educational trips until he wandered into one of the caravans as she was making the beds ready for their half-term visitors.

'Have you heard the news?' she said. She'd been dying to tell him and had been disappointed not to see him in the pub. 'I have a brother. His name's Lucas. He's twenty-four and he's training to be a plumber. Can you believe it?'

'Mum mentioned it. Congratulations.'

Corin bent to tuck a sheet under the mattress. He did a proper hospital corner, which might have impressed Mim if she hadn't felt so disappointed by his muted reaction to her news.

'Aren't you happy for me?' she asked. 'You know how much I've wished I had a family.'

'I know. But have you checked it out properly? Are you sure it's real?'

His words felt like a pinprick, puncturing her happiness.

'Why, do you think he might be a scammer, trying to steal my worldly goods?' she said. 'He's a daft one, if he is. The train fare down here probably cost more than everything I own. I can't think of any reason why he would make this up. He hasn't made it up, I know it.'

'Has he shown you any proof?'

'Yes. His dad – our dad – kept one of my nametags from the hospital where I was born. We have identical photos of me with my parents. It checks out. I thought you would understand what this means to me,' Mim said, thumping a pillow so violently that it looked flattened rather than plumped. Corin grasped her hand.

'I do understand. That's why I'm worried. I don't want you to be hurt.'

Mim looked down at their joined hands. His thumb stroked slowly across the back of her hand.

'Come to the Boat and meet him,' she said. 'He'll be in tonight. Then you'll see. It's not a con. He's not like that. He's quiet and sweet.'

Corin smiled.

'Are you sure he's related to you?' He laughed and let go of her hand. 'I'll be there.'

———————————

Lucas was becoming cheeky.

'Are you sure he's not a boyfriend?' he asked Mim for the third time since she'd mentioned that Corin wanted to buy him a drink that night. She couldn't be annoyed if he asked her thirty times. He was teasing her, in the way that Corin and Lia teased each other, and she loved that she had someone to do that to her.

'Absolutely sure,' she replied. 'You'll see why when you meet him. He's from a different world than us. He's so posh that it feels like talking to a member of the Royal Family.'

'What does he want to drink with us for then?' Lucas asked. 'Aren't we too common for someone like that? Or does he like showing off by flashing his cash around?'

'No, he's not like that at all.' Her response was instinctive and Mim had to smile; she was defending Corin from exactly the assumptions she'd made about him when she'd first met him. Her opinion could hardly be more different now, after months of getting to know him. How could she begin to explain? 'He's nice,' she concluded, feeling the full inadequacy of her words. 'You'll like him.'

She hoped it was true, but she needn't have worried. Although Lucas looked uneasy when Corin shook his hand and started to speak, within a few minutes he appeared more relaxed, and by the time that Mim took them a couple of fresh pints, they were chatting and laughing like old friends.

'I'm taking Lucas out on a fossil hunt tomorrow,' Corin said. 'It's not my day for a public tour, so we'll just look on the village beach but we might find something. We'll have to set off around eight. Why don't you come?'

'I can't. I'll be swimming then.' Mim couldn't hide her disappointment. 'Will there be time for me to join you after that? I'm still determined to find a proper ammonite. You will wait for me, won't you?'

'Don't let Lia catch you sounding so enthusiastic,' Corin said. 'She'll think I've poisoned your mind.' He smiled at her, a warm smile that reflected in his eyes. 'I promise we'll wait. We won't leave the beach until you've finished your swim.'

The noise struck Mim first, even though her head was partly in the sea and water was clogging her ears. It started as a low rumble and turned into a roar, ending in a crash like the longest, loudest clap of thunder that Mim could imagine. Her feet found the sea bed and she wiped the water from her face so she could see what was going on. In the distance, on the far side of the beach beyond the village, a huge cloud of brown dust rose into the air, covering the shore.

'It's a land slip,' she heard Karen shout. She didn't wait to hear any more. She waded out of the sea, ignoring the tired ache in her legs, and started to run down the beach, slipping and sliding on the pebbles, struggling for each breath but determined not to slow down. Lucas had gone that way with Corin on their fossil hunt this morning. She had waved at them when she arrived to swim, happy that they were getting on so well. Where were they? Were they safe? Water ran down her face and she wiped it away, but it made no difference. She couldn't see them. She fixed her eyes on the distance, willing them to appear, but there was no movement at all. Her heart thumped against her chest. She'd only just found a brother. She couldn't lose him now.

'Lucas,' she yelled. Her foot slipped off a stone and she fell to her knees with a painful bump. She got straight back up again. 'Lucas!'

She hobbled on, concentrating now on where she placed her feet so a few seconds passed before she looked up and saw a figure running in the opposite direction, away from the dust. She hesitated, trying to work out who it was, then picked up speed again until she met Lucas near the path back to the village centre. She threw her arms round him, not caring how wet she was, and hugged him tightly, relishing each ragged breath she could feel shuddering through his chest.

'Thank God,' she said. 'You're alive. When I heard the noise…' She closed her eyes and rested her head against his, unable to finish the sentence. Memories of Corin's safety talk at the fossil hunt had rushed back in as soon as Karen had said the words 'land slip'. All she'd been able to think about was those pictures of huge fallen boulders and how Corin and Lucas might have been crushed underneath something similar. She shivered, horrified by the idea of what might have been.

Then she opened her eyes and looked over Lucas's shoulder. Corin… She'd assumed that he had followed Lucas. She'd assumed they were both safe. But all she could see behind Lucas was a huge pile of rubble and the dust that continued to billow everywhere. There was no one else in sight. Her heart wasn't thumping now. It seemed to be frozen.

'Where's Corin?' she shouted, pulling away from Lucas. 'Lucas, what's happened to Corin?'

'I don't know. He was further down the beach. He yelled at me to run this way and I did.'

Mim didn't stop to think. She started running again,

on towards the huge pile of rocks that now created a barrier over halfway across the beach, ignoring the shouts of Lucas, Karen, and Heather urging her to turn back. Her legs ached down to the bones and every breath was a struggle, but still she pushed herself on. She had to find Corin. She would find him. Corin couldn't be under those rocks, she told herself as she ran, skirting towards the sea and well away from the cliff, because he knew about geology and things like that. Corin couldn't be under the rocks because he was far too clever to be caught. She'd heard him warn people to stay away from the foot of the cliffs, so he wouldn't have been there himself. Corin couldn't be under the rocks because... The truth struck her with the speed and force of her own emotional rock fall. Because she couldn't imagine life without him if he was.

She ran past the barrier of rocks towards the next section of beach, waving her hands to shift the dust that was still flying in the air. She picked her way forward across the pebbles, looking up and down the beach, desperately scanning the shore again and again. He wasn't there. She couldn't see Corin anywhere. He wasn't in the sea and he wasn't on the beach. That only left...

Mim sank down onto the stones, wracked with coughs as the dust caught in her throat. This was her fault. She'd insisted that Corin stay on the beach until she'd finished her swim. She remembered the warmth of his smile as he'd promised to wait for her. Had he been trapped because he was keeping his promise to her? How would Bea and Bill ever get over this? How would she?

And then, as she became aware of a crowd gathering on the beach from the village, she heard a quiet bark. Dickens! She hadn't given him a thought. She scrambled up towards the foot of the cliff, hardly caring whether it was safe or not, and as the dust finally settled she saw a sight that made her heart flicker back to life. Corin was sitting close to the fallen rocks, cradling Dickens in his arms. He looked dazed, dirty and undoubtedly alive.

'Dickens strayed too close to the cliff,' he said. There was the slightest shake in his voice. 'I couldn't leave him. He mustn't have paid attention to the safety talk.'

Mim stared at him. Was he making a joke, at a time like this? He smiled. She hadn't thought she would see that smile again.

'Where's Lucas?' Corin asked. 'Did he get past? Is he okay?'

She nodded. She couldn't speak. The relief was too great. Relief and something more, something she didn't recognise and had no name for, something that scared her more than anything else that had happened today. He was the same old Corin, though the smile seemed more fragile than usual. His hair was sticking out as it always did, despite the particles of dust that weighed it down. He looked the same but she wasn't seeing him in the same way. She wanted to weep with thankfulness that he was alive.

He stood up, put Dickens on the ground, and walked towards her.

'Are you crying, Mim?' he asked.

'No.' Treacherous eyes. How had that happened? She scrubbed her face. 'It's the sea,' she said. But what chance was there that he'd believe her when her voice wobbled on every word?

He came closer and drew her into his arms.

'All's well,' he murmured into her hair. 'Don't worry. You're safe now. Everything's going to be fine.'

Chapter Twenty

The rock fall was the only topic of conversation in the village for days. Mim couldn't complete a shift in the Boat without having to give an eyewitness account to either locals or fascinated tourists, who seemed thrilled to have arrived in the area at such an interesting time. There had even been a brief paragraph about it on the BBC website. Mim was worried that it would put people off holidaying in the caravans, but Bea disagreed.

'Bill couldn't find a space in the village car park yesterday,' she said. 'Daytrippers are thronging to the beach. I can't bear to go near it. When I think about Corin down there...' Bea shuddered. The recent events had taken their toll on her; Mim noticed the tired lines around her eyes. She was a subdued version of her former self, evident even in the plain clothes and glasses she was wearing. 'The sooner he gives all that up and takes over the business, the better. He'll be safe in an office.'

Safe but not necessarily happy, Mim couldn't help thinking. Which was better? Bea was out of luck if she thought Corin was going to let the rock fall put him off the beach. He'd been back within an hour of it happening, helping the police and fire service who had arrived to assess the scene. Mim had wanted to drag him away but what business was it of hers? None at all, even though memories of those moments when she had thought Corin was under the rocks still haunted her several days later.

Lucas was dwelling on his close shave too. He visited Mim one day when she was going round each caravan, adding a notice to the information packs warning of the dangers of rock falls and giving advice on how to visit the beach safely.

'You don't have to worry about this on Blackpool beach,' he said, pointing at Mim's leaflet. 'The only dangerous part is crossing the tram tracks, and at least you can see when a tram is coming.'

Mim laughed.

'It's not a great alternative, is it, being flattened by a tram rather than a pile of rocks?' Her smile faded; it was still too distressing to joke about. She was usually capable of putting awful events behind her and looking forward, so why was she struggling so much with this one? 'I'll have to come and visit you in Blackpool and compare the beaches for myself.'

'You should definitely come,' Lucas said. 'There's a proper beach in Blackpool, not just stones. It's not dead like this place either. You'll love it.'

Lucas's imminent departure was another cause of distress to Mim. He had taken two weeks off work to look for her and their time was almost up already. His return train journey was booked for Saturday and the deadline loomed over their blossoming relationship. She liked him more each day, but they were still getting to know each other and learning the similarities and differences between them. Lucas had shown her lots of photographs of their dad and there was a clear resemblance between the three of them. Mim loved making the connection and discovering the roots that she'd missed out on for so long.

'I wish you could stay longer,' she said to Lucas, not for the first time, when he called in to the Boat one night. Their relationship felt too fragile and too precious to bear a separation so soon. 'Is there no way you can manage another week? There should be the equivalent of paternity leave for finding a sister instead of having a baby.'

'I can't. My boss is off next week for the school holidays and I need to be in work.'

'Then I'll have to save up and come and visit you as soon as I can,' Mim said. She sighed. 'It might not be until autumn though. Howie tells me it can be packed in here over summer.'

Lucas picked at the label on his bottle of lager.

'There is another option,' he said. 'Why don't you move back to Lancashire?'

'Move back?' Mim was tidying behind the bar but that made her stop in her tracks. She hadn't seen that coming. 'Do you mean for good? To live there?'

'Why not? It's your home, isn't it?'

Home. The word filled Mim's head as she served another customer. Lucas had inadvertently found her most vulnerable spot. A home and a family – those were the two things she'd always wanted. She'd found one. Could the two go hand in hand? She instinctively felt that it couldn't be that simple, not now. Returning to Lancashire hadn't crossed her mind since the first week of arriving here. Was she willing to do that? To leave behind everything she had found in Devon? To leave behind everyone?

'I wouldn't have a job or anywhere to live,' she said, when she wandered back over to Lucas. She tried to focus on the practical objections; the emotional ones were harder to deal with.

'I've discussed it with Mum,' Lucas said. 'You can stay in our spare room, at least to start with. That's better than an old caravan, isn't it? And we're in Blackpool.' He laughed. 'There are hotels and bars everywhere. You belong in Lancashire with us. It's what Dad would have wanted.'

Mim went back to the caravan that night and looked around the space that had been hers for the last five months. It wasn't just an old caravan to her. This place had been a lifeline, offering her comfort and safety when she'd been at her lowest point. She loved living here, especially now the weather was warmer and she could throw open the doors and windows instead of huddling under the duvet. She loved being able to spend her spare minutes sitting on the cliff tops, watching the waves down below and the gulls circling overhead, enjoying the sort of peace that had been missing in her life until now. But she had to be realistic. The caravan had only ever been meant as a temporary place to stay. At some point she would need to move on and find a permanent base. Did it make sense to make that base in Lancashire, now that she knew Lucas was there? Was it really what their dad would have wanted, for his family to be together? She'd never had the chance to know him but perhaps it wasn't too late to make him proud.

Her gaze fell on the college prospectuses, lying open on the courses she'd flagged as possibilities. Something else she would have to leave behind if she went back north. She ignored the sudden twist of disappointment. There would be similar courses in Lancashire. It would be fine. She would have Lucas to cheer her on and encourage her, instead of the Howards.

The Howards. She'd been trying not to think about them but now they crowded into her head, loud and large as life. Bea and Bill, Lia and Ros. Corin. They had drawn her into their world and it was a wonderful place to be. The last few months had been some of the happiest of her life. But that was because she'd had no one else and nowhere else to go. Much as she loved the caravan, it wasn't a proper home. Much as she liked the Howards, they weren't her proper family. She wasn't really one of them and she never could be. It had been a brilliant adventure staying here, one she would never forget, but was it time for the adventure to end?

She met Heather and Karen for their regular swim the next morning, after a night of tossing and turning over her decision.

'Late night, was it?' Karen asked, smiling. 'You still look half asleep. What have you been up to?'

'Nothing as exciting as you're suggesting.' Mim grabbed a slice of coffee cake and told them about Lucas's suggestion that she go back north.

'You're not really going to leave, are you?' Heather asked. 'I thought you were settled here now. We'd miss you.' Mim would miss them too. They were the first real friends she'd ever had. But now she knew that such friendship existed, she could find friends in Lancashire, couldn't she?

'We wouldn't have to make as much cake,' Karen

said. She smiled and reached out to pat Mim's hand. 'We've all become fond of you.'

'I love it here,' Mim said. 'But it's not a permanent sort of life, is it? It's been like an extended holiday from reality. I can't still be living in a borrowed caravan in twenty years' time, even if Bea and Bill didn't mind. I have to think of the future. I love working in the Boat but I don't earn enough to afford a place of my own, especially somewhere round here. It's much cheaper to live in Lancashire. I'd have better prospects there.'

'That's true,' Karen said. 'Everything is more expensive down here. We get better weather though, most of the time. I wouldn't relish living in that caravan over winter, however cosy it looks now. You were lucky there was no snow this year.'

'Don't encourage her,' Heather said, nudging Karen to shut her up. Mim smiled. This was exactly what she would miss. 'Okay, there are some practical arguments in favour of going. But there are lots of reasons to stay, too. You're earning money and not paying rent – that's not something to give up lightly. You've made friends here and become part of the village community. And what about the charity? You're a trustee and you've put so much work into it. The first guests are about to arrive. Don't you want to see it through?'

'Yes. I want to make sure it's a success. It would be one of the hardest things to leave behind,' Mim said. 'But the idea of the charity is to allow families to spend quality time together and make memories. Shouldn't I be doing that with my family? You live in the same village as Bobby. You wouldn't want to move away from him would you?'

Heather hesitated then shook her head with obvious reluctance.

'No, I wouldn't. When Carmel died, I couldn't have managed without him. He was my rock. There's nothing like having the support of your family when you need them.' She smiled. 'I'm not helping persuade you to stay, am I? What's your heart telling you to do?'

'I haven't a clue,' Mim said. 'I think mine is purely functional. It's never spoken to me yet.'

'Perhaps you need to make time to listen.'

'I don't have time. Lucas is due to leave tomorrow.' He had pressed her for an answer and she felt terrible that she hadn't given him one yet. She'd come close many times but something had held her back, sticking the words in her throat. 'I keep coming back to the same point. He's my family, like you and Bobby. That means everything to someone like me. If I let him leave, I'll always wonder if it was a mistake and what our relationship might have been.'

'Can't you make it a holiday?' Karen asked. 'Go for a week or two and see if it works out.'

'Give it a trial run to see if I like having a family? How would I explain that to Lucas?' Mim smiled. 'I don't do half measures. I either commit in full or not at all. If I go, it *will* work out. I'll make sure it does.'

'It sounds to me like you've made up your mind,' Karen said.

Mim gazed out across the Littlemead car park, towards the clifftops and the view of the sea beyond. There hadn't been a choice – not really, not since the moment Lucas had asked her to go. It was the first chance she'd had to prove herself as a sister, and she wasn't going to let him down. Heather's words had only confirmed it for her; Lucas needed her and her place was with him. She had vowed to be the best possible sister, hadn't she? She had to follow that through, whatever the cost.

'I have to go back to Lancashire,' she said.

It was easy to dismantle her life in Devon. Mim was well-practised at moving on at short notice. But it had never been so painful before.

She broke the news to Howie first, apologising that she was about to leave him in the lurch as peak tourist season was getting underway. His unequivocal support for her decision and genuine sorrow to see her go almost made her cry. And that was before she'd told the Howards. How was she ever going to bear saying goodbye to them?

Mim wandered along the track to Vennhallow shortly after lunch, when she hoped she might find the family together. She was in luck. Bea, Bill, and Lia were sitting outside in the garden. Bill was snoozing in his chair, his moustache rippling with each snore. Bea was reading a book and Lia was scrolling on her phone. Mim lurked in the shadows of the house for a moment, locking in this memory of them to savour when she was gone.

'Hello Mim.' Bea looked up from her book and smiled. 'Have you had lunch, my dear? There's another bowl of salad in the kitchen and Mrs Dennis has made a heavenly Victoria sponge. You won't say no to that, will you? Is Lucas with you? There's plenty for him too.'

'No.' Mim came forward and joined the family on the terrace. 'Lucas wanted to do some more sightseeing before he leaves.'

'Is it tomorrow he goes?' Bea asked. 'It's gone so quickly. It's a shame you've had so little time together when you've only recently found each other.'

'It is.' Mim sat down on an empty chair. Bea had given her the perfect opening. 'That's why I've come to talk to you.'

Bea's smile faded. She had guessed. Mim could see it in her face.

'You're here to say goodbye, aren't you?' Bea said. She reached across to Bill and shook his arm to wake him up. 'I had an awful sense that this might happen and that we might lose you.'

'Goodbye?' Lia looked up from her phone. 'What are you talking about? Where are you going?'

'Back to Lancashire,' Mim said.

'But darling, why would you want to do that? Your life is here now.'

'It was. But now I have a brother and he'll be there.'

'Brothers are totally overrated.' Lia smiled. 'What about As You Like It holidays? Our first guests are arriving tomorrow. We need you.'

'I'll be here.' Mim had already worked out an answer – not a perfect one, but better than nothing. 'Lucas had booked a train for tomorrow, but he'll stay on an extra day and we'll drive north together on Sunday. Heather has offered to take over the cleaning duties between guests. I hope you'll still let me be involved in some way. I can deal with the emails and the admin from Lancashire. I can spread the word about the charity in a whole new area too.'

'We'll be sorry to see you go,' Bill said. 'I'll come with you to the garage and fill up your car.' He raised a hand when Mim tried to protest. 'It's the least we can do. You only came down here because of us.'

'Don't encourage her, Daddy,' Lia protested. 'We need to persuade her to stay here.'

'If I know Mim, she won't be persuaded once she's made up her mind,' Bill replied. 'If she's given Lucas her word, she'll stick by it. Isn't that right?'

Mim nodded.

'Is there no one who could persuade you?' Bea asked softly. 'No one at all?'

'No.' Mim smiled, thought it was the hardest smile she'd ever given. 'Think of the positives. You have an extra caravan to use for the holidays now.'

'We won't use it,' Bea said. 'That caravan is yours whenever you need it. Who knows when you might want a holiday yourself and come back to see us?' She walked over to Mim and took hold of her hands. 'Do come back and see us, won't you? You're one of us, Miranda Brown, wherever you are and whatever you do. Don't forget that. There will always be a home for you here.'

Behind her gaudy glasses, there were tears in Bea's eyes. She squeezed Mim's hands and then muttered something about 'another bottle of wine' and hurried into the house. Bill stood up.

'I should follow her,' he said. He held out his hand to shake Mim's. 'It's been a bigger and better adventure than we expected, eh? Don't you worry about us. You deserve your chance at happiness. If you believe that's waiting for you in the north, I'll wish you the best of luck. You know where we are if you need us.'

He followed Bea into the house. Mim moved over to sit on the bench next to Lia.

'You don't really need me,' Mim said to her. 'Look what you've achieved with the charity. All the ideas and initiatives were yours. You obtained most of the donations and all the sponsors for the caravans. I've done some donkey work but anyone could have done that. You have vision and drive and creativity. Now you know you can succeed at anything you put your mind to. I'm going to watch out for whatever brilliant thing you do next.'

Lia leaned against Mim.

'Don't go,' she said. 'I do need you. You're the only person who judges me for what I do now, not because of who I am or who I was.'

'I'm not the only one.' Mim couldn't resist the opportunity to meddle. 'There's a certain young gardener who seems very impressed by everything you've done.'

Lia sat up.

'Bobby? Do you think so?'

'I'm sure of it. He likes you. How could he not? But you know, it must be hard for him to look at all this and believe he has a chance. Perhaps you need to give him some gentle encouragement.'

Lia threw her arms round Mim.

'You are the best sister I never had,' she said. 'You know I'll be on the phone to you every day, until you're literally sick of hearing from me. I may even have to figure out where this Lancashire place is so that I can visit you. Do they have any five-star hotels there, darling?'

Mim squeezed her back, determined not to cry. And now there was only one person left she needed to tell...

Mim sat on the beach, enjoying the view before her last shift started at the Boat. She loved this view – the way the bay curved upwards on both sides, as if the village lay at the centre of a smile; the way the cliffs rose in a sharp climb on one side and a gentle slope on the other; the way the sea changed every day, never the same twice. The raw, natural beauty soothed her soul, despite the evidence of its danger in the closed-off section where the rock fall had taken place.

She'd called at Corin's house on the way here, but he hadn't been at home. She couldn't decide if it was a relief or a disappointment. As unlikely as it had seemed at the start, his friendship had become a precious thing to her over the last few months, as precious as her relationship with Lia. Maybe even more. She owed him a proper goodbye, but the thought of going through with it made her feel like there was a huge pile of rocks hovering over her chest, ready to fall and crush it. Perhaps Bea or Lia would have told him by now and spared her the trouble? Then they could simply meet and wish each other well for the future…

A wet nose nudged her hand. Dickens had stopped at her side and, looking up, she saw Corin striding along the beach towards her. He smiled and came and sat down beside her on the stones.

'This is well met,' he said. 'I was on my way to the Boat to see you.'

'Were you? What for?' Mim asked. He looked remarkably jolly. If he knew she was leaving he clearly wasn't bothered.

'There's a 6k wild swim taking place on Dartmoor in August. I thought we could join in. What do you say? Shall I sign us up?'

'That sounds great,' she said. She couldn't meet his eye and reached forward to stroke Dickens. 'But I won't be here in August.'

'Won't you?' She heard the puzzlement in his voice. 'Where will you be?'

'In Lancashire.'

She risked a glance at him and caught the return of his smile.

'Visiting Lucas? The swim is right at the start of the month, so perhaps you can fit it in before you go. Unless you're chickening out of the 6k after all…'

'I won't be visiting him.' This felt like torture. Mim decided to spit it all out at once. 'I'll be living there. I'm moving back. We're leaving on Sunday.'

The silence stretched, broken only by the sound of the gulls with their urgent calls as they wheeled overhead. Dickens was sitting at her feet, staring at her. She suspected that Corin was doing the same.

'This Sunday?' he said at last. 'In less than two days' time? When were you going to tell me?'

'I called round earlier. You were out.'

'I was at the factory.' He picked up a pebble and twisted it round and round in his hand. 'You're not serious, are you? You're not really leaving for good?'

'Yes. I am.'

He stood up and walked off to the water's edge. He threw the pebble into the sea, where it landed with a violent splash. When he didn't return, Mim followed him.

'What about me?' he asked, still looking out to sea. 'What about us?'

'You've been a brilliant friend,' Mim said. The words sounded inadequate even to her own ears; he deserved more than that, much more. But now he was here in front of her, and she had to say goodbye, she didn't know how or where to start. She tried again. 'It's been the most precious friendship of my life. I can't begin to tell you the difference you've made. These past few months have shown me how rich life can be and that I can enjoy those riches too. I'm not going back to the life I had before. I'll be looking for college courses in Lancashire, so your encouragement wasn't wasted.' She smiled. 'Perhaps I can send you updates like Benite.'

'Like Benite?' He turned to face her, frowning. 'Is that what you think? That I see you as a charity project?' He shook his head and took a step nearer. 'Isn't it obvious, Mim? I love you.'

Love? Corin loved her? For a few seconds, the sound

of the waves whispering onto the shore, the calling of the gulls, the breeze ruffling her hair, all disappeared and Mim was aware of nothing but Corin's eyes on hers and a breathless sense of hope and possibility. And then the world came rushing back in, bringing a reality check with it.

'Don't be daft,' she said.

Corin's frown deepened.

'Is that the way you always react when someone tells you they love you?'

'I wouldn't know,' Mim said. 'No one has ever told me before. Obviously, it's the way I'd react if someone like you said it.'

'Someone like me?' Corin stepped forward to avoid a wave. 'What does that mean?'

Mim hardly knew. Nothing was making sense right now. Words tumbled out of her mouth without thought.

'Well, look at you. Look at me. We're not a good match, are we?'

'Why not?'

'You should fall in love with someone who says baath.' She exaggerated the long vowel. 'With someone who attends posh dinner dances, not who serves the drinks at one. Someone who went to the right school and university and who is bright enough to scrape more than one A level. You shouldn't fall in love with someone who sleeps in their car. And not with someone who has this and everything it stands for,' she added, twisting her arm so that the puckered, scarred skin was facing towards him.

He took her arm in his hand and gently ran his finger down the damaged flesh. Mim could hardly breathe.

'That's not who you are,' he said. 'I fell in love with someone with extraordinary strength and resilience. Someone honest – brutally so, at times. Someone who can smile and laugh and work to help others even when she has nothing. Someone who is beautiful, inside and out. That's the Mim I see. How could I not fall in love with you?'

Did he mean it? She could still hardly believe it. He looked sincere. There was softness in his eyes, warmth in his expression that corroborated his words, and it invited Mim to let go and bask in it. He took hold of both her hands.

'Well, Mim? I have to ask the obvious question. Do you love me?'

'I don't know.'

What else could she say? He'd just praised her for her honesty, so how could she give him anything but an honest answer? She'd never experienced love. She didn't know if what she felt for Corin was love or not. But she could see from the pain etched on his face that this time her honesty had been too brutal. He leaned forward until his forehead was touching hers and she felt the disappointment in his sigh.

'Can't you stay and we can find out?' he murmured.

'I can't,' she said. And then his lips met hers as if he was trying to stop the words leaving her mouth. It was a kiss like no other – full of tenderness, full of love, and full of the promise of what could be. But she'd made a promise of her own to Lucas and she couldn't break it, even for kisses like this. Especially not for kisses like this. She forced herself to pull away, though it felt as though she were tearing herself in two.

'I don't want you to go,' Corin said. 'Surely we can work something else out? Find Lucas a job here, or split our weeks…'

'I have to go.' Mim held one of his hands between both of hers. It wasn't the hand of the idle, rich man she'd once assumed him to be. They were the rough, worn hands of a man who had spent years helping others to improve their chances and to live their best possible life. She willed him to understand that she needed to live hers now. 'You of all people should understand why. You left Africa when your family needed you. There are no compromises. Family comes first, whatever your own wishes might be.' She squeezed his hand. 'I have to be with Lucas. He's family, and that means everything to me. I'm not on my own anymore. I belong with someone. It's all I've ever wanted. Please understand. I have to choose him.'

Corin pulled her into a hug. His heart thudded against her chest and his breath was warm in her hair.

She had no idea how long they stayed that way; time had ceased to exist.

'Be happy,' he said at last and gave her a final, haunting kiss.

He drew back. Mim couldn't stop herself. She reached up and ran her hand down the side of his face, exploring for the first and last time the softness of his hair, the smoothness of his cheek, the firmness of his chin.

'Be safe,' she said. 'Stay away from those cliffs.'

He nodded, then he walked away along the beach, Dickens at his side, his head bent low, and Mim watched until his figure disappeared on the horizon.

Chapter Twenty-One

L ucas was not impressed with the Volvo.

'The radio doesn't work,' he said in disgust, after fiddling with the buttons in vain to try to find Radio 1.

'How can there be no air-conditioning,' he asked, half an hour into their journey, when the sun was beating down on them and the temperature in the car was becoming uncomfortable, even with the windows open. Windows that had to be wound open manually – another source of derision.

Mim hardly noticed his complaints. She was busy concentrating on every last detail of the Devon countryside, to remember over the coming months and to stop her focusing on some of the more painful scenes of the last few days.

It hadn't all been painful. The arrival of the first

official guests of As You Like It holidays yesterday had been a joy and a privilege to witness. Four families and one couple had arrived at various times throughout the day, looking fraught and weary, and Mim had witnessed their spirits lifting as they saw the caravan site bathed in sunshine and breathed in the sea air. She hoped that they could find a fraction of the happiness that she had experienced staying there.

Saying a final goodbye to her friends had been the hardest moments. Karen and Heather had insisted that Mim join them for one final swim on Sunday morning, and it had been perfect. The sea was calm and as warm as it had ever been, and Mim had floated on her back knowing that she would never forget the last few months. They had changed her life. She had learned the meaning of true friendship. She had discovered that there was more kindness in the world than she had thought. She had gained the confidence to try to improve her lot in life. And she had found a brother. All this from that impulsive decision to help two strangers on a cold December night. She felt as if she had been repaid a thousand times over.

As for saying goodbye to the Howards... Mim had asked them not to make a fuss, but of course they had ignored her and the full family gathered on the drive to wave her off, even Ros and the children. Mim was amazed that Olly hadn't been dragged down from London for the occasion. She was showered with unexpected gifts: Bea gave her a new wetsuit so she could continue the wild swimming; Ros handed over a bag of clothes that no longer fitted her bump; Lia gave her a drawing, showing Mim as a phoenix, rising from the flames. Bill tried to hand over money but Mim drew the line at that. They all hugged and kissed, and some held back tears and some didn't. Corin kept his distance, lurking with Dickens at the corner of the house, looking on with a face bleached with tiredness and despair. It was too painful to see; Mim felt as if the rocks she'd imagined hovering over her chest had fallen, crushing her heart. Was this what love felt like? It was too late to find out. She'd made her decision and it was the right one. She had to make it work.

It was raining by the time they reached Lancashire – fat, heavy drops that pounded on the roof of the car, inevitably reminding Mim of staying in the caravan. Mim followed the signs for Blackpool and Lucas directed her to a smart detached property on an estate of new-build houses. Mim pulled up outside and looked up at the house. This was where her dad had lived. This was where Lucas had been brought up, in comfort and safety. It was a far cry from the places she had stayed. There was one obvious problem though.

'Where's the sea?' she asked, peering all round. She'd never visited Blackpool before, but everyone knew there were miles of beaches at the resort.

'We're a couple of miles away from the front,' Lucas

said. 'You can drive there in a few minutes or catch the bus.'

'Great!' Mim said. That was further away than she'd expected, but no doubt it was an advantage to be away from the hustle and bustle of the town centre. Blackpool was bound to be quite different to Littlemead. She spotted a figure lurking in the front window of the house. 'Is that your mum?'

'Yeah. I texted to let her know we were almost here. Come and meet her.'

Mim followed Lucas into the house. A small porch led through to a narrow hall where his mum was waiting. She looked around fifty, and was tall and slim with a neat blonde bob and a warm smile. She approached Mim.

'Hello, love. You must be Mim. I'm Carol. Is it okay to hug? We're family, after all.'

Mim nodded and Carol gave her a hug. She smelt delicious, of some exotic perfume. Mim wasn't sure whether she felt more relieved at the friendly welcome or intimidated by Lucas having such a glamorous mother.

'Let me look at you,' Carol said, stepping back and holding Mim at arm's length. 'You definitely have the look of Martin, and of Lucas. I can't tell you how glad I am that Lucas found you. But let's save the chat for later. You look done in after that long drive. How about I show you your room and then we can have a cup of tea? Stick the kettle on, Lucas.'

Carol led the way upstairs and into a bedroom at the

back of the house. It was a pretty room, decorated in pale blue and with a double bed filling the centre and a white wardrobe in an alcove. A vase of flowers sat on a dressing table under the window.

'What do you think?' Carol asked. She twitched a couple of flowers into place, though the arrangement already looked perfect. 'Will this be okay? If there's anything you need, just shout.'

'It's lovely,' Mim said. 'Thanks for letting me stay. I hope I won't be in your way for too long. I'll look for somewhere else as soon as I can.'

'Stay as long as you like,' Carol said. 'This was the guest room. Now it's yours. It should always have been yours. If I'd known...' She smiled, too brightly, and tears glittered in her eyes. 'The bathroom is next door. Come down when you're ready and we'll have that tea.'

While they drank their tea, Mim flicked through Carol's old photograph albums and listened to stories about her dad. There were videos of him too – playing football with a young Lucas, singing karaoke in a hotel bar, cooking Christmas dinner with a paper crown on his head... It was strange and wonderful to see the man that the sixteen-year-old boy in her photograph had grown into; to hear her father's voice for the first time, to hear him laugh, and to recognise bits of herself in him. Carol and Lucas spoke of him with obvious love. He looked like a good, kind man. So Mim had to know ... why had he never contacted her?

'Did he ever mention me?' she asked.

'No. I'm sorry, love. Not until the end,' Carol said. She sighed. 'Ours was a whirlwind romance. We were married after four months and Lucas was a honeymoon baby. He said there was never a good time to tell me. And then when we struggled for years to have another baby, he thought it would hurt me to know that he already had another child. He was wrong. I would have welcomed you with open arms. I wish we could have spared you what you went through.' Carol wiped her eyes. 'I'm finding it hard to forgive him. You should have been part of this family. I would have loved you like my own. It hurts that he could have doubted that.'

'I'm here now and that's all that matters,' Mim said. She took Carol's hand – a gesture that she wouldn't have made before spending all those months with the Howards. But she mustn't think of them now. 'I want to be part of this family, if you'll have me.'

'Gladly,' Carol said. 'This is your home, for as long as you want it. We'll always be here for you from now on.'

Carol was a teacher at a local primary school and as she was off for half-term, she offered to show Mim round the local area. They started with a day trip to Blackpool as Mim was keen to see the sea but she had to hide her disappointment. The golden sand stretched for miles and she sank into it when she walked, but she missed the crunch and roll of pebbles under her feet. The air smelt of fish and chips, not the tangy saltiness of the sea. There were swarms of people everywhere, and noise and cars and bright lights, and even a huge theme park. She'd looked forward to living by the sea but this wasn't like Littlemead. There was nothing wild and natural here, nothing that touched her soul.

She couldn't resist going to look at Gordon's hotel again now she was back in Lancashire. She'd lived there for so many years, years that had transformed her and made her who she was. She drove to Burnley one day while Carol and Lucas were at work, but the building she found wasn't her familiar hotel any more. Developers had bought it and were turning it into flats, according to the advertising board outside. The building was covered in scaffolding and it looked like the place was being gutted. She peered into a skip on the drive and it was full of pieces of her past: the carpet from the main stairs, the light fittings from the dining room, even the old office chair that she'd sat on. Some of the windows had been removed from the building, and the curtains from her attic bedroom flapped against the stone exterior of the hotel. This was the closest she'd ever come to finding a place to call home and now it was truly gone. She drove back to Blackpool with tears in her eyes and an emptiness in her heart.

Mim borrowed Lucas's laptop so she could keep on

top of the emails and admin for As You Like It holidays. It was a bittersweet job. She was thrilled that donations continued to arrive, as well as nominations for families who would benefit from a break. Lia had set up a Facebook page full of glorious photographs of the caravans, the local area, and the first families enjoying their holidays, including a heart-wrenching thank you letter written by a young girl who had experienced her first holiday at Vennhallow. The charity was thriving, just as Mim had hoped it would. But she couldn't see those photos without an aching feeling of loss that she wasn't there. She scoured the images for faces she recognised, hoping to catch a glimpse of Ros with a new baby, or Bill tinkering with a new invention, or Dickens chasing imaginary rabbits across the field, or Corin just being Corin, so she knew he was there and that he was well. And then she felt horribly guilty that she was thinking of the Howards when she was here with her real family.

The Howards hadn't forgotten her either. Bea sent her regular messages, checking how she was and whether she was eating enough cake. Lia bombarded her with several texts each day and telephone calls that tore Mim between laughter and sadness. Then, when Mim had been in Lancashire for almost eight weeks, Lia surprised her with a video call one Saturday morning.

'Hello! Isn't this a surprise?' Lia's smiling face filled the telephone screen. 'I absolutely had to see your reaction when I told you my news.' Lia frowned and she appeared to be studying the screen at her end. 'Darling, what is that ghastly thing you're wearing? Ros didn't give you that.'

'It's my uniform for the chippy,' Mim said. She'd managed to get a job in a fish and chip restaurant, which would have been good news if it didn't bring back so many painful memories of the Easter swim with Corin and the sight of him in a wetsuit. She waved the phone up and down so that Lia could see the full effect. 'Be glad you can only see and not smell it. I don't think I'll ever be free of the stink of grease and vinegar again.'

She laughed and Lia wrinkled her nose.

'Can't you find a better job?' Lia asked. 'You would look so pretty on the reception desk at a luxury hotel.'

'I'm still working on it. Until I'm offered that job, I'll make do with the ones I have. It's not just the chippy. I clean a couple of B&Bs and work a few nights in a bar as well. I'm lucky to have found so much work. There's no time to be bored.'

'Oh darling, that sounds beastly. When do you have time for fun?'

'The bar can be fun. It's not quiet like the Boat. You should see some of the hen and stag parties we have coming in. You wouldn't believe half of what goes on.'

'I think I'd rather go to the Boat,' Lia said with a grimace. Mim had to agree. Working in the bar in Blackpool made her feel horribly old. Every night she had to stifle the wish that she was leaning on the bar in the Boat, sharing a beer with Corin.

'Anyway, what's your news?' Mim asked, shaking off that image. She was trying not to think about Corin but it was harder than she had ever imagined. Reminders of him popped up everywhere. 'Where are you? I can see lots of trees behind you.'

'That's the wrong question.' Lia laughed. 'You should have asked who I'm with.' Lia swivelled round and stretched out her arm so Mim could see more of the background. Bobby was there and as Mim watched, he walked behind Lia and put his arms round her. He gave a sheepish wave to Mim. Mim gaped at the screen.

'There.' Lia grinned. 'I knew you'd be surprised, darling. Isn't this the most utterly glorious news?'

'Yes.' Mim laughed. 'It really is. Are you going out now?'

'This is our first official going out date.' Lia brought the phone nearer to her face and winked. 'There may have been a couple of staying in ones already.' She zoomed out again and Mim was sure she could see the blush on Bobby's cheeks. 'We're going for a walk and having a romantic picnic.'

'A walk?' Mim repeated. It didn't sound likely. 'What have you done with the real Lia, Bobby?'

'This is her,' he said. 'She's even bought new walking boots.'

The phone pointed down briefly to show Lia's feet

wearing what were clearly a new pair of expensive boots. That sounded more Lia.

'This is all thanks to you, darling,' Lia said. 'I'm so happy I could literally burst.'

Mim couldn't doubt it. Neither Lia nor Bobby had stopped smiling yet.

'I need to return the favour,' Lia continued. 'Everyone should be as happy as we are. When are you going to come back and see Corin?'

'Corin?' Mim repeated.

'Now, remember I said you were the only one who didn't treat me like an idiot?' Lia laughed. 'He's moping down here. He rarely smiles and he hasn't teased me once. Even Dickens is better company. I never thought I'd say this but I miss my irritating big brother. Don't deny that there was something between you because it was obvious to everyone – even to me, and you know how utterly self-absorbed I am. You were made for each other. And if you're with him, you get me as a real sister, and wouldn't it be worth putting up with him for that? Come home, darling. We all miss you and want you back.'

———————————

'Are you happy here, Mim?' Carol asked, as they sat in the garden a few days later, enjoying a glass of wine. It was Mim's night off from the bar and she'd hoped to catch up with Lucas, but he had gone out with friends.

Their working hours weren't proving compatible. Mim spent all weekend in the fish and chip restaurant when Lucas was off and on the nights when Mim was free, he was usually out with mates or with his girlfriend. It wasn't how she'd expected it to be but his life had been established here long before he knew about her and she supposed she had to fit around it where she could. She was here with him, available if he needed her, and that was what mattered.

'Yes,' Mim replied at once. 'Of course I am.'

Carol laughed.

'Now give the question a moment's thought and let me have your answer,' she said. Mim smiled.

'It's the same. I love getting to know Lucas. Everyone has been kinder and more welcoming than I could have hoped.'

'We love having you here,' Carol said. She topped up their glasses. 'Don't take this the wrong way, will you? I've sometimes wondered if you're missing Devon more than you admit.'

'Who needs Devon when we have gorgeous weather like this?' Mim asked, pointing at the perfect blue sky over their heads.

'What about the people?' Carol was being annoyingly persistent and didn't fall for Mim's attempt to change the subject. 'When you were telling me about your conversation with Lia, you were different. You lit up. You do miss them, don't you?'

'Yes.' Mim sighed. 'I'm sorry. That seems ungrateful, doesn't it? I don't regret the decision to leave. Getting to know Lucas, and you, has meant everything to me. I do want to be here.'

'But you want to be there too?' Carol smiled. 'What about the man you keep mentioning? Corin. Do you miss him too?'

'I don't keep mentioning him, do I?' Mim asked. She'd thought she had that under control by now. Obviously not.

'Only once or twice a day. Was he your boyfriend?'

'He was a friend. A good friend.' Mim looked at Carol. She hadn't tried to mother Mim, like Bea had, but they had become close, and the temptation to confide in her was irresistible. She leaned forward. 'Before I left Devon, he said he loved me, but I didn't know if I felt the same. I've not had much experience of love. I don't know what it feels like. How are you supposed to know?'

Carol reached across and squeezed Mim's hand.

'How does it feel to be away from him now?' she asked.

'Horrible,' Mim admitted. It was a relief to be honest, with herself as much as with Carol. 'I keep hoping he's going to wander into the bar, in a woolly jumper full of holes and with his dog at his side. I think of things to tell him but he's not there. My chest feels all heavy and crushed when I think about him. It's like there's something missing – a gap where he used to be.'

Like a piece of her world was missing... Bea's words about Bill echoed in Mim's head. She'd thought that Lucas was the missing piece, but if that were the case, why did she feel this physical ache, as if she'd been wrenched away from an essential part of her being? Unless... She emptied her glass. Had she made the biggest mistake of her life?

'That sounds very much like love to me. It was how I felt when Martin died. How I still feel,' Carol said. 'I'd give anything to have more time with him. Don't you want to be with Corin?'

'I can't.'

'Do you mean because of Lucas? You don't have to live in the same house as him to be a good sister. You don't even have to live in the same county. That's the beauty of family. He'll be your brother wherever you are and whatever you do. He has his own life. You're allowed yours too.'

'But wouldn't Dad have wanted us to be here together? I don't want to let him down.'

'He would have wanted you to be happy, that's all. And he would have been so proud of who you are, Mim. You could never let him down.' Carol took Mim's hands in hers. 'Your dad lived and died full of regret over what he'd missed. Please don't do the same.'

Should she stay or should she go? It was the same dilemma, only this time it was the opposite way round as she tried to decide whether her future lay in Lancashire or Devon. She hadn't expected to make the decision again; she'd been determined to make it work in Blackpool, whatever it took, and she'd given it her best shot. But Heather had told her to listen to her heart and she couldn't ignore what it was saying any longer. Bea's words about Bill echoed in her thoughts. Mim had lived without money, lived without a roof over her head, but this challenge had defeated her. She couldn't live without Corin.

She dreaded telling Lucas after he had made such an effort to find her. She waited until they both had a free evening and invited him to the local pub. They were on their second round of drinks before she plucked up the courage.

'There's something I have to tell you,' she said, clutching her pint glass in both hands. This was even harder than she had thought. What if he hated her for leaving him, after such a short time? 'I have to go back to Devon. I'm sorry.'

'You're moving back?'

'Yes. I know I agreed to live here and I've loved staying with you and your mum, don't think I haven't, and I hate to be letting you down, but…' Mim stopped. Lucas was grinning at her, which wasn't the reaction she had expected.

'It's because of Corin, isn't it?' Mim nodded. Lucas grinned even more widely. 'I knew he was your boyfriend.'

'He isn't...'

'It was obvious to me that something was going on and I only met him twice.'

'Obvious to you and everyone except me.' Mim laughed. 'I really am sorry. You're still going to hear from me all the time, though. You're stuck with me. And if you ever fancy starting a new life in Devon...'

'No, I'm settled here. I wouldn't say no to a few free holidays, though. I'm saving up to move in with Jessie as soon as we can afford it.' He smiled. 'Don't look so guilty. I'm glad I found you. You're all right.'

Everything was going to be okay. Mim couldn't stop smiling. For years, she'd wanted to be part of a family more than anything in the world; now she had two, one created with blood, and one chosen with love. She was luckier than she had ever thought possible. She was sad to be leaving Lucas but it didn't compare with the devastation she had felt when driving away from the Howards. And the sadness couldn't survive against the overwhelming excitement of seeing Corin again. She remembered the moment he had said he loved her – the dizzying sense of hope and possibility – and it all came flooding back. She couldn't wait to be with him.

She drove back to Devon at first light on a Friday morning in early August, trying to avoid the holiday rush. She ticked off the signs as she had done on a dark winter's evening seven months ago: Birmingham, Bristol, Exeter... Despite the toil of a long and busy journey, her heart swelled as she pulled on to the country lanes she had come to know so well, noticing how green everywhere had become in her absence, and how the hedgerows danced with flowers. She knew beyond all doubt, as she drove down the hill into Littlemead and saw the sea glittering in the distance, that she had made the right decision. This was where she belonged.

She wasn't sure of her welcome at Vennhallow, despite Bea's words when she left, so she parked in the village car park, grabbed her bag and set off along the coastal path towards the caravan field. The sun was already warm and she stopped to catch her breath at the top of the hill. She would never tire of this view. This was the seaside she loved and that filled her heart with joy.

There was activity around the caravans: a couple of young children were chasing each other through the field and outside the accessible caravan a man in a wheelchair and his companion were eating breakfast. There were no signs of life at Mim's former home and the sign bearing her name still hung from the veranda, so she unlocked the door carefully and peered in, wary of disturbing anyone inside. The place was empty but spotlessly clean, and a vase of fresh flowers sat on the table, which was a mystery; she hadn't told anyone she was coming back. She locked the door again and set off across the lawn towards Corin's house.

She was only halfway when she saw him, striding across the grass with Dickens scampering at his side, just as she had pictured him so often during the lonely hours in Blackpool. The moment he saw her was obvious. He froze and then he ran towards her, scooped her up in his arms and swung her round. If she hadn't already been sure she loved him, the expression on his face would have sealed it. As Lia might have said, he looked as if he might literally burst with happiness. And it was all for her, Mim Brown. That look of love was for her and it was unbelievable and magical and something she wanted to see every day for the rest of her life.

'I love you,' Mim said, when he put her back on the ground. 'Sorry it took so long to get there.'

He laughed and kissed her and it was the best kiss in the world.

'What are you doing here?' he asked. 'How did you get here? Why didn't you let us know?' He smiled. 'No. Don't answer any of that. Tell me again what you said.'

'That I'm sorry for taking so long?'

'The other part.'

'I love you.'

He kissed her again, for longer this time. Mim was about to say it a third time to see what would happen when he took a step back.

'Are you staying?' he asked.

'I was going to but is someone else using the caravan? It's been cleaned and there are flowers in it.'

'They're for you.'

'But you didn't know I was coming.'

'I've put flowers in it since you went away, in the hope you would come back.'

Mim couldn't reply to that. Love was proving to be the strangest thing. She didn't know from one second to the next whether she wanted to laugh with utter joy or cry her eyes out. Corin grasped her hand.

'Come to the house,' he said. 'I have something for you.'

That sounded intriguing. Mim stole another kiss and let him lead her to his house. There was an overnight bag and a box of Dickens's belongings in the hall.

'Oh,' Mim said, dropping her own bag to the floor. 'Have I interrupted? Were you going away?'

'Yes. I was on my way to Lancashire.' He slid an arm round Mim's waist. 'I've spent the last few weeks thinking about what I have and what I want. About what you might want. And then when Lia said that you were moping, I knew I had to try again.'

Moping? Mim suppressed a smile. Clearly Lia had been hard at work.

'You were coming to see me?' she asked. She grinned. 'Have I ruined your grand gesture? Try it now and let's see how you get on.'

He pulled her closer.

'I was going to tell you about some changes to the family business. We've agreed that I'll job share with Lia. She's done fantastic work with As You Like It. We'll both run the business when Dad retires.'

'So you can carry on fossil hunting? That's brilliant. I know how much you love it.'

'I love you more,' Corin said. 'I've done this so we can split our time between Devon and Lancashire. I know you want to be with Lucas and I want to be wherever you are.'

He was going to do that, for her? Mim discovered another strange thing about love. It didn't have any limits. Her feelings for Corin just kept growing.

'That's lucky,' she said. 'Because I want to be wherever you are. But you don't need to give anything up for me. I'm moving back to Devon.'

'For good? Are you sure? Lucas...'

'Is a grown man and doesn't need me watching him all the time. He's looking forward to holidays down here as often as he can.'

Corin studied her, as if deciding what to do next. He smiled. 'I think it's definitely time for this.' He went into the bedroom and Mim followed, laughing.

'So this is what you meant when you said you had something for me... Smooth work, Dr Howard.'

'It wasn't. But hold that thought.' Corin smiled at Mim in a way that made it difficult to think of anything else. He opened a drawer in a cabinet that sat under the window. It was empty. Corin took Mim's hand. 'This is for you. I want you to feel that you belong here. I want you to know that this will always be your home. This is for your emergency box, when you're ready.'

Here came the tears again, hot on the heels of the laughter. Mim was undone. He understood her. He knew who she was, what she was, and what she needed. Everything she'd been through over the last thirty-four years had led to this moment and made it more precious than she could ever say.

'I know it's not much,' Corin said, when Mim didn't speak. She shook her head.

'It is. It's the Taj Mahal.' She squeezed his hand and he answered with a smile that brought more tears. 'Are you asking me to move in with you?' she asked. 'Just so we're clear?'

'I'm asking you everything. Move in with me. Marry me. Let's make our own family.'

'Are you sure you're up for that?' Mim asked, wiping away her tears. 'Your children might have common northern accents.'

'I'll risk it if you'll take the chance that yours might have posh southern ones.' He smiled. 'I love you, Mim. Nothing else matters.'

Mim leant against him and studied the cabinet. Some might see an empty drawer, but to her it was already full of everything she'd always wanted: love, understanding, security. Corin was solid and warm at her side, promising the future she had never dared to hope for, and there was only one possible response. She collected her emergency box from her bag, and emptied the contents into the drawer.

She was home.

Acknowledgments

My thanks to all at One More Chapter for their hard work in bringing this book to publication. Special thanks to my editor, Hannah Todd, who championed the story from the first idea.

I hadn't planned to write a book set in Devon, but after spending time there on holiday, I couldn't resist writing about this beautiful part of the country. Corin's fossil walk was inspired by a similar walk we took, led by Martin Curtis of www.jurassiccoastguides.co.uk. I'm siding with Mim rather than Lia, and think it's a fascinating way to spend a morning, even though I was disappointed not to find an ammonite! Any mistakes in the details are mine.

The writing life would be impossible without the support of my writer friends. I still can't believe how lucky I was to find the Authors on the Edge: Mary Jayne

Baker, Sophie Claire, Jacqui Cooper, Helena Fairfax, Melinda Hammond, Marie Laval, Helen Pollard and Angela Wren. I hope our Hebden Bridge meetings can resume soon! Thanks also to the Beta Buddies for providing laughter, understanding and unfailing support. I'm especially grateful to Jennifer Young for taking an early look at *Finding Home* and telling me exactly what I needed to hear. It seems a fitting coincidence that this book is about how wonderful Geographers are!

Thanks to Rachel Gilbey for doing a brilliant job in arranging blog tours for my books, and to all the book bloggers who take part, or who independently read the books and write such incredible reviews. It makes a huge difference in helping readers find books, and I'm grateful for the support.

After years of writing in secret, for my eyes only, it still seems amazing – and scary! – that other people are reading my stories. Thank you for choosing to read *Finding Home*. If you've enjoyed it, please do consider leaving a review on Amazon or on the website from where you borrowed or bought the book, as it will help other readers find it and will brighten my day! I love to hear from readers who have enjoyed any of my books, so please do get in touch on Twitter at @katehaswords or through my Facebook author page at KateFieldAuthor.

ONE MORE CHAPTER

One More Chapter is an
award-winning global
division of HarperCollins.

Sign up to our newsletter to get our
latest eBook deals and stay up to date
with our weekly Book Club!
<u>Subscribe here.</u>

Meet the team at
<u>www.onemorechapter.com</u>

Follow us!
 <u>@OneMoreChapter_</u>
 <u>@OneMoreChapter</u>
 <u>@onemorechapterhc</u>

Do you write unputdownable fiction?
We love to hear from new voices.
Find out how to submit your novel at
<u>www.onemorechapter.com/submissions</u>